TWIN DRAGONS' DESTINY

DRAGON LORDS OF VALDIER BOOK 11

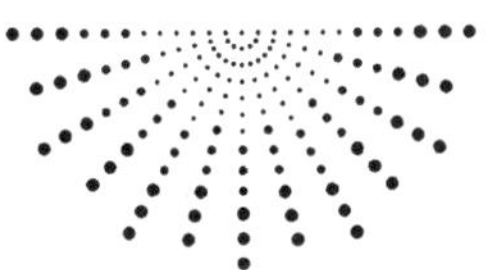

S.E. SMITH

CONTENTS

ACKNOWLEDGMENTS

I would like to thank my husband Steve for believing in me and being proud enough of me to give me the courage to follow my dream. I would also like to give a special thank you to my sister and best friend, Linda, who not only encouraged me to write, but who also read the manuscript. Also to my other friends who believe in me: Julie, Jackie, Christel, Sally, Jolanda, Lisa, Laurelle, Debbie, and Narelle. The girls that keep me going!

And a special thanks to Paul Heitsch, David Brenin, Samantha Cook, Suzanne Elise Freeman, and PJ Ochlan – the awesome voices behind my audiobooks!

– S.E. Smith

Science Fiction Romance
Twin Dragons' Destiny

First E-Book Published April 2018
Cover Design by Melody Simmons

Summary: Twin Dragon warriors are given a second chance at life, but time is running out because even second chances come with a deadline.

ISBN (paperback) 978-1-944125-15-8
ISBN (eBook) 978-1-944125-28-8

Published in the United States by Montana Publishing.

{1. Fantasy Romance – Fiction. 2. Paranormal Romance – Fiction. 3. Action/Adventure – Fiction. 4. Fantasy – Fiction. 5. Romance – Fiction.}

www.montanapublishinghouse.com

SYNOPSIS

Scorching hot stories set in science fiction and paranormal worlds that come alive in your hands. Don't miss out on stories that readers say they can't get enough of!

The line between life and death is sometimes blurred...

Barrack and Brogan have memories of their death – and it isn't a pleasant one. When the Goddess Aikaterina gives them a second chance at life – and at finding their true mate – they are willing to do whatever it takes to change their destiny. What they don't expect is that it would be so difficult! It turns out that their true mate is a human, a species they have limited knowledge about, from a planet they have never visited. With time running out, it doesn't take them long to realize that this may be one battle that will take all of their skills to win.

Delilah Rosewater is haunted by dreams of her death. She doesn't understand why the dreams feel so real, or why she knows with growing certainty that time is running out for her. Her feelings of frustration strengthen as she searches for the one person she feels could understand her increasing panic - Sara Wilson. She is shocked when instead of finding Sara, she comes face-to-face with two irritating men who claim to be from another world!

Caught in an unexpected snowstorm in the Appalachian Mountains, Delilah doesn't know what to think of the two men and their wild claims of a powerful Goddess, alien worlds, and new destinies. Will Delilah open her heart to the twin dragons and accept the second chance that the Goddess has given them before time runs out for all of them?

AUTHOR'S NOTE:

For those who have not yet read the Dragon Lords of Valdier series, here is a little background.

The Valdier are dragon shifters. Only the Valdier and their mates can bond with the mysterious and powerful golden symbiots, who are, yes, symbiotic creatures, and they are stand-out characters all on their own! Each Valdier consists of three parts: the dragon, the man/woman, and their symbiot companion. They are friends with the Curizan (a species able to harness the energy around them) and the Sarafin (a cat shifting species).

The following is a character guide for those new to the series:

CAST OF CHARACTERS:

Delilah Rosewater: Human
Barrack: First of the Twin Dragons
Brogan: First of the Twin Dragons
Barrack's Symbiot: Whiskey
Brogan's Symbiot: Gin

Delilah's Rottweilers: Moonshine and Rum

Amber Delilah Rosewater: Delilah's mother
Daniel Alvin Rosewater: Delilah's father
Bane **mated to** Lesann: Barrack and Brogan's parents
Merck – younger brother to Barrack and Brogan

Zoran Reykill, Leader of the Valdier
true mate to Abby Tanner:
one son: Zohar
Zoran's symbiot: Goldie
Zohar's symbiot: Truck

Mandra Reykill **true mate to** Ariel Hamm:
one son: Jabir
Mandra's symbiot: Precious
Jabir's symbiot: Munch

Kelan Reykill **true mate to** Trisha Grove:
one son: Bálint
Kelan's symbiot: Bio
Bálint's symbiot: Tag

Trelon Reykill **true mate to** Cara Truman:
twin daughters: Amber and Jade
one son: James
Trelon's symbiot: Symba
Amber's symbiot: Treat
Jade's symbiot: Trix

Creon Reykill **true mate to** Carmen Walker:
twin daughters: Spring and Phoenix
Creon's symbiot: Harvey
Phoenix's symbiot: Stardust
Spring's symbiot: Little Bit

Paul Grove **true mate to** Morian Reykill:
one daughter: Morah
Paul and Morian's symbiot: Crash
Morah's symbiot: Princess Buttercup

Cree and Calo Aryeh **true mates to** Melina Franklin:
one daughter: Hope
Calo's symbiot: Teddy
Cree's symbiot: Bear
Hope's symbiot: Rainbow

Vox d'Rojah, King of the Sarafin
mated to Riley St. Claire:
one son: Roam
twin daughters: Sacha and Pearl

Viper d'Rojah **mated to** Tina St. Claire:
one son: Leo

Asim Kemark **true mate to** Pearl St. Claire

Ha'ven Ha'darra, Prince of the Curizan
mated to Emma Watson:
one daughter: Alice

Adalard Ha'darra, Prince of the Curizan/younger brother of Ha'ven
mated to Samara Lee

Jaguin, Valdier tracker **mated to** Sara Wilson

Olis 'Ray' Lister married to Mabel Lister, real estate tycoon
Earl Helman – Mabel Lister's brother

DeWayne Davis – Attorney at Law

Bubba Joe – friend of Delilah's
Rudy – DeWayne's cousin

Mason Andrews **married to** Ann Marie, Paul Grove's Ranch Manager

Aikaterina: Unknown species; accepted as a Goddess to the Valdier, she is the oldest and most powerful of her kind.
Arilla and Arosa: Unknown species, still young for their kind, they are twins and thought to be Goddesses.

PROLOGUE

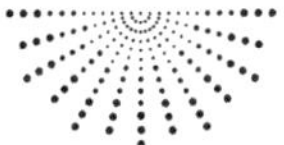

**enturies before:**

Aikaterina sat beside the river of gold, her fingers caressing the growing symbiots that would one day form a living companion for a dragon warrior. She drew strength from them, knowing that the essence of her blood would keep the dragons of Valdier safe for many centuries to come.

The Valdier considered her a 'Goddess,' but she wasn't. Her species were wanderers, having no true home but the universe. They lived off of the energy around them. It was the essence of life to them and without it, they would perish.

She knew her species was probably more dependent on the Valdier than the dragon-shifting race were on her. When she first came to this world, it had been to die. The courage and spirit of the Valdier gave her new life. As a gift, she gave them a touch of her essence—the living gold symbiots. And, in time, she found others of her kind who were weak and dying like she had been and brought them to this world to heal.

A smile curved her lips when she saw Arosa and Arilla frolicking in the stream. Although the twins were thousands of years old, she still thought of them as infants. They reminded her of newborn stars. She had witnessed the creation of many celestial bodies and still found a star's birth fascinating to observe. Centuries ago when she had found Arosa and Arilla out in the cosmos, they had been struggling to survive—barely clinging to life.

Arilla looked up with a frown and slowly moved her hand through the air as if she could feel something. Confusion turned the young Goddess's eyes a darker gold. Arilla looked at her and tilted her head.

"What is it that I feel, Aikaterina?" she asked.

Aikaterina looked up, feeling the disturbance as well. She closed her eyes and focused on the stream of energy flowing through the river. A great sadness filled her as a vision appeared in front of her. It was caused by the death of a rare set of twin dragons, the first to be born. She felt the intense pain of their symbiots as they watched the men and the dragons who gave them life die.

Bowing her head, she allowed the wave of grief to pierce her. She called to the orphaned symbiots. Rising to her feet, she opened a portal for them to return to her. Behind them, she could see the smoke-filled remains of a village and hear the wails of grief. Two identical dragons lay dead amid the carnage.

She looked from them to the two young boys pressed against the side of one of the huts. Their words would forever haunt her because deep down, she knew this was because of her interference. She was the one who had gifted the twins to the village for protection. She did so not long after she brought Arilla and Arosa to this world with her.

"Do you think...?" the young boy named Calo whispered, staring at the smoldering remains of the green and white dragon.

"No. You heard him. We will die in battle, like warriors, before we let this happen to us. We will do the honorable thing before we hurt another," his twin brother, Cree, answered, his mouth tight with determination.

"We will die in battle," Calo agreed, watching as their father's symbiot healed him. "Or we will take each other's life before we hurt another."

The symbiots of Brogan and Barrack, the original twin dragons, fell weakly through the portal, unseen by the mortals in the village. Aikaterina caressed them, trying to give them comfort. The form she had taken shimmered and partially faded in response to the utter grief the symbiots shared with her.

This was a new feeling to her, one of excruciating pain and anguish. The constant search for hope only to have it ripped away time and time again—and the suffocating loneliness of knowing they would never feel the tender touch of their mate's hand. She had never understood the loneliness that the men and their dragons were feeling until now.

"What is it Aikaterina?" Arosa asked, floating over to her. "What is wrong with them?"

"Are they ill?" Arilla asked in concern.

Aikaterina gave the symbiots the command to return to the river. She was shocked when they resisted. They would surely perish if they did not return. She could already see their color fading until they were almost translucent. She gave the order again, this time a little more firmly. The creatures turned away from her, but they still did not return to the river. She watched with a puzzled expression as they retreated to a dark corner of the cavern and curled up around each other.

"The men given to them have died," Aikaterina murmured.

"Couldn't you have saved them like you saved us?" Arilla asked, not understanding why the species that gave them life and made their world so interesting should have to die.

"I fear that they have perished because of something I did," Aikaterina confessed, turning and floating over to the two symbiots.

She gently stroked them, giving them a large amount of her essence. They tried to resist, but she refused to let them fade away. Instead, she encouraged them to share with her everything they had experienced while with Brogan and Barrack. The more they showed her, the more certain she was that she was the one responsible for the devastation.

Eventually, she did the only thing she could to alleviate their distress; she sent them into a deep sleep. Floating upward, she crossed the magnificent cavern to the platform where she had created a portal to the universe.

"Can we go with you, Aikaterina?" Arosa asked with a hopeful look.

"Not this time, Arosa. This journey I must make alone," Aikaterina answered as she stepped through the opening.

Aikaterina walked through the burning village. As she did, time regressed itself. What she was doing would not be achieved without a personal cost to herself. From this moment forward, the energy it would require to hold this thread of the future would place a heavy toll on her.

Her initial trip was to the future to see if there was a way to undo the damage that she had unwittingly created. The chance of affecting the fabric of time in the universe, and the destinies of others who resided in it, was one of the reasons her kind remained merely observers.

Her species was born at the same time as the universe and was thrown outward with the explosion of the first atoms. During the millennia, they grew powerful enough to create worlds—and destroy them. However, no matter how powerful her species grew, they were also very vulnerable. They lived off the positive essence of all creatures. Most planets were devoid of life, thus over time, her species faded away until there were only a few of them left.

Aikaterina watched Brogan struggle with an older warrior at the door to a quaint cottage. His gaze was locked on a frightened young girl standing next to an older woman who she knew to be the girl's mother. Several other men from the village rushed forward to help the warrior protect his fragile family.

She lifted her hand and ordered the twin dragons' symbiots to restrain the twin brothers. Shocked expressions crossed all the warriors' faces when the symbiots suddenly surged forward and wrapped powerful bands around the twin dragons.

"Release me," Brogan demanded, struggling against the confines of his symbiot.

Barrack shifted into his dragon. The brilliant light green and white dragon strained to throw his symbiot off. Barrack roared in rage, trying to get to his brother.

"Barrack, Brogan, stop," a man begged, his eyes filled with grief. "Please, my sons, do not make us kill you."

"It is too late, Bane, the madness has overtaken their dragons. They can't control them any longer. Creja, fulfill your promise. Kill them before their symbiots either release them or they turn on us," one of the warriors demanded.

"Bane, they are right," Creja stated in a harsh voice.

"Look at my sons, Creja, but think of your twins. It will only be a matter of time before they reach this point. There are no true mates for them. It is better to strike them dead than to let them live knowing there is no hope," Bane replied in a tortured voice.

"She is our true mate! She approached us," Brogan growled, continuing to fight against his symbiot.

Creja shook his head. "Look inside yourself, Brogan, neither you, nor your dragon or your symbiot, desire the girl as a true mate. The same goes for your brother. Mula is not your chosen one. You will find that it is you who is trying to convince your dragon that she is your mate only to placate him," he argued, pulling his sword free from his side.

"Our dragons need her, Creja. The loneliness is too much. With a mate, we will fight to protect the Valdier. I have to take her. I no longer have a choice," Brogan argued.

Aikaterina lifted her hand, pausing time. She already knew what would happen from this point forward. She recognized the emotion in Brogan's voice from what their symbiots had shown her. Her understanding of these emotions had grown over time and was one of the things that attracted her to this world.

The Valdier were a fierce, proud, and passionate species, but in order for them to find their true mate, all three parts of who they were needed to agree and connect as one with their destined partner. It was a safeguard that she'd created to keep them from believing themselves all powerful with the symbiots by their side. Perhaps it was another flaw on her part, but it was one she did not regret for it gave life to her species in a different way.

She stopped between the two warriors. Their symbiots shimmered with color, knowing she was there. She swept her gaze over each of the twins.

"Release them," she murmured to the symbiots.

The golden bodies melted and reformed in the shape of Werecats. Both symbiots sat protectively next to their men. Aikaterina transformed and grew solid. While the form she took looked like a Valdier maiden, she retained the essence of who she really was—a Goddess among the Valdier and creator of the symbiots.

"Awaken warriors," she ordered with a wave of her hand.

Brogan stumbled forward while Barrack turned in a graceful circle, his dragon searching for those who were about to attack them. Both man and dragon froze when they saw her. Their expressions changed, pulled from the edge of madness that gripped them, to stunned disbelief.

"What...?" Brogan started to growl, his voice fading when he saw everything around him held in suspended animation.

Aikaterina watched Barrack shift back to his two-legged form, his gaze warily following his brother's. They looked around them, noticing several dragons frozen in mid-flight while on the ground men, women, children, and animals were frozen in different phases of motion. She studied their faces when both men turned their gaze back to warily stare at her.

"Walk with me," she instructed, turning away.

Barrack looked at his brother. The slight edge of madness had faded to confusion. He could feel his dragon retreat in submission, something he could never remember happening before.

"Do you feel it too?" Brogan asked under his breath.

He gave a sharp nod. He ran his gaze over the woman's figure as she walked away from them. Their symbiots docilely walked on each side of her.

Barrack started forward, following the woman from a short, safe distance. He kept his eyes fixed on her back, confused by his dragon's deference to her. Brogan fell into step beside him.

They looked intently around as they walked. Remorse filled Barrack when he saw the terror on the faces of those he had always thought of with respect. To see the women and children seeking refuge and the fear on the warriors' faces told him of the cataclysmic effect their presence had on the village.

"I have done this," Brogan commented in a harsh, rough voice. His eyes fixed on the anguished expression on their mother's face as she rushed forward - her hand held out to Creja, father to a set of young twin dragons. "I have brought dishonor to my family."

"We both have," Barrack agreed with a heavy heart.

Barrack could feel his brother trying to withdraw from him so he couldn't feel his emotions. It was impossible, of course. Brogan shutting him out would be like trying to cut himself in half.

No matter how hard they tried to shield each other, their connection was too strong. That bond is what led to their downfall today. The loneliness that they felt was magnified by that of their dragons. Their symbiots fed off their combined emotions and had become depressed and listless over the last few months to the point that nothing they did helped the creatures.

Shame coursed through Barrack. He knew that the young maiden Brogan became fixated on was not their true mate. He was not even physically attracted to the girl, nor was his dragon or his symbiot. He knew Brogan really wasn't either. Despite that, he had looked the other way. He'd hoped that if their dragons were convinced she was their mate, it might stave off the relentless emptiness gnawing at them and would give them time to search other villages and cities for their true mate.

Brogan was the more volatile and, while he might deny it, emotional of the two brothers. His dragon had been pushing him to claim a female, any female, to fight off the madness. Unfortunately, Mula was the one to cross Brogan's path several months ago. The young girl had flirted with both of them, unaware that Brogan's dragon would consider her innocent, albeit blatant, invitation as serious. It was only when the girl realized that to flirt with one twin meant she received the attentions of both that she had retreated in panic.

Barrack did not blame the girl for her fear or for being unaware of what her light-hearted fun would provoke. He and Brogan recognized the impossibility of finding a true mate. They both understood that dealing with one dragon warrior was difficult enough. It was unheard of to find a woman who could handle two of them as mates. In the end, the best they could hope for was to die in battle before they both completely lost control. Today proved their hope was for naught, and their worst nightmare had come true.

Focusing on the woman in front of him, he clenched his fists. Perhaps she was here to end their misery. If so, why not just do it and get it over with? After seeing the pain he was causing, he knew that neither he nor Brogan would resist.

"Who are you, and how did you do that?" Brogan finally demanded, coming to a stop several feet away when the woman paused on the bridge that crossed the river.

Barrack's eyes followed the wave of his brother's hand. The village looked surreal while frozen in time. He swallowed, unable to comprehend the power such a feat would take. In the back of his mind, he wondered if he and his brother were not already dead.

"You are not," the woman murmured, gazing out along the river.

"I'm not what?" Barrack asked.

"Dead – yet," she answered in a serene voice.

"Who are you?" Barrack demanded. His voice was hoarse with astonishment at the realization that, whoever this being was, she could read his mind.

"I am called Aikaterina by your people," she replied, turning to look at them. She reached out and tenderly caressed the head of each of the symbiots. "I gave you a part of myself to help protect you."

"Curse us, you mean," Brogan retorted, his eyes growing dark with anger.

"Brogan," Barrack warned before he turned to look at Aikaterina. "Are you telling us that you are the Goddess Aikaterina?"

Aikaterina bowed her head. "Yes. Your brother is correct. My gifts to you have become a curse," she replied, lifting her hands from the symbiots' necks. "The threads of time are not easy to manipulate for a reason. To change time is to change the fate of the future. Sometimes those paths cross each other and will right themselves, creating a future that will continue relatively undistorted. But, at other times, the threads become tangled or they break. If that should happen, the changes can have unexpected outcomes."

Barrack frowned, trying to understand what the woman was telling them. Brogan growled under his breath that the woman talked in riddles. He reached out and gripped his brother's arm when he started to turn away. Something told him that they would not be given another chance.

"What kind of unexpected outcomes? As in bad ones?" Barrack asked, his gaze locked on the woman's face.

A small smile curved her lips. "Perhaps," she responded.

"Perhaps? I thought you were all powerful. Anyone who can do this has to know what is going to happen," Brogan impatiently snapped.

She turned her intense gaze on Brogan. "Even the most powerful cannot predict what a species with free will would decide if they are given a second chance." Her gaze moved to the village. "If you knew there was a true mate for you out in the universe, would you wait for her?"

"Yes!" Barrack was surprised when he heard Brogan's strident response.

"Yes," he replied, echoing his brother's reply in a softer tone. "If there is such a woman," he added.

"There is... but...," her voice faded and her eyes grew distant.

"I knew it. She is just giving us false hope, Barrack. There will never be a female who can handle us, much less our two dragons and our symbiots. This imaginary true mate would have to be accepted by all of us—and accept all of us in return," Brogan growled in frustration.

"You are wrong, warrior. There will be one, but she, too, is destined to die young," she replied, reaching out to touch their symbiots again.

"Die? How? Where is she?" Barrack demanded, stepping closer to her.

"I can change your fate, which will change hers, but like all things, nothing is guaranteed," Aikaterina explained.

"Which means exactly what?" Brogan asked in a hard tone.

A shiver ran through Barrack when Aikaterina turned to look at Brogan. He saw Brogan's head snap backwards, as if he had been struck. The sound of his brother's hiss exploded through the air before he fell back several steps. Barrack automatically reached out to steady Brogan when his back hit the stone wall lining the bridge.

"You have a long wait ahead of you, warrior. I hope you learn to calm your temper before you find your mate, or she might calm it for you," Aikaterina warned.

Barrack would have expected the warning to come with a touch of anger or even a little admonishment. The last thing he expected was the warning to come with a small, pleased smile. If he didn't know better, he would almost think that Aikaterina hoped Brogan failed.

Turning his head back toward the Goddess, he narrowed his eyes. He didn't understand what had just happened, but he could sense that whatever Aikaterina showed Brogan deeply shook his brother.

"What do we do now?" Barrack stated.

Aikaterina looked at the village. He followed her gaze. She was looking at their mother and father.

"You must leave," she stated quietly.

"How... how will we know when our true mate is born?" Brogan asked in a surprisingly calm voice.

She turned to look at both of them. Barrack saw her caress their symbiots again with a gentle hand. Both of the Werecats purred and rubbed against her.

"Your symbiots will know when it is time. Look for a warrior named Jaguin. His mate Sara will know where you can find your mate," she promised with a smile.

Barrack was about to ask her how but the words remained frozen on his lips. Aikaterina transformed. She no longer looked like a Valdier maiden, but something vastly more ethereal. Her body was the same color as the symbiots, but he could see through it. She was slowly rising from the bridge.

"Go, warriors, before your village wakes," she softly ordered. "If they see you, then your fate will remain unchanged, as will your true mate's."

"Shift, Brogan," Barrack said, feeling the urgency of his dragon pushing at him.

Brogan nodded. In seconds, both warriors had shifted to their dragon forms. Lifting off the ground, they flew over the village heading north. Their symbiots flowed into one another and transformed into a large golden spaceship. Within seconds, the symbiots had reached the fleeing dragons.

Barrack felt the symbiot flow over his dragon form, pulling him inside the spaceship. A moment later, Brogan was beside him. They both shifted again, unsure of where they would go, but knowing that they could not remain on Valdier. For as long as they remained on their home world, they—and their future true mate—would be in peril.

"There are Spaceports on the edge of the galaxy that are seldom visited by our kind. We could hire out," Brogan suggested.

Barrack nodded, taking a seat in the chair that his symbiot formed.

"We will stop and retrieve our stored items and leave before anyone is the wiser," he agreed.

They had moved deep into the mountains several years before when they first felt the edge of madness come upon them. Minutes later, they landed outside of the crude cottage they had built at the foot of the mountain near a wide river. They retrieved their clothing, food, tools, and weapons before returning to the symbiot spaceship.

Barrack looked down as their symbiot ship rose. He reached up and rubbed his chest. This was the only home they had ever known. They had lived, worked, and fought here. He wasn't sure if they would ever see Valdier or their parents again.

"We will return," Brogan said, looking down at the forest where they had made their home.

"How can you be sure?" Barrack asked, looking at his brother.

Brogan met his gaze. Barrack was shocked to see a haunted expression in his brother's eyes. He reached out, shocked again when he felt an unfamiliar wall blocking him from seeing Brogan's thoughts. He looked back at Brogan with a confused frown.

"What did Aikaterina show you, Brogan?" Barrack asked.

Barrack watched Brogan blink and turn his head to stare out the window as they accelerated out into space. He waited, unsure if Brogan was going to answer him. Brogan stared into the vastness of space as they moved farther away from Valdier.

"She showed me our mate," Brogan finally said, rising to his feet.

Barrack turned and followed Brogan with his eyes as his brother disappeared through the doorway. For a moment, jealousy ate at him. He wanted to see their mate. He wondered why Aikaterina didn't share the image with him. Then, the moment faded as he remembered the haunted look in Brogan's eyes. There was something else Brogan was not sharing with him, something important.

Rising to his feet, he gazed out into space with a frown. This was the first time they didn't share a secret. For some reason, Aikaterina must have decided only Brogan should know something about their true mate.

"We will find her," he murmured.

I wait. Goddess say she need us, his dragon replied.

Barrack blinked in surprise, feeling a warmth and excitement in his dragon that he had not felt in decades.

"Yes, our mate will need us," he agreed, a satisfied smile curving his lips.

~

Aikaterina watched over the village. The villagers would remember killing the twin dragons. Their memories would be fragmented, blurred, but there would be the knowledge that the twin dragons were dead. There would be grief, and she would need to pay close attention to the young twins. She had seen their mate and knew that they would be strong until they finally met her.

The original twin dragons' destinies were not yet set. They had centuries more to wait before their true mate would be born. She would have to give a guiding hand to help the threads of their lives intersect.

Unfortunately, that thread would be very short-lived. The threads of time would once again be restored and the incident that would have occurred today in the village would become their reality if the twin dragons could not convince their true mate that they belonged together—and if she did not accept them unconditionally and of her own free will. If they tried to force Delilah against her will, the natural course their union would negatively react, creating ripples that could have devastating effects. If that should happen, she would be force to release her control on the threads and allow history to continue in the natural order it had begun.

Aikaterina rose in the air, allowing the gentle breeze to carry her. She must return to the Hive, the home she had made in the cavern offshore, and rest. She could feel the strain of holding the fabric of time. For her, time was irrelevant when calculated in the terms of years. Still, she would feel this strain until the twin dragon's mate was born. She only hoped that the twin dragons, especially Brogan, would survive that long.

CHAPTER ONE

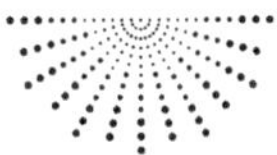

Outer rim of Valdier - Centuries later:

"Are you sure we were supposed to return here?" Barrack asked, pacing back and forth in the engine room of their spaceship.

"You felt the pull as well. Our symbiots said this was where we were supposed to go," Brogan's muffled voice snapped in irritation. "Hand me the splicer."

Barrack grimaced and looked through the array of tools spread out across the floor. Currently, he could only see half of his brother's body. The top half was under the power console that controlled the main engines.

"I thought you already repaired this," Barrack commented, handing Brogan the splicer.

"I did. The damn part that two-faced Tiliqua sold to me was faulty. I knew I should have looked somewhere else. Those two-headed bastards are always looking to make a quick credit," Brogan grumbled.

"I told…." Barrack started to say before he clamped his lips tightly together when Brogan slid out from under the console and shot him a heated glare.

"Not one word or I'll let you repair it this time," Brogan threatened.

Barrack gave his brother a sour look. "You know I hate working on machines. They hate me too," he retorted.

Brogan snorted. "'Hate' is a really mild version of the word I would use to describe you and anything to do with this spaceship," he replied before pulling himself back under the console.

"I can't believe after all this time, we are finally going to meet our true mate," Barrack said, lowering himself down until he was sitting on the floor next to his brother.

"What you really mean is you can't believe my dragon and I have kept our heads together this long without losing it," Brogan said.

Barrack chuckled. "That too," he admitted, leaning his head back. "What do you think she looks like? Is she from our village or the city? Do you really think that she can handle both of us? Goddess! Just the thought of her between us makes me hard."

Brogan listened as his older brother, by mere minutes, speculated on what their true mate would be like. He could understand Barrack's excitement. If his brother's dragon was bouncing around inside him like his was, then it was amazing that they had not shifted and destroyed their transport ship by now.

The image he kept close to his heart nearly choked him. Despite the passage of time, the image and the softly spoken names of those who would guide him and his brother to their true mate were the only things that had kept him sane.

Not that I was all that sane to start with, he thought, thinking of the long scars that ran down the side of his face and neck. He'd kept them deliberately to remind himself of the dangers he and his brother faced if they weren't careful.

The scars were the result of a fight he had with a group of youths from the village. They had separated him from his brother and his symbiot in the hope of killing him. The youths had listened to the fears of their parents. He hadn't understood at the time that his sometimes volatile temper had fed into their fear.

He had broken free and escaped, but not before he was injured. Their father had decided against punishing the youths, fearing it would cause more attacks. Instead, he had cautioned Brogan and Barrack to never be caught alone again or without their symbiots. Brogan decided he would leave the scars to remind him of the dangers he and his brother would face if they weren't careful.

Brogan had a tighter grip on his control now, because of her. He focused on his mental image of their mate's eyes, her sun-kissed, creamy mocha skin, her full lips, and her shoulder length black-brown hair streaked with gold. Throughout the years, he had clung to that image instead of the other one the Goddess had also shown him—the one of their mate lying peacefully upon the pristine white silk inside a small box, her young life cut short when it had barely even begun. Two threads of life revealed – one when Delilah was older and one when she was a child. Only they had the power to change her path.

"She is beautiful," he said.

"Tell me again," Barrack ordered.

Brogan's lips curved in wry amusement. If he had a credit for every time he had heard Barrack ask him that, they could have afforded a fleet of transports. He had tried to share the image, but nothing worked. It was strange. He could share everything else with Barrack except this.

"She has sun-kissed skin the color of the bark of the strongest trees in the forest, yet as smooth as the finest silk," he began.

"Meaning she can handle the fiercest storms," Barrack said.

"Yes. Her hair reaches just below her smooth shoulders where the dark strands are threaded with gold streaks," Brogan continued, knowing what his brother would say next.

"The touch of the Goddess to guide us to her and let us know that she is ours," Barrack replied with a sigh.

Brogan chuckled. "Yes," he agreed.

He bit back another chuckle when he felt Barrack kick his foot.

They'd had this discussion a million times before, yet Barrack was acting as if it was the first time. He winced when Barrack hit his leg.

"Ouch! Be careful, my leg is still sore," he stated.

Barrack grunted. "It wouldn't be if you'd let your symbiot run over you again. You should have known there would be another mercenary hiding behind the counter," he stated.

"It's still mad at me for refusing to wear my armor. Is that why you let me go in first, so that I would get the knife in the thigh instead of you?" Brogan demanded, wincing when he scraped his knuckles on the edge of the console. "Why do they make these panels so damn small? Do they think only the Tiliqua work on these things?"

"Probably.... Tell me about her lips," Barrack said.

Brogan finished splicing the wires together and pulled himself out from under the console. He sat up and laid the splicer next to the rest of his tools. He gave his symbiot a rueful smile when the gold creature trotted into the room.

He lifted his bleeding hand. The symbiot snorted, but melted. Warmth surrounded his hand, healing his new cut before moving up his arm and down his body, repairing the bruises and the deep cut on his thigh, which he had sealed as best he could with a portable medical kit.

"Her lips were made for us. They are full and lush while her eyes are dark and inviting. They glitter with determination and amusement. She loves to laugh," Brogan said, leaning his head against the edge of the console and breathing a sigh of relief as the dull ache in his thigh faded. "Her breasts...."

"Her breasts were made to fit in our hands," Barrack finished, lifting his hands and studying his palms. "I wonder if she will mind that my hands are rough."

Brogan raised an eyebrow at that comment. "Don't get all regal on me. I doubt our mate expects to meet nobility," he dryly stated.

Barrack shot him an exasperated look, then rolled to his feet. Brogan grinned at Barrack. His brother shook his head at him and gave him a sardonic smile.

"I don't think you'll ever have to worry about being mistaken for nobility," Barrack stated, "but we are wealthy in our own right. We will have enough to build our mate a home anywhere she wishes, and we will buy her gowns—which, of course, we'll rip off her luscious body—and then we'll buy her more gowns and anything else she desires."

"Why buy her gowns to rip off when we could just ask her to go naked?" Brogan asked, rising to his feet and collecting his tools. "My dragon would be happy if she remained in her dragon form for at least a century!"

"We could ask her about that," Barrack agreed with a grin. "She could either remain naked or in her dragon form. Either would be acceptable."

"I wonder if...," Brogan started to say before he shook his head.

"You wonder what?" Barrack asked, helping Brogan put the tools back in the storage cabinet.

Brogan paused and looked at his brother. "I wonder how she will react when she meets us," he said.

"She will love us at first sight," Barrack said with confidence before he chuckled and slapped Brogan's shoulder, reminding him of another bruise he forgot about. Brogan muttered a silent thank you to his symbiot when the creature moved over the tender spot. As he took the last of the tools from Barrack, the memory of their mate's determined eyes flashed through his mind. Brogan wasn't quite as confident as his brother about their reception. He wasn't so sure what she had been looking at in the glimpse of her that the Goddess had given, but something told him that he and Barrack didn't want to be on the receiving end of whatever had put that look in her eyes.

Earth: Alleghany County, NC - Current Day:

"DeWayne Davis, you'd better get your butt out of here before I load it full of lead," Delilah Rosewater swore, pointing the empty shotgun at the small-town lawyer from West Jefferson.

"Now, Delilah, you can't go pointing guns at people," DeWayne sputtered defensively as he raised his hands and stumbled back down the uneven steps of the large wooden farmhouse. "I've got legitimate business here."

Delilah nodded at the small sign nailed to the railing of the front porch. "For a lawyer, you sure don't know how to read very well. That sign says 'No Soliciting'. That means you, DeWayne," she said, taking another step across the worn front porch.

"I've been authorized to make you an offer, Delilah. I know how much this house and property means to you, which is why I'm working to get you a good deal," DeWayne explained, stumbling on the uneven stone walkway at the bottom of the steps.

"I'm not interested in selling. I don't owe nobody nothing, – and the fact that you've just pissed me off even more by making me mad enough to be talking like I don't have a college education has just infuriated me even more. I don't have time for this. Now, get in your car, DeWayne, and get off my property," Delilah demanded.

DeWayne clenched his free hand while his other gripped the leather satchel. He glared up at where she was standing on the porch. She knew from the way his jaw tightened that he wasn't going to go this time without having his say. For once, she wished she had actually loaded her grandfather's old shotgun.

"Mountain View Properties wants to make an offer on your property. Mr. Lister is willing to pay you twice the amount it's worth, Delilah. I could write you a check by the end of the week if you agree," DeWayne said, reaching into his worn, brown leather satchel.

"I tell you what, DeWayne, if you take those papers and put them in my burn barrel on the way out, I won't think about shooting you in the ass. For the last time, I'm not selling my grandparents' property. Not now, not ever! You think I don't know what it is really worth? They aren't offering me a fraction of the value! All they want to do is cut down all the trees on the mountain and turn the meadow into a golf course. It... is... not... happening," she snarled the last part slowly so he could understand once and for all that she wasn't interested.

"Delilah, listen… I can make a counter offer. You know the price of land has been going up. Lots of city folks are buying property in the mountains nowadays. You've got a lot of valuable land just sitting here going to waste. The views—well, if this were in California, you'd be a millionaire a dozen times over. Just think about it! You've still got your folk's old house in town. You could sell this place and move back there. Hell, you work at the library! It is practically across the street from that house," DeWayne said.

Delilah's mouth tightened. That was his second mistake, thinking he could sweet talk her with the promise of money. His first one was coming out here. His third one was taking a step closer.

"You've been warned, DeWayne. For such a big shot lawyer you sure don't pay attention. I'm surprised that I have to remind you – again – that you should read the signs before you step on someone's property, especially after they told you not to come back again after the last time you were here," she commented, bracing the heavy gun against her side and reaching for the front door. "I'll count to three before I open the door."

Delilah smiled when she saw DeWayne's eyes flash to the second sign under the first one. The huge red letters were written twice as big as the No Soliciting sign—Beware of Dog. She smothered a chuckle when she saw him swallow and shove his papers back into his bag.

"One," she called, gripping the doorknob.

"Delilah, the sheriff….," he started to argue as he stepped backwards.

"Won't do a thing, DeWayne, you know that. You're trespassing. You passed a dozen posted signs on your way up here," she said. "Two."

"Come on, Delilah. At least listen to the offer," DeWayne begged, his eyes moving between her and the door.

"Time's up. Three," she warned, thankful she had propped the screen door open otherwise she would have been adding a replacement door to her budget. "Get him, Moonshine. Sic-em, Rum."

"Aw shit! Delilah!" DeWayne cursed as he turned on his polished heel and took off clumsily toward his car.

Delilah stood back as the two massive Rottweilers tore through the open door, cleared the front porch in two steps, and leaped off. She crossed to the steps and watched as DeWayne yanked open the passenger door to his car and dove inside. She chuckled when she saw that he barely had time to pull the door closed before Moonshine jumped up, slamming the door shut the rest of the way. The loud and impressive snarls, foaming white slobber, and sharp rows of teeth sent DeWayne scrambling over the center console into the driver's seat.

Afraid that DeWayne might hurt the dogs in his haste to depart, Delilah raised her fingers to her lips and loudly whistled. The two dogs' heads immediately turned toward her. She raised her hand, giving the silent command to come.

From the porch of her grandparents' house, she watched in satisfaction as DeWayne took off down the long, winding driveway. If he didn't slow down, he would miss the curve about three quarters of the way down and end up in the creek.

She propped the gun up against the railing and waited, listening just in case she needed to call the sheriff. Breathing a sigh of relief when she didn't hear anything, she looked down at the dogs with a grin. They whined and wagged their little tails at her with affection.

"You two did very well. I think that deserves a treat," she laughed, scratching each dog behind the ear. There was no need for DeWayne to know that the only thing these two would do was sit on him and lick him to death. "Come on. Daylight is burning, and I still have a lot of work to do," she said, picking up the old shotgun, which she wasn't even sure worked anymore, and heading for the front door.

She pulled the screen door closed behind her as she went inside. The house was still a bit musty from being closed up, so she left the front door partially open. She propped the shotgun next to the door and walked across through the foyer to the back of the house. Placing her hands on her hips, she looked at the work she had already finished so far. It wasn't bad, even if she said so herself.

She shivered as a draft of cold air swept through the house. She had left the kitchen and mudroom doors open to get a cross ventilation. The mudroom was currently a storage room for most of the items from the kitchen she was renovating.

Some people would call her crazy for rebuilding a house that should have been torn down forty years ago. By the time she was done, city folks would pay her a fortune for a retreat like this from their hectic lives. She honestly didn't give a damn about anyone's opinion since she didn't plan on selling the house or the property. This was her heritage, and she was going to keep it. Hopefully one day, she could pass the house and land on to her kids.

"If I ever have any," she grumbled under her breath as she pulled on the long rubber gloves and got back to work.

Late that night, Delilah was stiff, sore, and beyond exhausted, but she felt good. All the kitchen cabinets were sanded and prepped for a nice coat of varnish. The house had been breathtaking when she was little. Her grandparents had kept it immaculate. After their death, her parents tried to keep it up, but between the lack of money and their health, the house was eventually boarded up.

The one thing Delilah had always been thankful for was that her mother insisted that the house and property would be passed down to her. For the past year, she had been working on it. Her job as the county librarian paid her an adequate amount if she watched her budget.

She had kept her dad's old truck. It was old enough that she could repair most of the stuff on it without having to hook it up to a computer like the newer trucks. The property and her grandparent's old house, along with the house in town, were paid for. Her mom had left her a small life insurance policy that she had never touched. It wasn't much, but twenty thousand dollars was a nice rainy day fund.

Life was good - for the most part, she thought with a sigh.

She sat wrapped up in a thick throw on the front porch swing, sipping hot chocolate, and gently swaying back and forth with both dogs by her feet. All around her, fireflies twinkled in the trees. With all the lights off inside the house and no street lights, the night was so dark that without the full moon she wouldn't have been able to see her hand in front of her face.

Leaning her head back, she listened to the lonesome howl of a coyote. She wasn't worried about the coyotes or bears. The two dogs would give her warning as well as scare away any critters that tried to get too close.

"Well, give me another six months, and I think the house will be like new—for a hundred-year-old house," Delilah wearily chuckled and then let out another sigh. "I need to get some sleep, but I don't want to."

She looked down at Rum when he raised his head and whined. The dogs helped, but they couldn't protect her from the nightmares that were plaguing her dreams night after night with growing intensity.

She twisted her lips in sardonic amusement. Well, not all of her dreams were nightmares—as long as she didn't mind the fact that there were two very hot, sexy, and extremely horny guys in them. She shook her head. She really should quit reading those romance novels the ladies in town kept donating and start reading up on things like how to fix a fifty-year-old furnace so that she didn't have to buy a new one. Of course, the romances were much more interesting to read. Hell, even a few of the men were hooked on the stories—for the action and adventure, not the romance, of course.

"Can you believe seventy-three-year-old Mr. Cooks has an eReader now?" she told Rum. "I wonder if the dreams will go away if I stop reading those books. What do you think?"

"Woof," Rum responded.

Moonshine stood up, whined, and nudged her hand. Delilah laughed and shook her head. It was past their bedtime. The dogs were funny. They had routines and bedtime was at ten o'clock. If she was late, they would bug her until she gave in.

She gripped the blanket around her and rose from the swing. Walking across the porch, she tested a spongy board under her foot with a grimace before she continued to the front door. Opening the screen door, she pushed open the front door and waited for the dogs to enter. She followed them, closing the screen door and hooking it before she closed and locked the front door behind her.

She followed the dogs up the narrow stairs to the second level and down the hall to the master bedroom. Stepping inside, she smiled at her concession to modern times—a new bed that was big enough for her, as well as Moonshine, and Rum. She had decided on a King size bed after discovering that a full size just wasn't big enough given that the two dogs tended to forget that it was *her* bed not just theirs.

"Oh, no! You two are *not* stretching out on my side. You have your comforter on your side of the bed. The other side is my side. Move your big asses over," she ordered as she headed to the bathroom.

"I'm soaking tonight. You two don't get into anything and stay out of the bathroom," she playfully ordered.

Moonshine mouthed off. She wasn't sure if it was because she banned him from her side of the bed or the bathroom. If she wasn't careful, the two boneheads would try to climb into the claw foot tub with her again. The one and only time that had happened, it had been an uncomfortable, very wet and extremely messy incident. It was definitely not something she was eager to repeat.

Grabbing her nightgown and a pair of panties from the small suitcase she brought with her, she headed for the bathroom. Turning on the water, she breathed a sigh of pleasure as the hot water filled the large tub. She thought back to the renovations on the house.

After making sure the house's foundation and outside structure were in good shape, she had started on the roof and worked her way down. She had installed the new metal roof with the help of a couple of friends from town. The good thing about being the local librarian was that she knew most of the women in town, who knew most of the men. A few carefully shared comments and she had a dozen healthy men helping her one weekend.

There had been numerous strapping teenagers, a couple of fathers —to watch the strapping teenagers, one or two single brothers with matchmaking sisters, and three old-timers who came to oversee the entire project. Of course, that meant the women had to come and feed the men, which led to the rebuilding of the old corn crib and Model-T sheds, repairs to the porches and railings, and the removal of the old outhouse and chicken coop. The teenagers had handled the bonfire that followed.

It had been like the old days when the residents would get together to raise a house or barn. There had been a steady stream of visitors every weekend for the last six months. Some people stopped by to check in on her and make sure that she hadn't fallen off a ladder, while others stopped by in the hope of getting her to go out on a date with them—including DeWayne.

She shook her head as she pinned up her hair, so that it wouldn't get wet. Removing her clothes, she tossed them into the basket. She leaned over, turned off the water, then placed the towel within easy reach. Lifting a foot, she tested the water with her toes before she stepped into the steaming water.

"Oh yes," she moaned as she lowered herself into the tub.

She sank down, leaned back against the tub, and stretched out her legs, loving the fact that she could. Hanging her arms over the sides so that she didn't sink below the water, she sighed and looked up at the ceiling as the heat worked its magic on her sore muscles.

"Now, if I can just sleep without the dreams," she murmured, closing her eyes and trying to relax.

Her dreams were divided into two groups: erotic annoyances and terrifying nightmares. Out of the two, she preferred the first. Because the same dreams were occurring over and over every night, she had resorted to reading everything she could get her hands on in the library about the meaning of dreams. When that failed to solve the problem, she drove to Boone to see a psychologist.

She should have saved herself the money. Purchasing something for the house would have been a helluva lot more useful. First, the psychologist wanted to know what medications she was taking and if she was doing drugs—no. Then, the doc had asked about her recent or current relationships. Delilah had laughed at that one—none. Then, came the hang-ups about family—nope, nada. Yes, her parents died young, but they had always been a loving family. Her dad had worked too much but had a great sense of humor and loved her mom to distraction. Her mom had one of those quirky personalities that everyone loved, especially kids during story hour at the library. The most unusual fact about her family may have been that her dad was black while her mom was white—and no, Delilah didn't have any hang-ups about that either. It was life. Her parents had adored each other as much as they had adored her. Who could have a problem with that?

Delilah wondered if that was why she had accepted relatively easily that their deaths had happened so close together. Her dad had worked in the coal mines of Virginia and Kentucky, and he had suffered the effects of black lung as well as smoking too much. Her mom had died from undiagnosed pneumonia a few months after her father died, but Delilah thought if it hadn't been that, it would have been something else. Her father's death had truly sucked the life out of her mother.

Of course, at first, Delilah was heartbroken. It hadn't been until she went through a box of love letters that her mother saved that she realized the extent of the intensely close relationship her parents had shared. Every day that her father was away, he had sent a letter to her mother. Sometimes he had written poems to her interspersed with what he had done that day. Reading them with his letters, it gave her an image of her father that she never would have had if her mother had not saved the letters.

The psychologist had become frustrated when none of the usual diagnoses fit Delilah. How did you make a connection between two sexy guys who looked like something out of a wrestling magazine, dragons, and some kind of golden shape-shifting creatures _ all of whom wanted to do things that gave her hot flashes far too early in life – with her parent's deaths? When the psychologist couldn't figure that one out, she focused on the terrifying dreams of herself dying.

She finally told the woman she agreed that the dream of dying could be connected with her parents' sudden deaths. Delilah didn't believe it for a second, but it had been the only way to shut the woman up and get out of her office before she charged for another hour of her totally useless time. Frustrated, Delilah had decided to try to solve the problem on her own.

"Focus, Delilah. Pick the dream apart and see where it might have a connection to something going on in your life," she murmured, trying a technique that she read about in one of the books about dream therapy.

"I die younger than I am now, so it can't be real," she whispered, pulling up the image of her lying in the bed.

She smiled when she turned her head and almost saw the other little girl sitting by her side, holding her hand. She curled her fingers around the side of the tub. Sara Wilson—her best friend and sister-of-the-heart. Sara had slipped into her bedroom after the doctor had told Delilah's mom to keep everyone away.

"What's wrong, Delilah? Are you sick like the other kids?" Sara asked.

Delilah tried to nod, but she was too tired. Her fingers twitched when Sara wrapped her small hand around hers. It was so hard to breathe and her chest hurt.

"I'll tell them to let Auntie give you some medicine. These modern docs don't know nothing about healing people. Auntie has herbs that will make you feel better. She is teaching me," Sara whispered, afraid of being overheard.

"Don't... leave... me," Delilah pleaded, trying to draw enough air into her lungs. Her eyes closed and her fingers trembled. "I'm ... scared, ... Sara."

"I won't leave you," Sara promised.

Delilah could feel the tears slip down her cheeks. She opened her eyes and blinked. Perhaps this wasn't about her, but about Sara. Sitting up, she wrapped her arms around her legs. Sara had left when she was sixteen. They had kept in touch, sending emails back and forth. Sara moved to Columbia a couple years ago, and told Delilah all about her studies and life there, but a little over a year ago, all correspondence had suddenly stopped—when Sara disappeared.

"Maybe this is about Sara. Maybe I need to find her," Delilah said, raising a wet hand to wipe her cheeks. "Damn it! Why didn't I think of this before?"

Guilt washed through her. She had accepted the University and government's findings that Sara was dead, but what if she wasn't, and Sara was reaching out to her somehow? Delilah leaned forward and pulled the drain plug. She had immersed herself in the house renovations when she should have been devoting herself to finding her friend.

Cursing under her breath at her own selfishness, she rose from the tub and grabbed the towel. She had to go back to work tomorrow. She had no idea where to start, but she would figure it out. Hell, part of a librarian's job was to do research. She would start looking tomorrow. She had plenty of resources at her fingertips.

She dried off and dressed in an oversized nightshirt that said 'Bite me and I'll bite back' with a picture of a grinning Rottweiler on the front. Pulling off the hair clip, she ran her fingers through her hair. Confident that she was finally on the right track in resolving the issue of her dreams, she hung up the damp towel and walked into the bedroom before coming to an abrupt stop. She glared at the bed.

"Oh, hell no! I did not spend a small fortune for you damn dogs. Get your ass off my side," she growled, stomping over to the bed where the two Rottweilers were sprawled with their heads on her pillow.

CHAPTER TWO

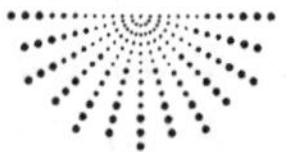

Barrack guided their transport toward the spaceport in orbit around Valdier. A muscle ticked in his jaw. This would be their first major obstacle to overcome.

"How much do you want to bet that we get stopped?" Brogan commented, sliding into the seat next to him.

"We should have used the symbiots," Barrack answered.

Brogan chuckled and cracked his knuckles. "I told you that before we left Kardosa. You should have listened to me," he said, leaning forward and staring out at the spaceport. "Their technology has changed a lot over the centuries."

"We already knew that from what we saw at the outer rim," Barrack retorted, ignoring his brother's jab.

"This is the Valdier Command Spaceport. State your business," a voice ordered over the communications system.

Barrack bit back a growl of frustration when Brogan reached forward and opened the link. As per usual, his brother wanted to charge into things without even considering a less intrusive method—preferably one that didn't require fighting or escaping from a prison cell. They'd had those results a considerable number of times over the past couple of centuries. The scar gracing Brogan's cheek was evidence of their last encounter with a Marastin Dow warship and the battle that ensued.

"We are looking for a warrior named Jaguin with a mate named Sara. Where are they?" Brogan demanded.

Barrack shook his head. "Smooth, Brogan, real smooth. Why don't you beat your chest as well?" he retorted.

"This is the Valdier Command Spaceport, please report to Dock A4-8 for clearance," the voice replied.

"Affirmative," Barrack replied, cutting the communications and following the lighted path to the docking station. "So much for telling them we are simple merchants."

Brogan shrugged. "I forgot. What does it matter? We must find this Jaguin and his mate, why not get it over with?" he said, pulling his laser pistol from the sheath at his waist and checking the weapon to make sure it was fully charged.

Barrack bit the inside of his cheek. If they were thrown in a cell because of Brogan again, he was going to leave his brother there. He wasn't about to lose their only chance of finding their mate because of Brogan's temper.

~

Zoran Reykill frowned as he purposely strode down the corridor of the Spaceport. His brothers, Creon, Kelan, and Mandra, followed. Crew members swiftly moved to the side and stood at attention as they passed.

Zoran paused as he reached a set of double doors. The two guards standing outside pressed their hands to their chest before opening the doors for him and his brothers. Trelon Reykill turned when he saw his brother enter and raised an eyebrow.

"I didn't expect all of you to come," Trelon commented, walking over to Zoran when the small group stopped.

"We were having a meeting when you notified us," Zoran said, glancing over Trelon's shoulder to the detention cell block. "Are you sure it is them?"

Trelon nodded. "There is no mistake," he said with a disbelieving shake of his head.

"Where did they come from?" Mandra asked.

"Kardosa Spaceport was the last place their ship was registered. They wiped everything else clean," Trelon answered.

Kelan frowned. "I could take a look," he suggested.

Trelon shook his head. "Cara already went over their system. Trust me, it is clean. She is impressed with the repairs done on the engines. She said some of the parts were shitty and they were lucky they made it this far," he chuckled.

"What about their symbiots?" Zoran asked.

Trelon shrugged. "They remained docile when we took the twins into custody," he said.

Zoran glanced at Creon, who was standing silently to the side, listening. The reason the four other brothers had come was partially out of curiosity, but mostly out of concern. Fortunately, Creon knew more about twin dragons than any of them. Not only was he close friends with Cree and Calo – twin dragons who had been children when Barrack and Brogan had supposedly died – he and Carmen also had a set of very young twins.

His brothers were determined to come with him, and not just to satisfy their curiosity; this was a matter of Valdier's defense. It would take their combined strength to defeat the seasoned original twin dragon warriors. The only other warriors who might stand a chance of defeating the original twin dragons were Cree and Calo—twin dragons themselves.

Twin dragons were not ordinary warriors. They were nearly unbeatable in battle, working as one with a skill and power that rivaled that of those of the royal blood. Zoran hadn't admitted to his brothers that he had been half expecting the twins. In truth, he hadn't been sure if the dream he'd had the night before had been real or not. He was about to find out.

"Take me to them," Zoran ordered. Creon stepped forward. "We'll go with you," he quietly said.

Zoran started to shake his head before he paused. He saw the determined expression on his brother's face and knew that Creon would not take no for an answer. Out of all of them, Creon knew more about twin dragons than any of them.

"Very well," Zoran said.

Trelon led them down the short corridor to a holding cell. Behind the clear shield were two men, identical except for the fact that one had several long scars running down one side of his face and neck. The men looked up.

"Open the shield," Zoran quietly ordered.

Brogan watched as the tall, powerful Valdier warrior entered the room. The deference of his dragon and his symbiot let him know this was a man of royal blood.

"I am Zoran Reykill," the man introduced himself with a nod of his head.

"I'm Brogan, this is my brother, Barrack," Brogan replied.

"We met your father once when we were young. He was a good warrior," Barrack quietly said.

"Yes, he was," Zoran replied, tightening his lips.

Brogan glanced at the source of his dragon's uneasiness - the man standing next to Zoran and the ones behind him. Zoran was certainly dangerous, but a good leader had to be tempered and wise. The man standing next to him had a roiling darkness within him that Brogan could relate to on a primitive, savage level. The others were on a varying level between the two men standing in front.

"This is Creon," Zoran said with a nod. "The others are Mandra, Trelon, and Kelan."

"Brogan, Barrack," Creon greeted with a brief nod.

"Now that introductions are done, we want to know where a Valdier warrior named Jaguin and his mate are located," Brogan stated in a blunt tone.

"Getting out of this detention cell and off the Spaceport would be helpful, too," Barrack dryly added.

Brogan shrugged his shoulders. "We can handle that. Do you know who this warrior is and where we can find him?" he asked.

Zoran raised an eyebrow, and Brogan thought that perhaps he should have rephrased his question so it didn't come out more like a command. Better yet, he should have let Barrack do the talking. His brother had a much better temperament for negotiating than he did, but Barrack had grown quiet the moment they had docked.

"Yes, I know Jaguin and his mate, Sara. I also know why you are here," Zoran replied.

"You… How?" Brogan demanded, taken aback.

Zoran's gaze held a seriousness that carried weight and his expression was stern. Once again, Brogan was reminded that he was no longer at the outer rim, but on Valdier in the presence of the powerful leader of all the dragon-shifting species.

"I received an unexpected visit in my dreams from a certain Goddess who appears to have taken a liking to you both," Zoran dryly replied.

"I can't imagine why," Creon muttered under his breath.

"Neither can I," Zoran agreed with an amused grin.

Brogan glanced at Barrack, who was silently standing near the wall.

"I have one more question that I hope you can answer," Barrack quietly interrupted.

Zoran turned to study Barrack's expression. "If I can, I will answer it," he replied.

Brogan saw a hint of indecision flash through Barrack's eyes. It took a moment for the image in his brother's mind to appear. When it did, he could feel his stomach clench.

"Do you know if our parents still live?" Barrack asked.

Creon spoke this time. "Yes, they both live in the same village," he said.

Brogan turned his head to look at Creon. "How do you know?" he asked in a voice that was rougher than normal.

Creon grinned. "Cree and Calo's mate, Melina, kicked your younger brother's ass," he chuckled.

"They are alive," Barrack repeated, a slow grin curving his lips.

Brogan blanched. "We have a brother?" he said.

"You have missed a lot since you have been gone, but your journey is not yet over. Come, we will return to the palace, and I will explain what I know and help you as best as I can," Zoran stated, signaling them to follow him.

Brogan looked at Barrack. "Cree and Calo have a mate," he said, his expression changing to remorse when he remembered his cruel words to the younger twins so long ago.

"If they found a mate, that means there really is hope for us," Barrack pointed out to him.

CHAPTER THREE

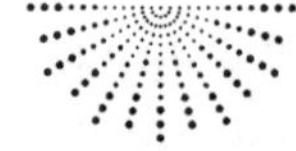

Barrack gazed around the palace grounds. Over the centuries, he and his brother had spent most of their time either on Spaceports along the Outer Rim of the Star System or alien planets that ranged from desert conditions to water worlds. Some had been brutal, while others had been beautiful, but none of them had given him a sense of peace like this one did. He was home.

We home, his dragon chortled, pushing at him to release him. *I fly.*

Not yet. We must learn where this warrior and his mate are first so that we can find our true mate, was Barrack's silent reply.

Want to fly, his dragon moaned in regret.

Barrack understood his dragon's growing restlessness. There was not a lot of room on a Spaceport, especially for a dragon. Their need to fly, to release their dragons had been one of the reasons they had been forced to visit other worlds.

In the end, their time on these worlds had given them a chance to see and do things most warriors would have missed. They had heard about the Great War between the Curizan and Sarafin, but never fought in it. The few Curizan and Sarafin they had met had been like them, nomads – a species without a home world searching for a place where they could survive until they were ready for the next phase of their life.

"My dragon itches to be released," Brogan muttered, rubbing at his arm where the scales were rippling up and down.

"Mine as well," Barrack quietly responded.

Barrack watched while his brother while he looked around the courtyard as they crossed to another building in the palace. They had transported down, leaving their spaceship above. Their symbiots trotted behind them, reflecting the brilliant colors of the plants and sky in their excitement.

"It feels good to be back," Brogan softly admitted.

Barrack gave a brief nod. They followed Zoran and Creon up the steps. He resisted the urge to look over his shoulders at the other two brothers who followed silently behind them. Only the one called Trelon had remained in space.

The small group paused and turned when the happy sound of squeals came from behind them. He watched as two small dragons, one red and pink, the other pink and red darted out from under a low hedge. A moment later, a small blue one emerged.

"Jabir," Mandra Reykill suddenly called.

The small, plump dragonling stopped so quickly that he tripped over his front feet and did a roll in the grass. Barrack watched in fascination as the huge prince hurried down the steps they had just climbed to the little dragonling.

"Are you alright?" Mandra asked, bending and lifting up the dragonling in his arms.

The dragonling growled down at the other two dragonlings when they peered through the bushes at him. A moment later the dragonling shimmered and shifted. The small, slightly chubby boy was the spitting image of the huge Valdier prince. The boy wiped his nose before he leaned forward and wrapped his arms around Mandra's neck.

"We are playing tags," Jabir stated. "Mommy and Aunt Carmen is looking for us," he added, looking over at the Barrack.

"Does you have dragonlings? They can plays with us," Jabir said with a smile.

"No, we have no younglings," Barrack replied, fascinated by the small dragonling."

"Mandra," a woman's breathless voice called.

"Barrack," Brogan murmured, stepping closer to his twin.

Barrack absently nodded his head. His eyes were locked on the same thing as were his brother's – the woman running toward them. Her white-gold hair was pulled back from her face. It swung behind her as she jogged up to them. A brilliant smile lit her unusual face.

"Sorry about that," she laughed, reaching her arms out for the little boy.

"Aw, Daddy. You got me tagged," Jabir complained, giggling when the woman tickled him.

"Now you get to tag me," she teased, lifting him into her arms.

Barrack stiffened in surprise when she drew back and smiled up at him and Brogan. The woman's eyes danced with mirth and a hint of curiosity as she looked back at him with a friendly expression. He could feel his brother's confusion as well. Every person they had met for the first time from the time they were younglings had looked at them with caution or fear. There was neither in this woman's gaze.

"Hi, I'm Ariel Reykill. This little guy is Jabir," she greeted.

"She's my mate," Mandra added, a slight growl of warning in his voice.

"Yes, I am. By the way, I just tagged you, too, so you get to cook dinner with Jabir tonight," she teased.

"Yay!! I wants worms!" Jabir exclaimed in delight.

"Not again," Mandra groaned. "We had worms last night."

"If it helps, we've had something called macaroni and cheese for three nights in a row," Kelan chuckled.

"Better than the stuff called peanut butter and jelly," Zoran muttered. "I have banned Cara from replicating any more of that disgusting mixture."

"Are you serious? The girls and I love the stuff!" Creon exclaimed, surprising the other men and causing everyone to laugh.

"You might as well forget it, Zoran. You'd have a rebellion on your hands," Ariel chuckled as she bent to set the little boy down on the ground.

Barrack watched as the little boy immediately shifted and took off after the two little dragonlings who had been watching them from the bushes. His gaze moved back to the woman when she released a sigh. In fascination, he watched as she reached up and brushed a lingering kiss against Mandra's lips.

"I'd better go. Amber and Jade have been constructing booby-traps throughout the garden. Carmen and Trisha are finding them while Abby and I chase the kids. I'll see you later, big guy," she murmured, her eyes flashing with an emotion that Barrack didn't understand at first until he saw the fire of desire burning in the other warrior's eyes. "It was nice to meet both of you."

Barrack's eyes followed the woman as she took off after the squealing children. His mind was still trying to process the fact that this female appeared unconcerned that she had been in the presence of twin dragons. He started when he sensed the others turning to continue to their destination. Brogan caught his attention and he could sense confusion in him as well. They had a lot to learn.

An hour later, he and Brogan stood in the empty conference room staring out at the garden. Their conversation had been brief. Zoran had not asked many questions, which had confused both of them. But there had been genuine sincerity in the other man's eyes that did not cause any sense of alarm.

"Do you believe him?" Brogan asked.

Barrack's mouth tightened for a moment before he shrugged. "We know it is possible," he replied. "I don't remember seeing women such as them before. They are not Valdier, yet they can shift into a dragon."

Brogan shrugged. "Lord Kelan called them a human. I have not heard of the species before. Perhaps they are dragon-shifters as well. Do you want a drink?" he asked, turning away from the window.

Barrack shook his head. He could feel his brother's impatience. While he was anxious to find Jaguin and his mate and retrieve his and Brogan's true mate, he was also curious about the scene in front of them. His lips twitched when one of the women suddenly shifted and began chasing two dragonlings. One was white, while the other was black. There was something different about the black dragonling. Her wings and tail reminded him more of a bird than a dragon. Both dragonlings squealed in delight and took off running with the female behind them.

"Brogan, look!" Barrack hissed, holding his breath.

Brogan looked up and walked over. He heard his brother's swiftly inhaled breath. The black dragonling rose up into the air. He noticed that when she passed through a shadow cast by a tree that she completely disappeared.

"The white one, Barrack," Brogan pointed out.

Ripping his eyes away from the black dragonling, he watched as the white dragonling began digging with incredible speed. One moment she was there, the next she was gone. The female dragon pounced on the hole and looked down.

Both men released a startled chuckle when the female dragon suddenly rolled to the side. Barrack's eyes narrowed when he saw the reason behind her sudden move. A large black dragon suddenly appeared. The female snapped at the male and they circled each other.

"She needs help," Brogan growled, placing the glass in his hand down on a table near the window.

"No, watch, there is something else," Barrack said, reaching out and grabbing his brother's arm.

Barrack felt Brogan's jerk of surprise under his hand when the female suddenly turned, wrapped her tail around the male's front legs, and pulled him off balance. The move caught the larger dragon unawares and he was flipped, landing on his back with his wings spread out. In a flash, the female was on top of him, her mouth wrapped around his throat.

"The younglings," Brogan muttered in concern when he saw the tiny black dragonling appear out of the shadows.

"They are family," Barrack said, watching as the white dragonling popped out of the hole, grabbed the ear of the huge male dragon, and began pulling on it. "Ouch!"

Unexpected pleasure washed through him when he heard Brogan chuckling. Long forgotten memories of themselves wrestling with their father returned. Along with those memories came a wave of regret.

"It is one of the Princes," Brogan murmured.

"Lord Creon. That must be his mate and younglings," Barrack stated.

Before their eyes, they watched the family of dragons shift. The two dragonlings transformed into little girls who looked as if they were the same age. One had the black hair of her father while the other had the sun-kissed gold of her mother. Two things hit the twin dragons at the same time, leaving them both shaken as they watched what could only be a miracle. First, there were two females – a rare sight from when they were growing up. The second was the knowledge that they were staring at twin dragons – female twin dragons.

"We have been gone far too long, brother," Barrack murmured. "I could use that drink after all."

CHAPTER FOUR

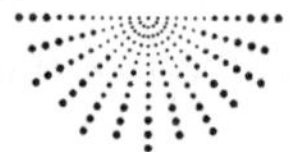

Several hours later, Barrack stood next to his brother at the edge of the forest. Excitement was building inside him along with an uncharacteristic nervousness. They would meet their mate soon. After centuries of waiting, the endless wait would be over. He and Brogan had done nothing but talk about what they would do on the entire trip here.

"She'll probably be less frightened of you," Brogan had said. "I think you should approach her first. You can explain to her that she is our mate, introduce her to me, and then we claim her."

"Aikaterina said she must accept us of her own free will," Barrack reminded his brother.

Brogan shrugged. "Once she sees your unmarked face, she will be fine. If I remember, you didn't have any trouble finding an interested woman," he remarked.

"I'd rather not remember," Barrack grumbled, thinking of some of the females who had propositioned him with a shudder.

"We can wait on the claim—for a day or two. You are right, she might be frightened at first," Brogan muttered with a frown.

"That warrior looks like the one Zoran told us about," Barrack commented, looking at the man who was quietly talking with a woman who had the same color hair as the one from the garden.

"You'd better do the talking," Brogan grunted, eyeing the warrior with an assessing gaze. "I'll cover your back."

Barrack nodded. Rolling his shoulders, he stepped out of the woods and began walking toward the warrior and the woman. They turned when they saw him and Brogan. His dragon woke with an intense awareness, eager to see his mate.

"You are the one called Jaguin?" Barrack called in a loud voice.

The man they suspected to be Jaguin turned to face them. He moved until he was slightly in front of the woman. It was obvious from his stance that he was her mate.

"Yes. Who are you?" Jaguin replied, his jaw tightening when he saw Brogan following slightly to the left.

Barrack studied the woman named Sara for a moment. She was like the women from the garden—a human. He could see her defiance and her fear. Zoran had warned him to be careful around Sara, explaining that she had been through things that would have broken the strongest warrior.

"I will personally slit both of your throats if you upset her," Zoran had warned.

Barrack had no doubt that the Valdier King meant what he said. Shame swept through him as he remembered their behavior toward Mula. Never again would they cause such a look of fear to appear in a woman's eyes.

He bowed his head. "I am Barrack. This is my brother, Brogan. We have need of a tracker." Barrack quietly said in greeting.

Jaguin stared at him with an expression of distrust. "Why?" he demanded, his eyes narrowing.

Barrack wanted to groan when his brother stepped forward. "To find our true mate," Brogan impatiently stated.

A touch of unexpected humor caused Jaguin's lips to twitch. "You have lost her?" Jaguin asked with a raised eyebrow.

"We have never found her," Barrack finally confessed.

Jaguin stared incredulously at them. "How do you expect me to find her if you don't even know who she is?" he asked.

Barrack's gaze moved over Jaguin's shoulder to the woman quietly standing behind him. He could sense her hesitation and agitation before he heard her draw in a deep breath. The man in front of her turned slightly toward her.

"Her name is Delilah. She was… is my best friend," she quietly said.

Barrack stiffened. Hope flared inside him. A quick look warned his brother that they needed to proceed with extreme caution. If their mate meant a lot to this woman, she would be very protective and careful of what she shared. He breathed through his nose to calm his dragon who was clawing to get out.

"Do you know where she is?" he asked, keeping his voice calm, almost gentle.

She shook her head. "Not for sure. I know that she is on my world. I heard her say that she was heading for a ranch in Wyoming. She is looking for me."

"Wyoming?" Jaguin said, turning to look at her. "Paul has a ranch in this place. We were at the ranch before I found you."

"You will take us there," Brogan ordered, stepping forward.

"Please," Barrack added with a sharp glance at his brother. "Please, we do not have much time."

"Jaguin, we have to take them. They…." She looked at Barrack and his brother with a worried expression. "…they are telling the truth. They don't have much time and neither does Delilah," she said, her voice breaking up on Delilah's name.

"Sara," Jaguin started to protest before he looked at Barrack, then at Brogan. The warrior turned back to his mate. "You are sure?"

She nodded and stepped closer to her mate, lifting her hand to touch his chest. "Look into my mind. I can see and remember things about Delilah that I shouldn't. It is foggy, like I'm not sure it is real, but I have memories of us together and those memories are becoming clearer than before, as if the past is rewriting itself," she murmured.

Barrack reached out and gripped Brogan's arm when his brother growled in frustration. He shook his head, breathing a sigh of relief when the warrior's shoulders relaxed and a small rueful smile curved Jaguin's lips as he wound his arm around his mate. Jaguin turned to look back at him and Brogan with a glimmer of determination in his eyes.

"We will need a ship. I think it is time I called in an old favor," he chuckled.

"Favor?" Barrack asked with a raised eyebrow.

Jaguin nodded. "I hope you like the Curizans," he replied with a wry grin.

~

Ten days later:

"I hate that female," Brogan groaned.

Barrack rolled over and tried to glare at him, but Brogan could tell that even that simple task hurt too much. As far as Brogan was concerned, he and Barrack had been subjected to ten days of torture far worse than anything the Marastin Dow or Antrox could ever inflict.

"Remember Rule Number One, and for Goddess's sake... *Don't let her hear you say that you hate her*!" Barrack choked, his eyes still closed.

"Why did we swear off killing females?" Brogan muttered, forcing his aching body to sit up.

"Because of Rule Number One," Barrack snapped. "Use your head, Brogan. If you keep mouthing off, the only thing that will happen is that we will still be lying here a month from now. The Curizan Adalard has agreed to take us and we had passed the last lesson until you opened your mouth. When will you learn to keep your mouth shut? I swear, if you frighten our mate, I will beat the shit out of you."

Brogan leaned forward and rested his forehead on his knees. His stomach clenched at the idea of frightening their mate. If there were any way to spare his brother and their mate the heartache of having to deal with him, he would have granted them that reprieve. He touched the scars running down his cheek. The words of the boys who had attacked him still echoed in his mind—monster, murderer, freak of nature. Those were the kinds of words they had used to describe him as they beat him centuries ago. How could any female love someone like him?

"I will not frighten her, Barrack. I swear on my life that I will not frighten her," Brogan swore, pushing up off the ground with difficulty. "I will be back."

"Brogan," Barrack called, struggling to sit up.

Brogan ignored his brother. He stumbled outside. He ignored the old Valdier warrior, Asim, who was tutoring them. He also ignored Asim's mate, Pearl. The human woman had been torturing them in the guise of trying to help them. He couldn't imagine why Aikaterina thought their mate would be anything like Pearl. Their mate would be gentle. She would never knock them on their asses like Pearl had!

Turning the corner, he called to his dragon. The beast was almost as weak as he was from the debilitating shock he'd received from the small device that Pearl used.

We must fly, he ordered.

You fly. You know everything, his dragon snapped.

Please, Brogan said.

I like Pearl's rules. You listen and we not feel this way, his dragon growled.

Enough! Brogan angrily replied. *Sleep, then.*

Gripping the thin band of gold hanging around his neck, he called to his symbiot. The creature appeared immediately. It sensed that he was close to the breaking point.

"Give me a skimmer," he ordered.

The symbiot shimmered and shifted into a long skimmer that hovered above the ground. Sliding his leg over to straddle it, he clung to the symbiot and bowed his head. He didn't care where they went, as long as he found solitude away from everyone else—including his brother.

"Go," he murmured.

The symbiot rose higher and took off. He would have slipped from the side if not for the golden bands that wrapped around his legs and waist. The symbiot skimmed through the forest before cutting through a deep mountain pass. Brogan quickly lost track of time and their location. In all honesty, he didn't care any longer. The farther he flew, the more he wondered if he should just keep going.

Finally, his symbiot stopped near a long river. It settled down on the ground and released the straps holding him to it. Stronger now, he slid his leg over the side and stood up. Immediately, his symbiot transformed into a Werecat and walked over to lie in the shade.

Brogan frowned in irritation when he realized that his symbiot had brought him to a quiet place, but it was not deserted like he wanted. Near the river stood an old warrior, fishing in the shallow, rushing waters. He turned when he heard a sound coming up from behind him.

Stumbling to the side, he watched as a symbiot—barely half the size of his— trotted past him to the old warrior. After several minutes, curiosity overcame his need for peace, and he slowly walked forward to stand next to the warrior. The old warrior glanced at him before he returned his attention to the pole he held.

"I wondered how long it would take for you to come over here," the old warrior said in a quiet voice.

"I... Do I know you?" Brogan asked with a frown.

The old warrior chuckled. "No. My symbiot told me you were here. It would appear your symbiot told mine that you needed someone to talk to," he said, looking over at his symbiot where it was trying to play with the other one.

"I don't need anyone to talk to," Brogan growled.

"Very well," the old warrior replied with a shrug.

"Grandpa Christoff," a young girl called.

Brogan turned at the sound of the girl's hesitant voice. He watched in stunned disbelief as she walked across the rocks with an uneven gait because of her prosthetic limb. He started to take a step forward when she stumbled, but stopped in surprise when the old warrior's hand shot out and stopped him.

"Let her do this," he said before turning his attention to the girl.

Brogan realized that the girl was older than he had originally thought. She eyed him with a suspicious scowl and lifted her head in defiance before she stopped several feet away. Brogan's lips twitched when she rolled her eyes at him and shrugged, as if dismissing him.

"Grandma asked me to tell you that dinner is almost ready," the girl said.

"Thank you, Crystal. I will be there shortly," Christoff replied with a gentle smile.

"'K, I'll wait for you to make sure that you aren't late," she warned, turning and slowly retracing her steps.

"What happened to her?" Brogan asked, unable to stop himself.

A sad look came into Christoff's eyes. "Too much for one so young," he said, turning his gaze to Brogan. "Would you join us for dinner?"

"Thank you, but no. I must return," Brogan said with a hint of unexpected regret.

Christoff looked out over the river. Brogan stood next to the old warrior, finding peace in the sound of the wind in the trees and the rushing of the water. Neither man spoke for several minutes, each lost in their own thoughts.

"Our lives are like the river," Christoff finally said, surprising him.

Brogan frowned and looked over at Christoff. "How so?" he asked.

Christoff smiled. "If our lives were straight and calm, they would be boring and not worth living. We are confined by the banks, but at times overflow them to see if there is another path that we can follow. Sometimes there is, but most of the time there is not, and we return to the path cut centuries before us to follow after our ancestors. As we wind through life, we try to find a way to understand the larger purpose of our existence. For a dragon warrior, finding our true mate is like discovering that all the mountains, rocks, and trees thrown in our path to stop us only make us stronger."

"What if we are not strong, but defective in some way? What if... what if we are destined to lose our way—or worse, that we are not good enough for our true mate?" Brogan asked in a quiet voice.

Christoff shook his head. "Even the strongest dam has a weakness or must give way to the river if it rises high enough. A river will always find a way, no matter how hard others may try to tame or defeat it. And love, just like a river, will overflow to heal even the most wounded warrior no matter how much we resist," he said before he bent over and picked up the basket of fish. "If you change your mind, my cottage is on the other side of the forest. If you follow the path you can't miss it. I think Crystal might enjoy a ride home. May the Goddess be with you, warrior."

Brogan watched as the old warrior walked over to the young girl where she stood stroking Christoff's symbiot. His eyes widened when Christoff said something that made the girl's eyes light up and chased the shadows away. She flashed him one last defiant glare before she turned her back to him. He didn't understand why until Christoff shifted.

Brogan knew he was staring, but he couldn't look away. The old dragon turned and winked at him before he knelt down so the young girl, who was missing one leg, could climb on his back. The girl sat in front of the small, deformed wings of the dragon. Christoff's symbiot rose up, shifting in the air, only to reform around the old dragon's misshapen wings.

Gripping the basket of fish with its front claw, the old dragon took several steps before the golden wings lifted the dragon off the ground as easily as if the wings were real. He ducked when the dragon playfully dived down toward him. The young girl giggled and wrapped her arms around the dragon's neck.

Brogan swallowed when his symbiot nudged his arm. Reaching down, he stroked his constant companion. Inside, he could feel his dragon sigh.

We broken too, his dragon mourned, growing very, very quiet inside him.

Brogan watched as the old dragon carrying the young girl flew over the treetops. The soft sound of laughter carried on the wind. He thought of the old dragon's words about life being like a river. He turned to look downstream. He could see the boulders and debris that were washed down after the last heavy rain. He could see the watermarks along the trees and banks showing how high the river was at one point during the spring rains, yet through it all, the water forged a path that continued to flow no matter how many things tried to impede its journey.

He also thought of the beautiful, defiant young girl who made her way through the forest to tell the old dragon that dinner was ready despite how difficult it must have been. Finally, he thought of the old dragon. He knew the old dragon would have been shunned because of his deformity, yet he still had found a true mate—and a family who loved him. He had also found a way to overcome his handicap.

We may be broken, but we are like the river. We will forge our own path and overcome the obstacles that we face like we always have. This time, the difference will be that I will accept the fact that while things may appear broken, like us, we are not without our own strengths. Pearl was right. I finally understand what she meant by her Unbreakable Rule. Friends and family do come first—and it is important to love them like there is no tomorrow, because you never know when life may build a dam to try to stop you, he quietly informed his dragon.

"Let's find Barrack. We have a true mate to find," he said, calling forth his dragon.

He lifted off the ground, his symbiot flowing around the form of his dragon. In the distance, over the treetops, he could see the faint spiral of smoke from a chimney. He would have to remember this place. When he and Barrack returned with their mate, he would like to visit the old dragon again—and thank him for his wise words.

CHAPTER FIVE

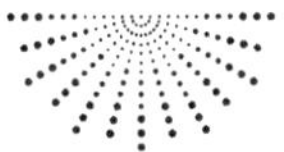

Earth – Paul's Ranch, Wyoming:
Four months later...

"I can't believe that you misplaced them! How in the hell can you lose twin dragons?" Jaguin growled, glaring at Adalard as they stood on the platform to beam down to the planet.

"Jaguin," Sara cautioned, reaching out to touch his arm.

"I'm not a ... What was the word Pearl used, Sara?" Adalard asked with a shrug.

"A babysitter," Sara murmured.

"Yes, a babysitter. They are grown warriors. When I searched for them, they were gone. I had no idea they would use their symbiots to escape from the ship before we all transported down. I don't know why you are surprised. It was obvious they were growing edgier the closer we got to this planet. I'm surprised they made it as long as they did," Adalard added with a pointed look.

"We should have locked them up. If they expose the fact that humans aren't alone, it could endanger future visits here," Jaguin reflected with a shake of his head.

"I'm sure everything will be alright. Barrack and Brogan both know that they can't be seen. You and Adalard drilled that into their heads on the way here," Sara gently reminded Jaguin, stepping up onto the platform next to him when the technician motioned for them to proceed.

Jaguin turned to lock eyes with his mate as they dematerialized. Within seconds, the brief disorientation of appearing in a new environment fogged his mind. It didn't take long to clear. He realized that his head was still turned toward Sara. He could see the look of worry in her eyes before she swayed. He quickly reached out and wrapped his arms around her to steady her.

"I don't think I'll ever get used to that," she moaned, raising a trembling hand to her forehead.

"I prefer a transport myself," Jaguin chuckled, holding her tightly to his body until she pulled away.

"Oh!"

They all turned when they heard the sound of a gasp. Standing in the doorway was a young woman. Her eyes immediately moved to Adalard. Her face paled, and she swayed before her lips tightened.

"Mason! Your house is infested with aliens again," the woman called before she looked at Jaguin and Sara. "Well, at least with two. I think you'll only need to exterminate one of them, though," she added, looking pointedly at Adalard.

"Samara," Adalard warned, taking a step toward her.

"Who is it this time?" Mason, Paul Grove's ranch manager, asked, stepping up behind Samara.

"Don't ask me. I prefer to keep my distance from the lot of them," Samara retorted, turning on her heel. "I've got horses to bring in. Let me know when they are gone."

"Samara," Adalard growled, taking a step to follow the young woman.

Jaguin heard Sara's smothered laugh when Samara raised her right hand and lifted her middle finger at Adalard. He now understood Adalard's distraction. He had noticed a growing restlessness in

Adalard the closer they got to Earth. In all honesty, he was beginning to think that Adalard was as bad as the twins.

~

Adalard watched as Mason turned sideways to allow Samara to pass. He winced when he heard the sound of the back door slamming. He had hoped that time and distance would heal the wounds he'd inflicted in his arrogance. Unbeknownst to Samara, he still watched over her from afar, each day a bitter torture.

He had known that she had returned to work on Paul Grove's remote Wyoming ranch. If she had left, he would have known at once and returned sooner – despite his promise to give her time. His carefully laid plans unraveled the moment he saw her.

"So, I recognize two of you—you're Jaguin, correct?" Mason said, looking at Jaguin.

"Yes. This is my mate, Sara Wilson," Jaguin replied.

"Ah, the mysterious Sara Wilson," Mason murmured before his gaze hardened, and he looked at Adalard. "What are you doing back here?"

A wry smile curved Adalard's lips. It was obvious that the human male still remembered him from his previous visit here. He wondered if Samara's brothers remembered him as well. If they did, he would have to remember to keep his shield handy and watch his back at all times.

"I promised I would return," he said, returning the other man's intense stare.

Mason's lips pursed together before he turned his attention back to Jaguin and Sara. Adalard was thankful the man kept his thoughts to himself. Seeing Samara so near damn near made him lose the tight control he was struggling to retain on the energy surrounding him.

"I take it that you are here because of the other two alien bastards who scared the shit out of me and Ann Marie earlier this morning," Mason said, folding his arms and moving so that he blocked the access to the back door.

Adalard could feel the muscle in his jaw twitch. He knew the human did it to prevent him from following Samara. What the human didn't know was that this time, there would be nothing that could prevent him from claiming his prize—except the prize herself.

Jaguin nodded. "Yes. Do you know where they are?" he asked.

Mason looked at them with a raised eyebrow. "You lost two of your own men?" he asked in an incredulous tone.

"Technically, he did. It was his ship," Jaguin replied with a grin and an accusatory finger point.

Adalard shot Jaguin a heated glare. Just because it was his ship didn't mean he should take all the responsibility. He shook his head.

"Don't blame me. I merely provided the transportation here to fulfill a debt. The twins were your responsibility. I've got enough to deal with without you adding more to thc list," he growled in defense, holding up his hands in a warding off gesture.

"All I know is that these two big-ass aliens showed up at the door, demanded to know where Delilah was, and left after I gave them the only information we knew along with a map. I wasn't about to argue with them," Mason said.

Deep down Adalard understood why Mason didn't want to argue with the two massive twin dragons, but he couldn't help but wish that the man had tried. The last thing he wanted to do was chase after the twins when he had business of his own to take care of – if Samara didn't try to kill him first.

"Then, you know where Delilah is?" Sara asked, stepping forward with a hopeful expression.

Mason nodded. "About a month ago this young woman shows up. She had a picture of you and was asking all kinds of questions. She was really vague about how she knew to look here. She said something about the University, a place in Columbia, and some guy named Cuello," he said.

Adalard heard Sara's harsh intake of breath and saw her face become pale. Mason realized at the same time that he had said something that was very distressing to Sara. He stepped forward, but Jaguin had already wrapped his arm around her waist.

"I'm alright," she murmured, looking down and shaking her head. She started trembling as she fought for composure before she looked up again.

"What... What did you tell her?" Adalard asked.

Mason looked at him with a frown. "I told her that we didn't know Sara Wilson, but if we heard anything we'd give her a call. She left her phone number and address. I gave the information to the two guys who came here earlier this morning. They said they knew you and that they were looking for a woman named Delilah. I figured there must have been some connection and honestly, I wasn't about to argue with them or those gold creatures you guys have with you," he stated.

Adalard nodded and turned to Jaguin and Sara. "So, what should we do now?" he asked.

"We have to go after them," Jaguin replied.

"Yeah, well, I wouldn't be in too big a hurry," Mason warned. "The East Coast is about to get slammed with a Nor'easter that they are calling the new hundred year storm. They are expecting up to fifty inches of snow in some parts with temperatures dropping well below freezing and winds in excess of one hundred miles an hour. We've got our own storm heading this way. It is supposed to hit this afternoon. We've been rounding up all the horses and trying to get the place ready to be snowed in for up to a week or more," Mason warned.

"Did Barrack and Brogan know about this?" Jaguin asked.

Mason nodded. "I told them, but they didn't care. I'm guessing maybe you aliens can handle this kind of extreme weather better than we can. Whether you can or not, they are still in for a rough journey," he said before his expression changed. "I'll have to admit, I'm glad you are here. We could use some extra help. We only have a skeleton crew on the ranch, at the moment. The few hands we have are working our Northwest range. That is where most of the cattle are, but that still leaves this section. With the weather, I can't safely take the helicopter up. There is only Samara, Ann Marie, and me to handle things. We've got more than five thousand head of livestock that will need to be taken care of. We've already moved them to more sheltered pastures, but they'll have to be fed," Mason said, shoving his hands in his front pockets.

Adalard shifted his attention back to the room behind Mason. A sense of satisfaction built inside him at the excuse to stay. He answered before Jaguin or Sara could.

"We will stay. The storm will shield the twins from sight. They know not to be seen and if Delilah is the sweet girl that Sara has described, she will appreciate having their assistance during such a storm," he reasoned with a shrug when he saw Jaguin and Sara's surprised expressions.

"Thank you. Whatever you do, though, just make sure that you stay away from Samara," Mason ordered. "I'll let Ann Marie know."

Adalard didn't answer. He would help, but he would also use the storm to show Samara that he wasn't the man she thought he was or anything like her brothers. He had promised Paul and Samara that he would give her time. That time was now up.

CHAPTER SIX

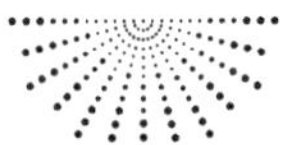

Near Saddle Mountain, North Carolina

"Move it, Rum. Damn it! Why is it every time I go to the grocery store you think helping me unload the car means getting under my feet? Moonshine, get your nose out of that bag, it isn't for you," Delilah growled in annoyance.

She placed the heaviest bags on the floor in the kitchen before turning to head back out to the truck. She was running behind thanks to the two black and tan clowns who thought playing in the snow was more fun than stockpiling supplies to weather the storm of the century. If she had been smart, she would have stayed at the house in town. The problem was that the old furnace there had decided to die in the middle of the night. The repair man told her that it was beyond help and needed to be replaced, and that wouldn't happen until at least a week after the storm passed because he was backed up.

Left with nothing but a small pellet stove in the living room, she wasn't about to try to weather the storm there. She decided she had two options. She could either go to the local school, which was open as an emergency shelter and wouldn't let her bring the dogs, or come up to a perfectly good house and have the entire mountain to herself.

She had plenty of propane for the gas fireplaces, emergency lights, a new roof, and insulated windows. She could spend the time working on some of the last-minute projects that she didn't have time to finish as well.

The dogs pushed past her, out the back door of the kitchen, and tripped over each other as they both tried to fit through the mudroom door at the same time. How two huge dogs could be so clumsy was beyond her. She suspected the reason the owner gave her the last two pups was because he had dropped them on their heads, not because he was moving.

She reached up and pulled her cap down over her ears. The temperature was beginning to rapidly drop, and the wind was picking up. She pulled the doors shut behind her so the house could heat up. Her thick boots crunched against the newly fallen snow. She tried to walk in the footsteps she made coming into the house.

Pulling open the driver's side door to the truck, she slid in. Turning the key, she started the ignition, thankful the engine hadn't cooled down completely and that there was still some heat coming out of the vents. She looked around to make sure the two dogs weren't standing near the truck before she shifted into reverse and backed the truck into the renovated Model-T shed.

Shifting back into park, she turned off the ignition and climbed out of the truck. Snow was beginning to fall in thick flakes outside the door. Delilah started forward before she remembered the snow shovel.

Grabbing it off the hook, she heard the dogs frantically barking. She hoped they hadn't found some poor rabbit searching for a last-minute meal before the storm. She jumped when the wind suddenly caught one of the shed's doors and slammed it shut. In the space of a few minutes, the scene outside was changed from that of beautiful fat flakes to a full-blown blizzard. She was barely able to see the house from a hundred feet away.

She grabbed the rope hanging from another hook and stepped

outside. She quickly closed the doors to the shed and slid the board across to secure them so they wouldn't blow open. Tying one end of the rope to the eye-hook screwed into the corner of the shed, she turned and began wading through the snow back toward the house. She held the rope in one hand, slowly releasing it while she used the shovel to keep herself from falling.

"Moonshine! Rum! Come on, boys. Time to go inside," she yelled above the wind. "I hope to hell you two did your business while you were out," she muttered, nearly breathless by the time she reached the house.

She propped the shovel up against the wall of the mudroom and tied the other end of the rope to the eye hook near the door. Testing it, she grunted in satisfaction. This way if she needed anything in the shed or needed to take the dogs out on their leashes during the storm, she could hold onto the rope. She'd heard one too many horror stories about people losing their way in a blizzard only to be found just feet from their door after the thaw.

Turning, she scanned the yard for the dogs. She couldn't see anything but white. With a grimace, she pulled off her glove and raised her quickly freezing fingers to her mouth. She released a loud, piercing whistle that was lost in the howl of the wind. Still, she could hear the muted sounds of the dogs barking.

Delilah rolled her eyes when she realized that the sound was coming from inside the house. The dogs must have finally figured out how to use the doggie door that she'd installed. She didn't remember unlocking it, but with everything else going on, that wasn't surprising.

She slid her glove back on and picked up the shovel. Pushing open the door, she looked down as she stepped inside. Her boots were covered with snow. She knocked off as much as she could before pulling them off and placing them on the shoe rack.

She propped the snow shovel next to the back door and bent to lock the doggie door. She froze when she saw the latch was still in the locked position. Straightening, she swallowed and turned. She could hear the dogs still barking.

Fear changed to anger which turned to being downright pissed off.

If DeWayne thought he could slink up here and find a way to get stuck in the storm with her, he was about to find out just how cold it was going to be. The bastard had probably locked the dogs in the front sitting room.

She wrapped her fingers around the shovel. She'd told DeWayne no again two days ago. She had done her research on the owner of Mountain View Properties, and he was about as low as a rattlesnake's belly. Olie Ray Lister had numerous lawsuits pending against him. These lawsuits ranged from not paying the agreed upon price for property, to not paying his contractors, to destroying the environment. She would try out her granddad's old shotgun on the man before she let him anywhere near her grandparents' property.

Silently pushing open the back door into the kitchen, she stepped inside. Her gloved hands slid along the yellow fiberglass handle of the broad shovel. She held it between both hands like a bat. Her thick socks silently slid along the smooth, polished wood floor. In the back of her mind, she couldn't remember what the law said about killing someone in your house. She wondered how much trouble she would get into if she did.

One more thing for me to research, she decided. *If nothing else, I'll have a shovel to help me bury the body!* She didn't plan on killing DeWayne no matter how tempted she actually was to commit the deed, but she wasn't above scaring the shit out of him. What really pissed her off was that she would undoubtedly be stuck with the jerk for a while. One thing she was determined to do was make it the most miserable time of the sneaky bastard's life. By the time the snow melted enough for him to safely leave the mountain he would be begging to get away from her and the dogs.

Walking down the narrow hallway leading to the front door, she tightened her fingers on the handle. She could see a man standing with his back to her near the staircase. Either the shadows were playing tricks on her eyes, or DeWayne had packed on some weight and height over the last two days. She decided he must be wearing snow boots and his entire wardrobe. That might work in his favor when she smacked him in the ass with the shovel.

He was looking into the front sitting room where she could hear the dogs whining. Lifting the shovel, she released a growl and charged at him. Her intention was to scare him. Her plan drastically backfired when the man turned, and she saw that it was not DeWayne but a huge stranger with eyes that glowed with a golden flame.

"Oh, shit!" she choked.

She instinctively swung her hands outward when he took a step toward her. The shovel was aimed for his head. He reached up with one hand and caught it in midair, bringing her forward momentum to a sudden stop. Their gazes locked in stunned silence at the same time as her foot connected with his unprotected crotch in a powerful kick. All those years of playing on the community soccer team paid off in that one unforgettable moment.

His eyes widened in shock and he released the metal end of the shovel. She lifted the shovel and tried to hit him in the head. The sound of the shovel connecting with something—or someone—behind her clanged in the narrow space of the hallway. She turned and thrust the handle of the shovel into the cheekbone of the man she had just kicked before driving the flat end of the shovel blade into the stomach of the man who was behind her. She swiveled around when the man she had kicked fell backwards over one of Moonshine's toys. Not waiting to find out who the men were or why in the hell they were in her house, she skirted around the man on the ground. He was holding his bleeding nose with one hand and his crotch with the other.

Delilah gripped the banister of the staircase with her right hand while holding her only weapon with her left. Her gaze went to the sitting room where the dogs were whining. A gasp escaped her when she saw that they were locked in a large golden cage.

She screamed when a man's face suddenly blocked her view on the other side of the railing. Swinging the shovel, she heard him utter what could only be a loud curse as he ducked. A rush of adrenaline filled her, and she raced up the stairs and down the long hallway to the master bedroom.

Grabbing the door handle as she entered, she slammed the door and twisted the old-fashioned key in the lock. Backing up, she realized that it wouldn't take very much for the two men to bust through the flimsy door.

Rushing forward, she placed the shovel within reach and pushed on the heavy antique dresser. She almost fell when it rolled across the wooden floor. Looking at the feet on the dresser, she groaned when she saw they were on wheels.

"Oh, for crying out loud," she hissed in vexation.

CHAPTER SEVEN

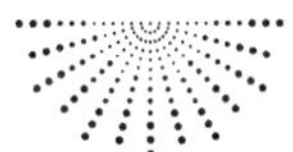

"Escape.... I've got to escape," she frantically muttered to herself when she heard the sound of footsteps on the stairs.

She pushed the dresser as tight as she could against the door. Picking up the shovel, she hurried to the window. Reaching up to unlock the latch, she stopped. There was no escape. Outside, the full force of the Nor'easter had arrived, and all she could see was white. Even if she was dressed in her warmest clothing, she wouldn't last more than a few minutes out there.

She jumped when she heard the knock on the door. Turning, she gripped the shovel with both hands and stared at the door in terror. She frantically searched the room with her eyes, trying to find a better weapon or some place to hide. Except for the bathroom or under the bed, there was nothing—not even a closet.

"Delilah, open the door," one of the men ordered.

She didn't answer. It wasn't the brightest plan, but she hoped that by not responding they would think she had slipped outside. If they fell for it, she could sneak down, release the dogs, and.... Her mind went blank after that.

"We know you are in there. You cannot escape with the weather like it is outside. Come out. There is no reason to fear us," he continued.

Padding silently over to the dresser, she sank down in front of the drawers and pressed her back against it. She laid the shovel over her lap and drew up her knees. Leaning her head back, she stared out the window at the falling snow. They were right. There was no escaping, but that didn't mean she couldn't go down without a fight. She reached into the pocket of her jacket for her cell phone. A quiet curse slipped from her lips when she remembered laying it down on the kitchen table with the groceries.

She bowed her head when she remembered that she didn't have the chance to put the cold stuff in the refrigerator. For the moment, the house was still cold. However, it wouldn't take long for some of the food to ruin once the house warmed up. She snapped her head up and made a face when there was another knock on the door, this one louder and harder than the first one.

"Open the door."

This voice was different. It was deeper, rougher, and held a touch of a growl that triggered a response in her that she wasn't expecting—awareness. The first voice soothed her, made her want to answer him. The arrogance in this guy's voice made her want to grab him by the ear and give him a piece of her mind. The visual image that came to her mind caused her to release an unexpected snort. She covered her mouth, but not before she knew they had somehow heard her.

"I knew she was in there. Let me break down the door," the rough-voiced man said.

"Brogan, have you forgotten everything that Pearl, Jaguin, and Sara told us? Human females are delicate. Plus, we promised Sara we would not frighten her friend," the calmer, smoother-talking man stated with a touch of irritation in his voice.

Delilah stiffened when they mentioned Sara's name. In her mind, she sorted through all the information that she had learned. Sara was kidnapped by a Columbian Cartel boss named Cuello. She had tracked down a reporter who said that an unidentified witness confirmed that Sara and another woman were being held and tortured by Cuello because of his thirst for revenge against a woman named Carmen Walker.

It turned out that Carmen Walker and her husband, Scott, were bodyguards. They were protecting a political family who Cuello targeted. They were both shot. Scott died, but Carmen lived. That was when the story got rather weird with the witness claiming that Carmen and three men had entered Cuello's compound and killed everyone but her before disappearing. Her best friend, Sara, and another girl named Emma Watson were never found. Neither were Cuello or the men in his cartel, but all evidence showed that the thugs were dead. As far as the rest of the story went, the girl swore that Carmen and the men turned into dragons and flew away. The reporter also swore that she found evidence to corroborate the girl's testimony, but no editor would believe - much less publish her findings - so she was forced to water down the article.

"You are the only one who knows what I really found. I've been keeping an eye on the ranch in Wyoming near where Carmen Walker grew up. I still live nearby and check when I can, but it is kind of hard to make a living and do that," Faith Sanders had said with a shrug. "My hope is one day to get a break. Who knows, maybe dragons really do exist!"

Did her research lead some of Cuello's men to North Carolina? The university wouldn't give her any information because she wasn't a blood relative. The only one she talked to was Faith and…

"The ranch…," she whispered, rising to her feet.

Was the man who worked at the ranch tied to Cuello and the Columbian Cartel? He didn't look like he was, but what did she know about an illegal business and dealing with drugs and stuff? These guys looked like they could easily kill someone. They also had an accent.

"Delilah, open the door, little fighter. We only wish to talk to you. I am called Barrack. I promise that Brogan will not break down the door. We apologize for frightening you. It was not our intention," Barrack said.

"You don't just walk into someone's house without their permission if you don't want to scare them," Delilah snapped.

"Have you not noticed it is snowing outside? It was cold. We knocked," Brogan replied. "Now, open the door."

"I didn't hear any knocking, and of course I know it is snowing! What do you think the weather forecast has been warning everyone about for the past week?" she retorted.

She glanced around as she tried to think of a way to get out of the house, down to the first floor, back in the house to rescue her dogs, and then figure out a way to get her truck out of the shed and down the mountain without dying. So far she was coming up with nothing. Any attempt to go out the window would probably result in a broken neck. The roof would be super slick with the snow and ice. A shiver ran through her. She had only turned on the fireplace downstairs.

She glanced at the one in her room. To light it, she would need to leave her spot in front of the dresser. Whether she liked it or not, she needed to turn on the heat upstairs as well. The house wasn't equipped with a central heating system. That was out of her budget.

"So, how much is Cuello paying you?" she asked, inching away from the dresser.

"Who is Cuello?" she heard Barrack murmur.

"He is the one that hurt Sara. Jaguin talked about him," Brogan quietly replied before he spoke louder. "He is dead. Carmen killed him."

"Carmen?" Delilah called over her shoulder.

She knelt in front of the gas fireplace and turned the valve. Twisting the knob to ignite, she winced when the igniter loudly broke the silence in the room when she clicked it. Thankfully, the pilot light lit the first time.

"What are you doing?" Brogan demanded. "I smell gas, which is a miracle since you nearly broke my nose."

"Oh, you're the one I kicked in the balls," she said, making a face.

Maybe reminding him of that wasn't a good idea. She turned the knob once the thermocouple began to glow a bright red. She sighed in relief when she felt the heat radiating from the fire. The room would warm up in no time.

"Yes, which I must tell you hurt a lot," Brogan retorted.

Delilah rolled her eyes and moved back to the dresser. "You poor baby," she replied. "So, if your boss is dead. Why are you here, and what do you want from me?"

"We answer to no one, *elila,* but ourselves and you. We have come a great distance and waited a very, very long time for you," Barrack answered.

"Why do you keep calling me that? Is it like some Columbian word for you're dead or I want to kill you or something? And you still haven't answered my question," she stated, leaning on the top of the dresser and resting her chin on her hand.

"*Elila,* means my heart in our language. You are our *elila,* our heart," Barrack said, his voice deepening and sending a shiver through her that had nothing to do with the cold.

"Yeah, right. You don't even know me, so the sweet talk doesn't work… *elila,*" she sarcastically retorted.

As crazy as it sounded, she was actually enjoying this little repartee. Maybe it was because they weren't trying to beat down the door, but she didn't feel threatened in a she-was-about-to-die sort of way.

Even though she was enjoying their exchange, especially now that her bedroom was warming up, didn't mean she was ready to open the door and let them in. They were still big guys with a funny accent who had yet to really tell her anything. Maybe it was time she asked a few pointed questions.

"Where are you from?" she asked, deciding that was as good a place as any to start.

"Valdier," they both replied at the same time.

She frowned. She'd never heard of Valdier. Of course, at the rate the world changed and with almost two hundred countries, she didn't know all of them.

"Where is Valdier? Is it near South America?" she asked.

"It is several million light years from here," Brogan answered. "We are from another star system."

"You're from…. Are you, like, saying you're from another planet?" she asked with an incredulous tone.

"Yes," they both answered again at the same time.

A shiver of unease went through her. "How do you know Sara?" she warily asked, bending over to pick up the shovel and lay it on the dresser.

There was a moment of silence before she heard them frantically talking to each other in a language she didn't understand. Every once in a while she would hear different names: Sara, Jaguin, hers, Pearl, Zoran, and Aikaterina. That was about all that she got out of their heated conversation.

"She is Jaguin's mate. He was with Carmen and her mate, Lord Creon, when they confronted the human male who killed Lady Carmen's first mate. Sara was tortured by this human. She would have died if not for their arrival. Jaguin returned to the ship with Sara where the healer onboard and his symbiot healed her," Barrack finally said.

Delilah tightened her grip on the handle of the shovel. She bit her lip to keep her horror at what they were telling her silent. This matched everything the reporter had told her. Her mind raced as she thought of some way of confirming that they actually knew Sara.

"There was… there was another woman with Sara," she started to say.

"Lady Emma. Lord Ha'ven's mate," Barrack acknowledged.

Delilah stared at the door. "How do you know about her?" she asked in a soft voice.

"Prince Adalard, Ha'ven's brother, is the one who transported us to your world," Brogan replied. "They are Curizans."

"What's the difference between a Curizan and someone from Valdier?" she asked with a frown.

"We are stronger and better looking," Brogan snickered, his voice filled with amusement.

"You are not helping, Brogan—even if you are right," Barrack replied, his voice laced with the same amusement. "The Curizans have only themselves to worry about when looking for a mate. We, on the other hand, have to find a woman who will be accepted by our symbiots and our dragons."

"Which is possible as Cree and Calo have proven," Brogan quickly added.

Delilah pulled the shovel toward herself and slowly backed away from the dresser and the door. She shook her head in disbelief. She didn't know what in the hell a symbiot was, but the 'our dragons' had her attention. Faith's voice came back to her.

"The girl had sworn she saw dragons, and I found their footprints in the sand along a cove..."

"I'm dreaming," she whispered, continuing to shake her head in disbelief. "I've fallen asleep in the snow, and I'm dreaming. There are no such things as dragons. There are no such things as dragons... or aliens or... or dragons."

She turned her head, looking around. Boots, she needed a pair of boots. There was enough snow on the ground by now that if she fell from the roof, she might survive. One thing was for sure, if she stayed here, the odds that she would make it out of this alive were dropping like a mob informant wearing a pair of cement shoes while swimming.

"Delilah... Delilah, please, little fighter, open the door. This conversation would be much easier if we could see you," Barrack said.

"And touch... without pain, that is," Brogan added.

Delilah ignored Barrack's muttered curse at his brother and the admonishment once again about not scaring her. She would have told him it was too late about twenty minutes ago, but she was too busy lacing up the boots she had retrieved from the shoe rack in the corner of her bedroom. Removing her jacket, she pulled on two more sweat-shirts with hoods. She'd take her jacket and put it on once she was on the ground.

She grabbed her jacket and the shovel and tiptoed over to the window again. Placing the two items down next to the window, she reached up and unhooked the latch. Snow, nearly six inches deep from the ongoing storm, butted up against the window sill outside. She estimated that there must be at least three feet of snow on the ground below the window. The roof sloped down to the wraparound porch, so she should be able to slow her descent a little before she went over the edge.

"Listen, I have a better idea. Why don't you two go back to wherever you came from and we can just forget all of this?" she said in a loud voice, hoping the sound would cover her opening the window.

"Ah, *elila*, I fear we cannot do that," Barrack responded.

"We do not have much time, Delilah. If you do not open the door, I will be forced to open it for you," Brogan said.

"I… Please, just give me a few minutes to think. I… I need… just… a few… minutes," she loudly pleaded, grinning as she slid first one leg than the other out the window.

"We will wait," Barrack reluctantly agreed.

"Thank you," she said, leaning down and grabbing her jacket and the shovel. "Ten minutes. I just need ten minutes. If you… wait right there, I'll open the door in ten."

"Five...," Brogan countered before she heard a grunt.

"We can give her ten minutes! We have waited centuries, what is ten minutes more if it makes our mate happy?" Barrack argued.

"She could do just as much thinking in five minutes," Brogan countered. "I need my symbiot. My nose and groin are killing me. You could use yours as well. You have a large knot on your forehead and I think your eyelids are turning colors."

CHAPTER EIGHT

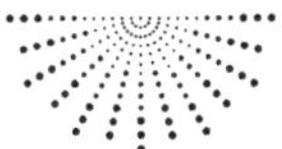

Delilah didn't wait to hear any more. Pushing off against the house, she half-scooted and half-slid down the snow-covered roof. She had to grit her teeth against the cold. This literally gave new meaning to having a frozen ass. Yet, it was still better than being tortured and killed by two madmen!

Her feet dug in when she reached the edge of the roof. Looking down, she could barely see the snow-covered ground. She swore that her eyelashes were beginning to freeze in the intense cold. The wind, snow, and sub-zero temperatures stung her cheeks and she was afraid if she opened her mouth that her teeth might freeze!

Refusing to think of all the things that could go wrong, she scooted forward until her feet were dangling off the edge of the roof. She closed her eyes and took a deep breath of icy air before she opened her eyes again and pushed off the edge. Her stomach dropped to her feet before ricocheting back up into her throat as she fell. She bent her knees as she hit the soft snow. She reached out to stop her forward momentum but did a face-plant when her feet sank and stuck into the snow.

She lay there a second to make sure nothing was broken before she popped her head up and gasped. It was freaking *cold*! She clumsily crawled to her feet. She moaned when her muscles protested. She was going to be sore as hell later.

Reaching for her jacket that lay on the snow next to her, she put it on. Even wearing five shirts and a set of heavy thermal underwear, she was still cold. Zipping up her jacket, she grabbed the shovel.

Now all she needed to do was rescue the dogs. She didn't know if it was the smartest thing to do, but she would be damned if she let some crazy lunatics hurt them. By her calculations, she had about eight minutes to sneak in, get the dogs, and run like hell.

Hurrying around to the front door as fast as she could in the blinding snow, she made sure she kept the house to her left. She stumbled when she reached the front steps. The timer was counting down faster than she liked. She estimated five minutes max before they started to break into the bedroom.

Holding onto the handrail with one hand and her trusty shovel with the other, she climbed the steps and crossed the front porch which had snow all the way to the door. She pulled the screen door open and gripped the doorknob before she remembered that it was locked. She was about to pull her hand away when she heard the slight click and the door moved inward.

"Duh!" she muttered under her breath. "Of course, it is open! How do you think Alien Lunatic 1 and 2 got in, Delilah?"

She pushed the door open and slipped inside, quietly pulling the screen door behind her so it wouldn't bang. She grinned when she heard the men quietly talking upstairs. She partially closed the front door behind her, promising herself that she would remember to thank Bubba Joe Wright for installing it and making sure that it didn't squeak when it opened.

Each step she took made a small crunching noise that was loud to her sensitive ears as the snow clinging to her boots fell off onto the throw rug in the foyer. The sitting room on her right opened into the dining room which then opened into the kitchen. She could grab the dogs and cut through the back rooms to reach the back door. She would have to take a chance that the old truck could make it through the snow.

If she had known she was going to have company, she could have attached her granddad's old snowplow to the front bumper. At least she had four-wheel drive! That would help a little.

Confident with her plan, she deduced that she had three minutes and counting until discovery, maybe a little more considering they would have to break into the room first. Of course, leaving the window open would probably give them a clue that she was no longer there, but what the heck. She could only do so much and jumping off the roof was the limit of her thought processes at the time.

She rounded the corner and stepped into the front parlor. A scowl darkened her face when she saw both dogs sound asleep as if nothing unusual were going on. Hell, they weren't even in the golden cage that had been in here earlier.

"Fine lot of protection you two are," she hissed in a soft voice. "Come."

Both dogs came alert the moment she spoke. With a hand signal, they both came to heel beside her. Once again, she thanked the stars that as the local librarian in a small town, she had access to tons of resources and plenty of time to read them. All those hours of watching dog videos and reading training books were paying off.

With renewed determination, she cut a path through the dining room, passed through the kitchen, and was out the back door with her dogs and her trusty shovel with a minute to spare. Grabbing the rope leading to the Model-T shed, she held onto it and struggled through the nearly thigh-deep snow to the shed. She gripped the wooden board that kept it closed and pulled with all her might. It would not budge. It was frozen in place because of the snow and ice.

Frustrated, she pulled the scarf up around her nose and mouth. Running a hand alongside the shed, she made her way to the side door near the back. It opened inward. She groaned when she realized that it had a brand new lock on it. There were three keys for it. One key was in the house, the other hanging on a nail in the shed and the last one was on a key ring—also in the shed because, of course, that is where you leave your keys during a snow storm—in the truck, under the driver's seat.

Glancing around, the only place where she and the dogs could hide now was an old smokehouse that her granddad had used. It was in piss-poor condition and on her list to be torn down and reuse the wood for something else. The problem would be finding it in a blizzard.

She reached down when she heard Rum whine. Both dogs were shivering in the mind-numbingly intense cold. Hitting the door with her shoulder, she groaned when it didn't move. Rubbing her arm, she decided it would be better to conserve her energy to find the smokehouse.

"Come on, boys. We can do this," she muttered, turning in the snow and struggling to take a step in what she hoped was the right direction.

~

"Should I have my symbiot heal my old scars?" Brogan asked, lifting his lip to test if the tenderness around it was gone.

Barrack looked at his brother and shook his head. "Do you think it will improve your personality?" he dryly asked.

Brogan chuckled and shook his head. "No," he admitted.

"If she is truly our mate, she will see beyond the scars. If they frighten her, then you can see if your symbiot can heal them. You know that it will not be able to completely erase them," Barrack stated, lifting a hand to rub his forehead. "That feels much better."

The symbiots looked at each other and snorted. Barrack knew that they were procrastinating, in part to give Delilah the time she needed to finally open the door. They decided that seeing them bruised and bloody wouldn't be a good idea, even if she was the reason behind it.

"Delilah, we have given you the time you requested. Are you ready to open the door now?" Barrack asked.

He frowned when there was no answer. He looked at Brogan with a raised eyebrow. Brogan leaned forward and knocked on the door.

"Delilah, time is up. Open the door," Brogan said. "I am really getting tired of saying that," he added under his breath.

"I am as well," Barrack responded. Turning to his symbiot, he motioned to the door. "Unlock the door and open it."

His symbiot shook as it rose to its feet. A thin thread of gold flowed out of its body and into the keyhole. He heard the sound of the metal key falling out of the lock and hitting the floor on the other side. With a twist, the symbiot unlocked the door.

He reached for the door once the symbiot withdrew. He paused when he felt the flow of frigid air through the narrow keyhole. A growl of warning echoed in the hallway as he twisted the doorknob and pushed the door inward.

He placed his shoulder to the door when it was stopped by something. Delilah had blocked the door. Brogan's voice ordering his symbiot to move the object registered at the same time as the blast of cold air.

The symbiot easily squeezed through the gap. A moment later, the dresser was moved. Opening the door completely, he stared at the open window across the room. Snow, blown in from the wind, slowly melted on the area rug thanks to the fire in the fireplace.

"Ten minutes…. She is smart. I believed her," Brogan grudgingly conceded, walking to the window.

Barrack's lips tightened. "In this weather, she will be dead," he bit out. Turning to their symbiots, he waved his hand at them. "Find her."

The symbiots shifted, their bodies becoming fluid as they flowed through the open window. Once outside, one shifted into a bird of prey while the other back into the form of a Werecat. Barrack touched the gold wrapped around his wrists.

We find mate. She in danger, his dragon growled, clawing to be released so it could go after Delilah as well.

Yes, we find mate, Barrack agreed.

Barrack watched as Brogan climbed through the window. A moment later, he followed, closing the window behind them. Delilah would be half-frozen in this weather if they didn't find her soon.

Sliding down the roof, his gaze narrowed on the depression in the snow that was quickly filling in. Brogan jumped off the roof, landing next to the spot and shifted into his dragon. Barrack glanced around.

The thick swirling snow made it impossible to see very far, even for him.

He jumped off the roof, shape-shifting before he landed. His dragon, fueled by fear for its mate, rose into the air. He connected with his symbiot. They had tracked her to the shed. Circling above, he glanced over at Brogan when his brother flew up to join him.

She tried to get into the shed but was unable to. There is a transport inside, but the doors remain locked, Brogan stated.

She headed into the woods, Barrack replied, his voice sharp with worry.

We will find her and when we do..., Brogan's voice faded.

Images of Delilah locked in a golden cage, covered in their symbiots, and a myriad of other ways to protect her flowed through Barrack's mind. He could feel his dragon adding to the list. His head turned at the same time as Brogan's when the image of a small wooden shack appeared in their minds. Brogan's symbiot in the shape of a bird of prey had spotted the snow-covered roof of the old smokehouse in a stand of trees not far away.

Barrack turned his head against the driving force of the wind and snow. Ice crystals formed on his eyelashes. The cold did not bother his dragon. It was more of an irritation because it separated him from his target—Delilah.

Brogan flew ahead of him, forging through the trees. All branches in his brother's way were either incinerated or snapped off and tossed aside. Brogan's symbiot swooped down and landed on a branch above the roof of the structure that looked like it was about to collapse.

He dropped down and shifted back into his two-legged form while Brogan landed near him and remained a dragon. There were tracks in the snow leading to the structure. Waving a hand to his symbiot, he moved forward to the door.

She there, his dragon said. *I hear her beasts.*

I know, Barrack replied, trying to remain calm.

He looked up at the metal roof. Rows of sharp icicles hung down from the thin corrugated metal like jagged teeth. The shed was creaking and bowing under the onslaught of the wind and from the weight of the snow-laden roof. The structure wouldn't last much longer.

Pushing the door open, he searched the small, dark shed. In the corner, Delilah huddled with her legs drawn up and her arms wrapped around each of the shivering dogs. Their soft whining told him that the two animals would not be a problem this time.

"Delilah, little fighter, what are you doing?" Barrack chided, his heart melting when he saw her trembling uncontrollably from the cold. "What are we going to do with you?"

She slowly lifted her head. All he could see were her eyes. He smiled when he saw her look of defiance.

"G... go... a... way," she stuttered through chattering teeth.

Barrack walked forward and knelt in front of her. He chuckled when she growled and snapped her teeth at him. She couldn't do much damage as her mouth was covered with a black scarf.

"You'll freeze and this structure is very unsafe and very, very cold," he observed, not wanting to frighten her, but wanting her to understand the danger that she was in.

"I... wou... wouldn't... be... be... here... if... you... had left," she mumbled, pulling her arms in and tucking them against her chest.

Barrack, the structure won't remain standing much longer. You must get her out of there, Brogan said, his words whispering through his mind.

I know. We are leaving in a moment, Barrack replied.

"Let us take you back to your home. It will be warm there," he encouraged, glancing up when he felt a whoosh of cold air sweep in blowing snow through the ceiling. "Delilah, the structure is about to collapse. You and your beasts are in danger."

She shook her head and buried her face in her knees. He motioned for his symbiot to enter and care for the dogs. The symbiot split into two and covered the dogs, sheltering each one in a warm cocoon.

He reached out and gently touched Delilah's hunched shoulder. The trembling in her body became worse, and he began to worry when she didn't look up. Sliding his hand forward, he wrapped his arm around her.

A smothered moan reached him at the same time that she turned into him. By nature, his body temperature was warm due to his dragon. He hissed when she placed her icy hands against his shirt.

Barrack, get out now! Brogan warned.

Barrack heard the snap at the same time as he heard Brogan's warning. His dragon sensed the danger as a nearby dead tree snapped because of the freezing temperatures and the increasing winds. He stood up, shifting as he did. His wings wrapped around Delilah to protect her as the tree hit the roof of the building and the structure collapsed around them, burying them in several feet of snow. The tree landed across his shoulder. He tucked his head and held Delilah safely against his body.

Barrack! Brogan roared.

Get the tree and debris off of us. I will carry Delilah back to the house once I am free. You and your symbiot take care of her beasts, Barrack replied.

He bent his head when he felt a small hand run up and down his chest. Tilting his head, his ear twitched to make out Delilah's softly mumbled words. A sense of calm swept through him, and he could feel its warmth filling the empty void that had haunted him and Brogan for as long as he could remember.

"I'm… just… dreaming, that's all," she mumbled as she stroked him. "Dragons… don't really… exist. It was supposed to be a dream."

Rubbing his chin against the top of her hooded head, he kept her shielded until Brogan and his symbiot cleared enough debris away that he could safely lift off. The storm was increasing in intensity. His dragon struggled against the wind to keep from crashing into the trees. He quickly realized that they were all in peril when several more trees snapped in half and fell, barely missing him.

I cannot protect her from the elements in this form, he said, trying to hold Delilah's shaking body against his chest and protect her from the driving winds and frigid temperatures.

Form a shielded transport, Brogan ordered, reaching out to the symbiots for help.

Barrack's symbiot melted, forming the transport and continued to lengthen. Brogan's symbiot brought the dogs inside the ship that was forming before it dissolved and melded with Barrack's until a sleek capsule-shaped golden ship was formed. Barrack swept down, disappearing into the ship when a section opened for him. He shifted, his arms still tightly wrapped around Delilah.

He turned and watched Brogan enter and shift. Within seconds, they were sealed inside the symbiot ship, protected from the outside elements. He stumbled when a blast of wind came down the mountain and buffeted the ship. Brogan reached out and steadied him.

"We need to get out of this," Brogan commented.

Barrack looked down when Delilah slowly raised her head. She looked at him before turning her gaze to Brogan. Barrack watched her eyes widen when she ran her gaze over the inside of the symbiot ship. Her lips parted and she took a deep, loud breath before her eyes rolled back, and she went limp in his arms.

"Does this mean we frightened her?" Brogan asked.

CHAPTER NINE

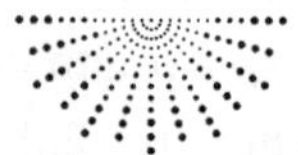

Delilah woke in stages. The first stage began with a loud sigh. It felt good to be warm. Hell, she felt downright toasty. She didn't think she would ever feel her fingers and toes again. In fact, she felt so comfy that she decided to roll over and sleep some more.

The second stage was a little trickier. Her bladder was telling her it was time to take care of business. She barely remembered pushing the warm, silky cover aside, much less padding to the bathroom and back to the bed. The dogs were curled up on their side. A glance out the window showed her that it was dark. She mumbled for Moonshine to scoot over when he stretched out.

"Move your hairy ass over, Moon," she grumbled, crawling back in the warm bed and pulling the soft, silky golden blanket back over her.

A section of her mind replayed her journey to the bathroom, noting that there was a piece of furniture in her room that she didn't remember adding. Since when did she add a huge dragon in the corner near the fireplace?

She shook her head. Her brain must be still in a sleep-induced fog. Lifting her head up, she saw that the dragon was gone. Rolling over, she wrapped her hand in the golden blanket and fell back to sleep.

In the third phase, she sat up in bed with her hand over her thumping heart. She sat still, trying to catch her breath. The remains of a vivid dream replayed in her mind like a scratched record.

"Damn, but that seemed real," she whispered in the darkness.

She turned her head when she heard a soft creak as if someone was shifting in a chair. She scrambled back on the bed when she saw a shadowy figure rise from her rocking chair in the corner near the window. She reached for Moonshine and Rum, only to discover that they were gone.

"You're real," she choked out.

A tall man with the scars running down his face stepped into the dim light cast by the fireplace. She swallowed when he walked closer to the bed. Her fingers curled around the thin, warm golden blanket draped over her.

"You tricked us," he stated, stepping forward.

A look of irritation flashed through Delilah's eyes. "Well, duh! You broke into my house," she retorted and nervously swallowed when he suddenly sat down on the edge of the bed. "What are you doing in my room?"

He raised an eyebrow. "Making sure you don't do anything stupid, like jumping off a roof or going outside in a blizzard," he replied.

Delilah looked out the window. Even though it was pitch-black outside, she could see the accumulation of snow against the window. It was nearly twice as high as it was before and still coming down. She could hear the howl of the wind.

"I've never done that before," she defended, turning her gaze back to him. "You're Brogan, right? The other one is called Barrack?"

A pleased smile curved his lips. "Yes," he nodded.

She narrowed her eyes. This guy was way too full of himself. Who cared if he was tall, dark, and looking good enough to eat? She'd read more than her fair share of romance novels in the library to know what they were really like!

The real men were like Bubba Joe. They were the guys who came with a beat-up truck, played country music, and could install a door that didn't squeak. Guys like this treated the woman like shit until the last few pages and expected the heroine to be all lovey-dovey and apologetic for wanting to kick their ass. Plus, they wouldn't know how to change a light bulb much less a door!

"Well, Brogan, you and your sidekick can get out of my house," she snapped, pushing the cover aside and rolling to the far side of the bed to stand up.

"There is a storm outside," he said, waving at the window.

She gave him a biting smile and shrugged. "Not my problem," she retorted in a sweet voice.

He frowned in confusion. "You would kick my brother and me out in a storm that came close to killing you?" he curiously asked.

"In a heartbeat," she bluffed, placing her hands on her hips. "I didn't invite you in. Just remember to watch the bend going down the road or you might end up in the creek."

"We saved your life. Surely that deserves some appreciation," he countered.

Delilah didn't even hesitate in her reply. She figured he'd try to play the 'save-the-heroine' card. All the heroes did in the novels, and so far, this was following the old Mills and Boon formula like a movie on the Lifetime channel. She wasn't falling for it. She liked the romances that didn't follow the formula but made its own.

"Which wouldn't have been in danger if you hadn't broken into my house," she pointed out. "So, you can add almost killing me to your list of bad decisions."

He folded his arms across his chest. Delilah tried to ignore the thick muscles straining the material of his white shirt. Hell, even his clothing looked like something out of a costume shop! What guy wore so much leather?

The white, long-sleeve shirt was tucked into a pair of dark-brown leather pants, which disappeared into knee-high black leather boots with thick straps running down the sides. He wore some type of elaborate leather utility belt that crisscrossed his chest. His black hair was tightly braided in several rows along his scalp and a carefully groomed mustache and goatee set off his strong jaw. What threw her a little until she decided he must have ordered some contacts online was the color of his eyes. They were almost the same color as the highlights Janie down at the salon added to her hair.

"What list are you talking about?" he asked, his expression twisting as his confusion grew.

Rolling her eyes, Delilah decided either Cuello really was dead or that he hired some really dense hitmen. Whatever the case, she wouldn't go down without a fight. There were some really great books on boxing in the library as well, and she read those too!

Boredom might be what saves my life! she thought.

She decided offense was the best defense. Lifting her hand, she started to tick off every offense that she could think of. Who cared if some of them might be a little far-fetched?

"You broke into my house. You put my dogs in a cage, terrifying them half to death...," she began.

Brogan scowled. "They were not afraid. They were jumping all over us," he interjected, his eyes narrowing. She blithely ignored his interruption, waved a dismissing hand at him and kept going.

"They were so petrified that they passed out. Moonshine and Rum are very sensitive," she snapped. Lifting another finger, she continued. "You tracked snow onto my front rugs. You unlocked the front door and left it partially open, allowing cold air in. You bent the end of my shovel with your forehead."

"You did that when you hit Barrack in the face," he pointed out.

"His face was in the way of me hitting you," she disagreed with a toss of her head and a dainty sniff. "You threatened me. Your presence forced me to jump out of a second story window into a pile of snow." She paused to take a deep breath and to think about what else she could lay on their shoulders.

"Are you finished?" he dryly inquired.

She tilted her head and glowered at him. "No, I'm taking a breath so I can continue," she retorted. "You made me forget my cell phone in the kitchen—which by the way reminds me, I hope you or your brother put the groceries in the refrigerator, or I'll really be pissed."

"Pissed? Why would not placing food in the cold device make you have to relieve yourself?" he asked, puzzled.

"Not that kind of pissed, the other one," she huffed, clenching her fists by her side as her cheeks flushed a delicate pink. Thank goodness for her darker coloring and the dim light. Her face assumed a stern expression, "The pissed as in I'll be mad. You don't want to make me mad. I know Judo," she lied.

Her hope of intimidating him faded when his expression changed. His lips tightened into a straight line, and his eyes flashed with an eerie glow that reminded her of what Barrack had said earlier about being from another world. A sense of unease filled her. What if they were serious and they were from another world? Even worse, what if they were and that meant that all of her dreams were destined to come true?

Perhaps I shouldn't have thrown the psychologist's card away so soon, she thought as doubt began to build inside her.

Her mind flashed back to the events of her escape from the collapsed smokehouse. The image of a warm massive body trickled through her mind. Her brain had become foggy by the time she made it to the shed with the dogs. She could never remember being so cold in her life.

The few hundred yards to the shed had felt like miles in the deepening snow and the horrific wind had cut straight through all the layers of clothing she had on to the bone. Her fingers and feet went from a painful tingle of cold to numb. It didn't help that she fell several times.

The dogs gave up trying to go ahead of her and had followed the best they could in the tracks she left behind. Just when she thought she was lost and doomed to die, she had stumbled again. When she looked up, she could see the outline of the shed not more than three feet in front of her.

If she hadn't been afraid of the tears freezing to her skin, she would have cried. Instead, she barely remembered crawling and half-staggering to the old, rickety wooden door. She had pushed the door in, uncaring if there were other critters inside.

The interior of the shed hadn't been much better than being outside as far as the cold was concerned, but at least it was a buffer against the wind and there was no snow. She and the dogs had staggered to the corner and sank down. Remorse filled her when she remembered how Moonshine and Rum were uncontrollably shivering. Huddling together, she hoped their combined body heat would help keep them alive.

Within minutes, the fog that was forming in her brain had settled to a thick whipped cream, so dense that she swore she could see the swirls in it. She didn't know how long they were in the shed or how the men had found them in the raging storm.

She shook her head when she remembered Barrack talking to her and that she argued back. Trying to communicate had finally been the last straw for her frozen body. She remembered laying her head down on her knees in the hope that her breath might warm her. Everything after that blurred and she decided she must have started to hallucinate.

Startled, she looked up at Brogan when she felt his warm hand under her chin. *When had he moved?* she wondered, blinking from the dim light.

"What?" she asked, her mind still focused on her memory.

"I asked who this Judo is?" he demanded in a soft voice that was edged with a hardness that made her wary.

Who was Judo? For a moment a confused expression appeared on her face then it cleared when comprehension finally dawned on her.

"Judo isn't a person. It is a form of self-defense, like boxing or karate," she muttered, pushing against his chest. "You… are in my personal space."

The wry grin that formed on his lips made her even more nervous. She grunted when her hands encountered only hard muscle. She quickly decided that retreat and strategic planning were her best courses of action for the moment. She ran her hand down his chest, surprised when she heard what sounded suspiciously like a purr, and stepped away from him. Delilah flashed him an easy grin to cover her nervousness before she turned on her heel and retreated to the bathroom.

She slammed the door harder than she'd planned and twisted the key in the lock. Leaning against the door, she tilted her head back and fanned her face. Damn, but he was hot.

"Why are the bad guys good-looking, while the good guys end up looking like Bubba Joe?" she groaned, thinking that baggy pants and butt-cracks could become all the rage if Brogan were wearing them.

"Who is Bubba Joe?" Brogan demanded from the other side of the door.

Delilah bit her lip to keep from laughing. Shaking her head, she elbowed the door to let him know she heard him. Looking out the window, she could see that it was getting light outside.

"Go away, Brogan. Better yet, make yourself useful. You can make sure all my groceries are put away and make some breakfast before the power goes out," she ordered, her voice laced with amusement.

"You are hungry? I will get Barrack to prepare a meal for you. Do not try to escape again," he warned.

She peered out at the mass of solid white and shivered. "Don't worry. If anyone is leaving the next time, it will be you and your brother. And don't hurt my dogs!" she added, wondering where, in the hell, her missing canines were and hoping that her imaginary dragon didn't eat them as a snack.

"They are annoying Barrack. I believe they like him better than me," Brogan stated.

Delilah chuckled. "I can't imagine why," she sarcastically muttered under her breath.

She waited until she heard the bedroom door open and shut again before she unlocked the bathroom door and peered out. Satisfied that the bedroom was empty, she hurried over to the dresser and retrieved fresh clothing.

She wanted a hot shower before the power went out. A quick glance out of the window told her it would only be a matter of time before a tree snapped and landed on the lines. She had a generator installed for the whole house along with a separate propane tank, but she wouldn't run it except in an emergency.

Retracing her steps, she returned to the bathroom and locked the door again. She turned on the water, thankful for the unending supply of hot water to melt the last of the chill from her bones. She undressed, stuffed her dirty clothes in the hamper, and crammed her hair into a plastic shower cap to keep it dry.

Sliding the door open, she stepped inside the steamy shower stall. She would have loved a bath, but decided a shower would be quicker. It wasn't until she reached for the bar of soap that she noticed the gold bracelets wrapped around her wrists.

She touched their intricate designs in awe. Three dragons wrapped around each other. On each side of them were stars and a round object that looked like a planet. At her touch, warmth spread through her fingertips and up her arm. She pulled away, shaken by the vision that popped into her head when she touched the gold. The vision was of the two men. The vivid colors were almost like seeing a movie in her head.

"Weird, totally weird, Delilah. I think you have frostbite on the brain, girl," she muttered before her stomach growled. A soft laugh shook her and she grinned. "You'd think if I was going to imagine something, it would be food. I'm starving!"

She hummed under her breath as she soaped her body. She scowled when she felt the hair stubble on her legs. She needed to shave. She was unaware that her simple, daily ablutions were causing feelings of such devastating frustration and growing need in the two alien warriors who were monitoring her every movement. If she had known, she might have had a bit more fun tormenting them.

CHAPTER TEN

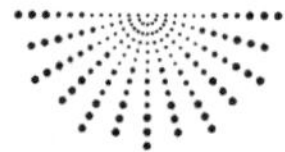

Barrack looked up when his brother stepped into the kitchen. He was studying the food packaging and wished there was a way to retrieve the food replicator from their ship. He turned the package over, trying to decipher how to prepare the food by the images.

"We should have learned to read our mate's language. This makes no sense to me," he grumbled.

Brogan looked over his shoulder and wiggled his nose in distaste. "It was difficult enough learning to speak it. There is not enough in that package to feed one, much less three people," he noted.

"I did not hear any screams," Barrack casually commented. "I assume that means she is no longer afraid of us."

He look at Brogan when he chuckled. An envious expression crossed his face. He had sat with Delilah the first part of the night before changing places with Brogan. It appeared that Delilah's two beasts had taken a liking to him. When the two dogs became animated and tried to play with his dragon, Barrack decided it would be better to leave the room so they didn't disturb their mistress.

"She has fire in her," Brogan said with a chuckle. "Where are her beasts? She has a great attachment to them and warned us to care for them."

Barrack nodded toward the front sitting room. "They like lying in front of the fire," he said.

He looked up when he heard the sound of an alarm. That alarm had sounded nearly a dozen times, mostly when a large gust of wind buffeted the house. He had traced the noise to a large box that was obviously used to generate power.

"Her power source is in danger," he commented.

Brogan nodded. "I noticed the same thing last night before I came up. The thin lines we saw leading to the house must supply it. I am surprised it has not gone off before now. I was thinking...," he said before his voice faded and his eyes became glazed.

Barrack stiffened at the same time as his brother. The connection with their symbiots now included Delilah. By the time he had lowered her onto the bed last night, he and Brogan's symbiots were already fluttering over her and claiming her. There was absolutely no doubt that Delilah was their mate. Even if Aikaterina hadn't shown them, their reactions to Delilah and that of their symbiots and dragons, sealed their fates.

He bowed his head, focusing on Delilah through his symbiot wrapped around her right wrist. Brogan's symbiot graced her left wrist. Half of his symbiot was also upstairs on her bed. It had formed a warm blanket that monitored her comfort throughout the night.

Their symbiots were the reason that they could give Delilah a little more space and time to adjust to their presence. If she tried to trick them as she had yesterday, their symbiots would alert them and then prevent her from doing anything that could endanger her life.

"Goddess, every time she brushes my symbiot across her skin I can feel it," Brogan hissed, his eyes closed.

"I know," Barrack replied in a strained voice as he experienced the same pleasure-torture.

Barrack turned his back to his brother, raised his arm and rested his forehead against it while leaning against the cold device where he had placed the food items. He moved his other hand to his cock, which became filled until he was afraid he'd embarrass himself. Closing his eyes, he concentrated on the images his symbiot was sending to him, for the moment uncaring that what he was doing was probably wrong.

After centuries of waiting, he justified his invasion of Delilah's privacy with the promise that he would confess—one day—about his lack of control. Until then, he was going to enjoy every nanosecond of his misconduct. In his mind, he replaced the image of the symbiot and Delilah's hand with his own.

His symbiot warmed with delight, understanding his need to experience this first moment of exploration. A soft groan slipped from his lips and he fought the urge to charge upstairs. He unwittingly rocked his hips forward when she slid her hand down between her legs. At that moment, he wished he was a bar of soap.

"Soap? Really?" Brogan snickered.

"Shut up and get out of my head. This is my fantasy," he muttered, returning to focus on the soap bubbles.

Ten minutes later, Delilah was toweling herself off. She cut short her deliciously hot shower when she noticed the light in the bathroom flickering. The last thing she wanted to do was to be stuck covered in soap bubbles with no running water. The idea of having to do a mad dash downstairs to the breaker box and back up again in a towel with two strangers in the house was also a great motivator.

She pulled off the shower cap and hung it on the hook in the shower to dry. Picking up her bra, she fastened it. She winced when she felt a slight tingle to her left nipple where the bracelet touched it. Glancing at it, she ran her finger along the smooth, silky surface looking for a reason. It was warm, but otherwise she didn't feel anything pointy. She looked down, gently probing her nipple, but didn't feel anything unusual. Shrugging, she finished pulling her bra on before grabbing the thigh-length burgundy sweater that she had found down at the Alleghany Cares thrift shop.

A shiver ran through her when a draft of cold air flowed out of the vent in the floor from the old furnace that piped heat through the house. She slipped on a pair of lace and silk panties and groaned in frustration. She forgot to grab a pair of thermal underwear to put on under her jeans.

Walking over to the door, she placed her ear against it. When she didn't hear anything, she unlocked the bathroom door and peeked out. Silence and warmth greeted her. She needed to install the small gas fireplace in the bathroom soon. It was still in the box down in the cellar. Up until now, she had been leaving the bathroom door open to allow some heat to enter the bathroom.

She opened the door, glanced quickly at the closed door to her bedroom and hurried over to her dresser. Pulling open the drawer where she kept her cold weather undies, she pulled out a pair of thermals and shut the drawer. Turning, she was about to step into the leggings when a movement on her bed caught her attention. She looked up and froze. A massive golden cat was lying in the center of her king-size bed. It rose to its feet, stretched, and yawned, revealing two canine teeth that had to be at least ten inches long, and as sharp as a butcher's knife.

Delilah released a bloodcurdling scream that would have made Fay Wray envious. The creature shook and the golden mane swirled around its head. Her mouth remained open even as the sound of the scream faded. She watched in astonishment as the creature sneezed and sat down like it was one of her dogs—*on her side of the bed!*

"Oh, hell no!" she growled, her eyes flaring as she glared at the creature when it rubbed its chin against her pillow that it had moved to the end of the bed. "That is my side! If you aren't going to eat me, then move your ass over to the other side of the bed—and quit rubbing on my pillow! God, you're as bad as the dogs," she groaned.

Brogan made it to the staircase a half second before Barrack. His long legs took the steps three at a time as he charged up to the second floor. His heart was pounding as he slid into the wall at the top and bounced off. Even though Barrack's symbiot was trying to reassure them that everything was alright, the sound of Delilah's terrified scream had sent a shockwave of fear through him.

He burst through the door, barely managing to keep from ripping it off its hinges. His wild eyes searched the room, stopping on Delilah who was pointing a shaking finger at something. Rotating on his heel to see who she was yelling at, he drew in a shuddering breath when he saw Barrack's symbiot turn its head and grin at him.

"What happened?" he demanded, taking a deep, calming breath.

"What happened? What happened? Do you not see that there is a huge… thing, on my bed? What in the hell is it?" Delilah demanded, stomping her foot. "I swear, ever since you two appeared in my house strange shit has been happening. Will you leave my damn pillow alone? I told you to get your ass on the other side of the bed," she turned and snapped.

Brogan watched with relieved amusement as Delilah reached forward and grabbed the corner of her pillow, jerking it out of the symbiot's reach. She held it, along with a pair of brightly colored leggings and a blue pair of pants against her heaving chest.

His gaze followed the movement of her breasts, remembering the small tweak he had given her nipple when she brushed his symbiot bracelet over it. The grin on his face was quickly hidden when he felt Barrack elbow him to the side so he could enter the room. He stepped aside, but his eyes hungrily moved over Delilah's bare legs.

"Eyes to the face, alien man," she ordered, snapping her fingers.

Brogan immediately raised his eyes to her face. He couldn't keep the grin from his lips when he saw the exasperation on her face. She pursed her lips and shook her head.

"Men! I swear, if you are aliens, then all of you come from the same place—Planet Horneywood! Now, will someone please tell me what in the hell that… thing is?!" she demanded again with a pointed look at him.

"Barrack's symbiot. Mine is currently watching your beasts downstairs," he replied.

"Barrack's symbiot—oh, well that explains everything," she sarcastically replied. "Can you expand upon that? My definition of a symbiot and yours may be slightly different. I want to know if I need to worry about that thing eating me or taking over my body."

"The only ones who will be eating you are us," Barrack replied, reaching out to stroke his symbiot when it shimmered.

Behave, Brogan warned the symbiot. *She isn't ready yet. Remember what Asim, Pearl, Jaguin, and Sara told us.*

The symbiot responded to his chiding by sending Delilah a vivid image of her between the two men. Brogan winced when he heard Delilah's sudden hiss. His gaze shifted from the symbiot to her shocked face. The intense desire to kiss her overshadowed his common sense.

He stepped in front of her and cupped her face. "You are so beautiful to me," he murmured before he started to bend his head.

The stars that swam before his eyes had nothing to do with the kiss and everything to do with her knee impacting his groin. This was the second time his manhood had received such abusive treatment in a matter of hours.

He removed his hands from her face as the intense pain registered. His knees trembled and he stumbled back, trying to remain upright when all he wanted to do was curl up on the floor. It would appear the Goddess was going to grant him his wish because when he leaned forward, Delilah delivered a powerful punch to his recently healed nose and a right hook to his jaw.

"What the... why did you do that?" Barrack asked in a startled voice.

"Two words—personal space—remember them," she growled.

"Where... where did you learn to fight like this?" Brogan groaned.

He rolled onto his back and looked up at her. He had one hand on his throbbing nose, the other on his equally pounding crotch, and his eyes were glued to a pair of black silk panties. She had dropped her pillow and her clothing when she hit him.

She flushed and gripped the sides of her sweater, pulling it tight as she scooted to the side. She bent over at the last second and grabbed the leggings and the blue pants from the floor.

"It's called boxing. I learned it from a book. You might want to try reading one about respecting other people's personal space," she snapped before she straightened and strode over to the bathroom door with a toss of her head. "And tell that thing to get off my side of the damn bed!" she added, before slamming the door and locking it.

Brogan turned his head and stared up at the ceiling. He released his nose and reached for the pillow that was lying on the floor next to him. Grunting, he shoved it under his head and relaxed before he commanded the symbiot wrapped around his wrist to heal his bruised body once again.

His chuckle blended with Barrack's. He shook his head. Their quiet chuckles turned to full-fledged laughter, drawing more groans from him as the small symbiot moved from one spot to another.

"She read it in a book," Barrack repeated, taking a deep breath and shaking his head in amazement.

"Personal space—I need to read.... Goddess, I don't know what hurts worse, my balls, my jaw, my nose, or my pride," Brogan admitted, closing his eyes. "She has a very strong punch for someone so small."

"As long as she takes it out on you, I'll be fine," Barrack retorted. "You should have seen your face, brother. I don't think I've ever seen such shock on it before."

Brogan tilted his head and looked up at Barrack. "Me? You should have seen yours when she hit you between the eyes with the shovel. She is upset you bent it, by the way. You will have to repair her tool," he said, wincing when he realized that he had a cut on his lip. "I never want to be kicked or kneed in the groin again."

"You could try wearing a cup," Delilah commented as she opened the bathroom door, completely dressed this time.

Brogan looked at her with a frown. "Why would I put a cup in my pants?" he asked.

He followed her with his eyes as she walked over to him and bent over his figure. She looked down at him and grinned, her eyes glittering with amusement. He warily watched her tuck a loose strand of hair behind her ear.

"Baseball, sweetheart," she said before she pulled her pillow out from under his head. "And my pillow is off limits to dogs, symbiots, and alien males."

He winced when the back of his head thudded against the carpeted floor. He guessed he should be thankful the floor underneath was wooden and his head was only a few inches from it. She straightened and tossed her pillow on the bed. Barrack quickly moved from her side of the bed when she glared at him. She turned on her heel and walked out of the bedroom door.

"Where are you going?" Brogan demanded, sitting up as she exited the room.

"To the kitchen," she called over her shoulder. "I'm still starving despite someone's promise of food."

For a moment, he sat on the floor watching her walk down the long hallway. He waved his symbiot away when it moved to run over the back of his head. He knew he had a stupid grin on his face, but he couldn't help it. Their mate definitely wasn't afraid of them.

I no have to read book to know how to bite, his dragon informed him with a gleeful sigh.

Oh, shut up, he muttered, grabbing Barrack's hand when his brother offered it to him.

CHAPTER ELEVEN

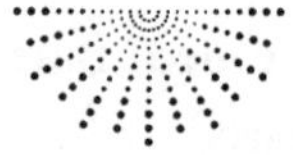

Delilah held onto the railing and skipped down the stairs. She couldn't keep the goofy grin off her face. For some reason, the knowledge that the men upstairs were aliens—though she was still trying to wrap her head around the fact that her dream of them was real—instead of drug cartel thugs should have scared her more than it did.

She paused at the end of the staircase and shook her head in disbelief. Moonshine and Rum were chasing more than a dozen flying golden dragons while a large golden version of the dogs watched from her refinished and newly reupholstered antique settee.

"Okay, I concede. I have aliens in my house. Fat lot of protection you two wimps turned out to be," she informed the dogs when they looked up at her with happy grins and their tongues lolling out.

She stepped down the last step and padded down the hall, looking up when the lights flickered again and then went out. Pausing, she sighed when the lights didn't come back on. They would be down for the count more than likely until after the storm. Thank goodness daytime was almost here and it was already starting to get light out.

"Well, as light as it will get," she said, looking out of the kitchen window at the overcast skies as she entered.

A glance around the room told her that her aliens had been busy. All of the bags of food that she had placed on the table, floor and counter were put away. Curious to see if they were able to figure out where everything went, she opened the refrigerator.

"Oh, my," she said, straightening and shaking her head.

Closing the refrigerator, she started opening the cabinets. She chuckled as she went through each of the upper cabinets where she kept her dishes, food, and her limited selection of spices. Completely intrigued, she walked over to the pantry door and opened it. She felt along the shelf for the battery-operated light.

Tapping the light on, she looked at the shelves. She was currently using the space for storing the tools and materials she used to renovate the house. It was more convenient than the basement and she didn't need a pantry full of food when she and the dogs were only here during the weekends.

"Wow!" she mused, shaking her head and staring at the shelves.

"What is wrong?" Brogan asked.

She looked at him and raised an eyebrow before turning her gaze to Barrack standing behind him. If she had to guess, this was the work of Barrack. Brogan struck her as the more impulsive of the two. She looked at the shelves one last time before she turned off the light and closed the door.

"Someone has some compulsive organizational issues," she replied, looking pointedly at Barrack. "I'll warn you now, I can organize a library like no one else, but don't expect my personal life to be as neat."

"Why do you say that? I think your home is very organized. Even Barrack commented that I should take a lesson from you since I would not listen to him," Brogan curiously asked.

"I'm not this good," she admitted with a laugh and waved her hand toward the pantry door, the refrigerator, and the cabinets. "Everything is organized by size, product, and all labels facing forward. I'm positively shocked that you didn't alphabetize them. You aren't falling down on the job, are you, Barrack?" she teased.

Barrack scowled at her. "We didn't learn how to read your

language or it would be," he retorted with a responding grin, looking pleased with himself that she noticed and recognized *his* touch behind the work.

"No worries. I think you did a good enough job without knowing the ABC's. I might have to get you to help me at the library," she playfully added before focusing on her rumbling stomach. "It looks like the power is out. I have a generator, but I'd like to avoid using it except for emergencies and running the pump for showers and such. It uses the same propane tank which I use for the fireplaces, stove, hot water heater, and dryer. I have a choice. I can run the generator for about a week or the rest of the stuff for at least three months depending on how warm I want the house. I'd rather not take a chance of running out with the crazy weather we've been having. Unfortunately, that means no pump; so no water. We can fill up some buckets with snow and let it melt to use in the toilets." She paused and looked at the men standing in front of her with an expression of uncertainty. "I mean, that's if aliens use the bathroom. Not that I really need to know if you have the equipment for it, just if you do, I want to make sure you guys are house-trained and know how to flush the toilets."

"We must relieve ourselves on occasion, and we do it using a facility similar to your own," Barrack retorted.

Delilah raised her hands. "That's all I need to know. I figured from Brogan's reaction when I hit him in his family jewels that you guys might have some of the same equipment down south, but it never hurts to ask just in case," she replied, her eyes instinctively moving to the area she was referring to.

She tried to keep her expression neutral, but from Brogan's muffled laughter, she must not have done a very good job of concealing her thoughts. She lifted her gaze to his and shrugged, once again thankful for her darker skin color that helped to hide her heat-filled cheeks.

Her growling stomach reminded her that she was hungry. She turned to look at the package lying on the counter. It was a package of Top Ramen.

Perfect! she thought with a sense of relief.

The noodle soup was quick, filling, and easy to fix. A pan of hot water and in five minutes, she would have a bowl filled with noodles and a mystery powdered broth packet that would either kill her eventually or preserve her body forever. At the moment, she didn't care. She was hungry. Besides, the stuff was ridiculously cheap and the dogs loved it too.

"So, I guess from the package on the counter, you guys want some soup. It is a good thing I can buy this stuff by the caseload. I might need one to satisfy you both. Do your gold symbiot things eat?" she asked, turning to bend over and grab a pot out of the bottom cabinet. "Wow, you've even done the pots and pans. Who knows, Barrack, you might give Bubba Joe a run for his money, after all!"

Straightening, she turned with a pot for the soup in one hand and a frying pan in the other. She could make a couple of grilled cheese sandwiches to go with the soup. A startled squeak slipped out when she discovered that both men were standing right behind her.

The fact that they had silently closed the distance was alarming enough, but it was the physical differences in their appearances that really shook her. Looking at their faces, she blinked when she saw that their eyes were glowing with tiny flames. If that wasn't freaky enough, it looked like they had scales rolling up their necks and across their cheeks.

"Holy Moly! You've got.... Both of you have.... You guys are like giant lizards!" she gasped. Swallowing, she gripped the frying pan tighter in her right hand, wielding it like a weapon. "Get... get back. I don't...."

"We are not lizards. The Tiliqua are a lizard species," Brogan stated, his eyes glittering with the golden fire.

Barrack nodded. "We are dragons. There is a huge difference," he added, twin flames burning in his eyes as well.

Delilah placed the pot onto the counter and pulled off the lid. Lizards, dragons, whatever—she didn't give a rat's ass what they were. They were aliens with scales. Every horror book she had ever read flashed through her mind. The scales that ran along their skin were light green with specks of white and actually beautiful.

If she wasn't so damn scared, she would have taken a closer look. Once again, horrific images amplified by her own vivid imagination of mutilation and people being devoured sent a wave of fight-or-flight through her. Since there was nowhere to run, her only recourse was to fight. She knew she could put them both on the ground. This time, though, she'd have to knock them out! With a growl of warning, she held the pot lid like a shield and jabbed at them with the aluminum frying pan.

"Get back," she ordered, her eyes glittering with determination. "I know how to fence."

Barrack frowned. "Our dragons will not harm you, Delilah," he promised.

"You even stroked him. Mine wants to feel your hand on him too," Brogan purred as his face started to change and a soft, rumbling sound emanated from his chest which made her start swinging at his head.

"No dragons in the house," she snarled. "Do you have any idea of the damage they could do to my wood floors? Out! I want you both out of my house now! Take your gold things, your dragons, and your alien selves back to wherever you came from."

Both men jumped back when she kept swinging the frying pan at them. They stumbled toward the back door that led out into the mudroom. Delilah saw them wince when she clanged the lid against the frying pan.

"Delilah...," Barrack tried to reason with her as he felt behind himself for the doorknob.

"Don't you Delilah me! For all I know you ate my best friend! Maybe that is why no one can find Sara!" she said, her eyes filling with tears at the thought. "I want you out of my house!"

Her lower lip began to tremble. She gasped when Brogan reached out and grabbed both of her wrists. He slowly pulled her closer to him, his gaze locked on her face. She tilted her head back and looked at him with a watery, defiant look that was ruined by her sniff. His gaze softened, melting some of her fear.

"We didn't eat your friend, Delilah. We live by a code of honor, something that we have not always been very good at, but we try. We will leave you alone, but our symbiots will stay with you. They will protect you, even from us if necessary," he gently explained.

Delilah could see the deep regret and sadness in his eyes. He looked lost and lonely. She parted her lips when he leaned toward her and pressed a brief kiss to her forehead. After he released her, their eyes remained locked for several seconds before he turned and murmured to his brother that he would be outside.

She watched as he opened the door. A frigid blast of icy air swept into the room. Barrack looked at her with the same lost, lonely expression before he stepped forward, ran the back of his fingers along her cheek, then turned and followed his brother outside, closing the door firmly behind him.

Trembling, she walked over to the window and looked outside. Her arms fell to her side. In the swirling snowstorm, she saw a truly magical sight – twin dragons. They each turned in a circle, their feet tamping down a spot for them to sit down. Her hand rose to her mouth when she saw Barrack tilting his head back, looking up at the sky, and then releasing an anguished roar that tore at her heart.

CHAPTER TWELVE

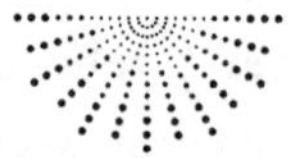

Brogan's dragon pawed at the snow. The wind had died down a little, but he could sense it was merely a lull in the storm as it changed direction. Thick flakes continued to fall but not like the blinding flurries of yesterday afternoon and throughout the night.

The snow was deep enough that in some places it rubbed against his belly. Hopping over the depressed section, he looked up at the roof. Long icicles hung from the eaves over Delilah's bedroom window.

She is lucky she not die, his dragon muttered, kicking at the white fluff.

Yes, she is, he agreed.

His dragon swept a wide circle in the snow with his tail, smoothing the area around him before he sat down. With a grunt, the large green and white dragon sat down in the center and irritably blew short blasts of fire at some flakes of snow that threatened to fall into his circle. Brogan sensed his dragon's disappointment. What concerned him the most was his dragon's acceptance of their failure.

We broken, his dragon mourned, drawing a claw through the snow.

Yes, but look at what Delilah has done to her home. It is old like us, but her love is healing it. She can do the same for us, he said, trying to encourage his dragon not to give up.

His dragon turned its head and looked at the house before returning its attention to blowing small flames at the falling snow. Brogan wanted to groan and shake his head. Instead of feeling sorry for themselves, they should be thinking of a way to get back in the house—this time with Delilah's permission.

Barrack..., he softly called, trying to connect with his more level-headed brother.

Go away, Brogan, Barrack muttered.

Brogan forced his dragon to turn around and face Barrack. It had made a circle the same as his. He could tell from the droop of the dragon's wings that it was feeling the same way, too.

What are we going to do? We can't give up now, Brogan insisted.

We scared her, Brogan. I saw the fear in her eyes just like.... Barrack's dragon lifted its head and roared in anguish.

She is a fighter. You saw her, Brogan argued, growing desperate as his own doubts began to build.

He wanted to reach out to his symbiot, but was afraid to in case it was feeling the same way. Hell, he could still feel her shock and horror when she saw the signs of his dragon rippling across his skin.

Mate no like dragons, his dragon stated, spreading his wings and falling backwards to stare up at the sky.

The realization that Delilah might never accept his and Barrack's dragon hit him hard. He thought they had a chance when she started teasing them. She wasn't afraid of their symbiot once she realized it wouldn't hurt her.

When she screamed earlier, he sensed that it was because she was startled. Those feelings were confirmed when he and Barrack entered her room to find her ordering the symbiot off of her side of the bed and away from her pillow.

What he felt in the kitchen was different. She was terrified—and repulsed. He opened his mouth and blew out a burst of fire, melting the snow which fell on him like raindrops. The temperature was so cold that the water droplets froze on his scales, making them look like they were captured in glass.

What are we going to do, Barrack? Brogan murmured.

Did they come so far and wait so long just to lose the one person in the universe who made the struggle worth fighting for? This was a fight they had to win—not just for their lives but for the life of their mate. Forcing his dragon to roll over onto its stomach, he lifted his head to growl in frustration at his brother when he didn't answer. Instead, he ended up with a snowball between the eyes.

Delilah watched the dragons in fascination. They didn't look anything like a lizard. Their scales shimmered against the falling snow and were quite lovely. Brogan turned in a circle, his tail creating a wide, deep rut and he sat down. She knew it was him by the scars on the left side of his face. How the dragon could have identical scars confused her.

"Heck, even how they change into a dragon confuses me," she muttered, leaning against the window sill and hugging the frying pan and pot lid to her chest.

She turned her head when the symbiots came in. They were in the same shape as the Rottweilers. Biting her bottom lip, she looked outside then back to them.

"Can you change into anything you want to?" she asked.

One of the symbiots nodded while the other shimmered and changed. Her mouth fell open when she found herself staring at a humongous teddy bear like one of Rum's squeaky toys. She snorted when the golden creature changed again into a miniature horse before shifting one last time into the big cat that had been on her bed.

"Wow! I saw some smaller ones earlier in the shape of dragons. Was that part of you or are there smaller ones around?" she asked, glancing out of the window once more before walking over to the two creatures.

She gasped when the other symbiot dissolved, and dozens of tiny dragons the size of a hummingbird swarmed around her. She couldn't control her giggles when several of them lifted her hair up. She held out her hands, marveling when more landed on her.

"Oh, my goodness," she breathed, watching them dissolve and form several more bracelets on her arms.

Her hand reached up to touch her ear when she felt them there before moving to her throat. Looking down, she saw that she now wore a necklace in the shape of a bird of prey. Warmth filled her, wrapping around her as surely as if the creatures were casting a magical spell. She could see images of Brogan and Barrack as children.

The flashes of their lives in vivid colors swept through her as if she was watching a television documentary. Over time, she saw their parent's joy and wonder turn to sadness. She didn't understand until she saw the people around them. Everywhere she looked there was suspicion and fear as they stared at the two young boys who just wanted to fit in.

"Some people really need their asses kicked sometimes, don't they?" she murmured, feeling the hurt and sadness in the creatures.

She reached down and hugged the symbiot when it reformed into the cat, minus the tiny bits of gold it left had on her wrists. A sense of calm washed through her and she turned and did the same thing to the other one. She was definitely a sucker for the underdog.

She heard a soft hiss in the kitchen when the symbiot she hugged last nudged her with its head. She followed the symbiots' gazes to the window. Turning, she walked back to the window and looked out into her backyard. Brogan was lying on his back, blowing small fireballs up at the snow while Barrack sat, with his back to his brother and the house, staring out at the desolate, snow-covered forest.

She looked at each of the symbiots when they came to stand next to her. If you could tell how a dragon was feeling by their body language, there was no missing that both of the brothers were feeling pretty low. She looked up at the sky. The snow was still falling heavily, but the winds had died down. It would still be 'freeze-your-ass' cold, but sometimes a girl had to suck it up and suffer through if she was going to set things right.

"Have you two ever played in the snow before?" she asked.

The symbiots snorted at her innocent question. She smiled at the memories of her childhood her parents and grandparents playing in the snow. It took a minute to realize that the two symbiots could see what she was picturing in her head just like she could see what they were showing her.

She blew out a loud breath. "I sure hope you guys really are the fun sci-fi type and not from the Twilight Zone," she muttered. "Breakfast will have to wait. Let me get my jacket, gloves, and boots on. We'll have to sneak up on them from the front. Are you two any good at sneaking around?"

The disgusted look they gave her made her laugh like crazy as she hurried to the front door. Grabbing one of her jackets hanging on the hall tree by the door, she slipped it on and zipped it up while sliding her feet into thick, lined rubber boots. She finished with a pair of gloves, a scarf, and a knitted black cap.

There was no way she would stay out long. Since she didn't really know how to talk to a dragon, and she wasn't sure exactly what she should say to the men—except, maybe, I'm sorry for being terrified of alien dragon-shifting men.

"You know, it isn't like I've ever really met any aliens before, so I have a right to be a little nervous," she informed the symbiots before she looked up and groaned. Standing in the doorway were Moonshine and Rum. It figured the two Rottweilers would wait until she was dressed to decide they needed to go out as well. "Come on."

It took her an extra five minutes to dress each dog in their doggie sweaters and the padded booties she had picked up at Ofelia's Boutique a few days before. She loved the fun stuff that she could find in town.

"You two don't get lost. I'm not chasing you down," she warned, opening the front door.

A frigid blast of arctic air almost had her doing a one hundred and eighty degree turn. If the two dogs and their new best friends hadn't charged past her, she might have considered it. Trying to be brave, she closed the front door and tucked her hands under her armpits.

"Go do your business while you can, boys," she ordered.

Freeing one hand, she made sure that the scarf covered her nose and mouth. In all her years living here, she couldn't remember the weather ever being this freaking cold. Walking around the wrap-around porch, she tried to step as quietly as she could when she reached the back side of the house. The porch narrowed where the entrance to the mudroom was before opening up again on the other side.

A sense of guilt swept through her. How she could order anyone out into this type of weather defied everything her mother and father had ever taught her about good manners and kindness to others. Since she was already feeling guilty and knew she would have to apologize for being a bad hostess, she decided she might as well make the apology worthwhile. The problem was – how did you get the attention of a dragon?

The solution came to her in the form of a little mischievous fun. If she wasn't brave enough to tap them on the shoulder with her hand, she'd do it with a snowball. Scooping a large pile of snow off the railing, she pressed it together to form a nice, softball-size snowball. She had not only read books on softball, but had played it as well. Silently stepping back, she wound up as best she could in the many layers of clothing and released the compact missile just as Brogan rolled over onto his stomach.

"Oh dear! Sorry about that. I was trying to get your attention, but you turned and well… You have to admit that was a good hit," she said with an apologetic smile when the snowball struck him right between the eyes.

She squealed in surprise when he flicked his tail and a small, bucket size amount of snow rained down around her. Her lips curved into a huge grin. She hadn't had a good snowball fight in years!

Reaching out, she formed another and threw it, this time at Barrack who had turned around when he heard her voice. She giggled when the dragon looked down at the snowball slowly sliding and dissolving down his chest. The feeling of lightheartedness grew when Brogan shook his head and gave her a toothy grin as he realized that she was having fun and playing with the dragons.

In all honesty, the book Pete's Dragon had always been one of her favorites. She had always wanted a dragon of her own as a child. Well, now she had two. Scooping up more snow from the railing, she moved along the porch firing snowballs at the two dragons who finally realized that she was playing with them.

Delighted snorts and rumbles echoed over the snow-covered mountain. Delilah ducked when Brogan tossed a tail full of snow at her. She squealed and took off as fast as she could along the porch. She was almost to the end when Brogan pounced out of his hole and landed near the steps.

Slapping at the snow on the railing, she sent a wave of the white fluffy mixture all over his face. Scooting by him, she made a dash around the house to the front steps. Behind her, she heard Brogan sneeze. A heated wave of air brushed past her, and she looked over her shoulder to make sure he hadn't set her house on fire. That would be horrible in more ways than one if he burned down their only shelter for miles.

Relieved when she saw that there were no flames, she focused on her escape. She didn't want to go inside yet. Besides, she needed to make sure the dogs were okay. She descended the stairs and had only taken two steps before she discovered that Moonshine and Rum were not only safe but had decided to join in the fun with a little help.

"Really?" she breathlessly demanded, watching the dogs standing on a golden symbiot sled pulled by the other symbiot.

A movement out of the corner of her eye made her squeal. Brogan was rounding the corner of the house with a devilish grin on his dragon face. Turning, she tried to run. It was impossible in the snow. Her feet sunk in the knee-deep fluff. It didn't help that her boots were a little big because she forgot to put on a second pair of socks.

After a dozen steps, she was hopelessly winded and in deeper snow than she realized. Her arms wind-milled two circles as she tried to keep her balance when her right boot stuck. Looking over her shoulder, she saw that Brogan wasn't having the same issues. He merely hopped to get where he wanted to go.

"Help!" she laughed, pulling on her boot.

She twisted and fell when her boot suddenly popped free. Lying on her back, she found herself staring up at the upside down face of Barrack. He had snuck around the other side. Her eyes softened when he spread his wings over her to protect her from the falling snow.

"I'm sorry," she said, tears suddenly burning her eyes. "I shouldn't have overreacted like I did. I've never met an alien before and, well… I shouldn't have acted that way."

Her arms lifted when he lowered his head and brushed his chin against her cheek. Delilah slid her fingers along his long jaw, amazed at how soft and warm his scales were. She sat up when he pulled back, scooting along the snow to keep her sheltered.

A nudge at the center of her back sent a wave of confusion through her until she realized that Barrack wanted her to move closer to Brogan. Reaching out her hand, she tentatively touched Brogan's outstretched claw. She held onto it as he helped her stand. A shiver ran through her when a gust of frigid air swept through the valley and up the mountain, cutting through the layers of clothing she wore.

Looking over her shoulder, she felt Barrack nudge her forward again at the same time as Brogan encouraged her to step closer. Understanding dawned when Brogan lifted his other front leg and curled it under her so that she could sit in his large palm. She held onto his claws when he lifted her to his chest and drew his wings protectively around her.

A sense of awe swept through her when she peered at Barrack through the opening Brogan left between his wings. Barrack stepped closer and lowered his head. With a puff of air, warmth filled the narrow, protected space they had formed with their bodies. They knew she was cold and were protecting her.

Stunned by the compassionate act, she slowly leaned against Brogan's chest. She reached down and pulled off the glove on her right hand. She reached up to touch him, but paused less than an inch from his chest as a wave of uncertainty hit her. What was she doing?

These were aliens, dragons, creatures who could burn her to a crisp, devour her, and no one would know.

Yet, even as those dark fears threatened to overwhelm her, the images of twin boys laughing and playing chased away the shadows. Their laughing eyes turned to confusion, then sadness before they hid their pain behind anger and indifference. They had been hurt by more than a physical blow. Their hurt came from a deeper, darker place —rejection.

She closed the distance and flattened her hand against his smooth chest. Beneath her hand, she could feel the steady beat of his heart. Curious, she leaned her cheek against the silken scales and closed her eyes. Around her, his sharp claws curved inward, holding her to him in a grasp gentle enough to hold the most delicate butterfly.

When Barrack nudged her arm, she opened her eyes and giggled when she saw his head partially in the cocoon that Brogan had made with his wings. He bumped her with the end of his nose again. It wasn't difficult to understand what he wanted—a little attention too.

She pulled her other glove off and turned so that her back was pressed against Brogan's chest. Swallowing, she leaned forward and cupped Barrack's long jaw with her hands. She gently ran her fingers along the underside, mesmerized by the power and nobility of such a magnificent mythical creature.

When she reached a sensitive spot his eyelids lowered and his rumble of pleasure shook the ground. She giggled and continued to scratch the spot. She was rewarded with the thud of his tail. Everything would have been fine if the two Rottweilers hadn't decided that Barrack's wiggling tail was a new toy. Her lips parted to warn him, but it was too late.

She fell back against Brogan when Barrack quickly pulled his head back and turned his gaze on the playful pups. Her arms strained to push Brogan's claws farther apart so she could escape. She had to try to protect her idiot dogs. They apparently didn't have an ounce of survival skills between them. Her fear that they were about to become dragon chow evaporated when, instead of toasting the pooches, he buried his tail in the snow with only the wriggling tip sticking up.

Of course, the dogs thought it was a fabulous new game of hide and seek. Barrack twisted back and forth, raising and lowering his tail until the dogs were covered in snow from trying to find it. Falling back in relief, she curled her arms around one of Brogan's claws and watched from her warm perch.

"I have a lot to learn about you guys," she acknowledged.

Brogan's chest rumbled again. She wasn't sure if it was laughter or satisfaction, but it was obvious from the way he bent to rub her hair that he approved of her comment. Now all she needed to do was figure out what in the hell was going on and why they were there.

CHAPTER THIRTEEN

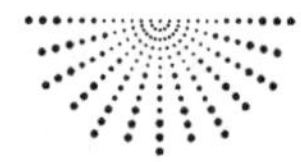

Thirty minutes later, they were all snug inside the house again. The eye of the storm had passed and the tail end of the Nor'easter had begun sweeping through the area. The sound of the howling wind and snapping trees echoed through the air, sending a shiver through her.

Picking up a small brush she used for the dogs, she ran it over them. She brushed as much of the snow off as she could before she brought the two Rottweilers in through the mudroom. She bent over and pulled off their booties and sweaters and shook the snow off of them, too.

"Do all beasts require clothing?" Barrack asked, watching her towel off Moonshine.

"What?" she asked in confusion, rubbing Moonshine's back paw before reaching for Rum.

"Your beasts... Do all of them wear clothing, and if so, how is it possible to dress all of them?" Barrack asked, watching her.

Delilah shook her head in amusement. "No, not all dogs wear clothing. I saw these sweaters and booties at Ofelia's and they were just too cute to pass up. It gets cold around here and Rottweilers aren't the furriest dogs. I guess some would think I'm crazy for putting sweaters and booties on them, but I don't want their feet to get frostbite," she explained.

She looked up when the outside door opened again. Brogan stepped inside and shook the snow from his hair. She lifted the towel to protect herself. Barrack wasn't as lucky and was coated in the cold flakes.

"You did that on purpose," Barrack growled, wiping a hand down his face and looking at his brother.

"Yes," Brogan replied with a grin before he turned to look at her. "There was a dead tree near the other shed. I removed it so that it would not fall on it."

She lowered the towel and looked at him in surprise. "Thank you. Bubba Joe was supposed to come up and cut it down for me last week, but his momma had to have surgery," she said.

Brogan's face darkened and his lips twisted. "You have mentioned that name several times," he commented.

Delilah shrugged. "He's been awesome," she said. "Let's go inside. The dogs are dry, and I'm freezing."

She hung the towel up on a hook and gathered the sweaters, booties, and her gloves. Pushing the kitchen door open, she waited for the dogs and the symbiots to enter before she followed them. Barrack and Brogan hesitated a moment before they followed, closing the door behind themselves.

She could see the indecision on their faces, as if they weren't quite sure what to do next. The rumbling in her stomach that had started before the sun came up was at a full-fledged military salute. She glanced at the clock and saw that it was almost eleven thirty in the morning.

No wonder I'm starving, she thought.

"Why don't you two go dry off or whatever. I need to hang these up and freshen up before I make an early lunch for us. After lunch, I'll show you where you can sleep. Fortunately for you, I have beds in all the bedrooms," she said over her shoulder.

Not waiting for their reply, she hurried down the hallway to the front door. A quick glance in the sitting room showed that the dogs and the symbiots had already confiscated the room. It looked like the human/aliens would be restricted to the other parlor, dining room, or kitchen.

There was a small sitting room upstairs, but it would be too cramped for the three of them. She liked to use it during the summer because the breeze coming down from the mountain would keep the room cool. She hung the dogs' sweaters and booties to dry on the hall tree before removing her outerwear and hanging them as well. Sitting down on the bench seat, she removed her boots.

Wiggling her sock covered toes, she sighed in relief. She hated wearing shoes. The boots were comfortable as long as she wore double layers.

"What is wrong? Are you in pain?" Barrack asked, leaning against the doorframe to the sitting room.

"Geez, you scared me!" she exclaimed, lifting a hand to her chest. She could actually feel her heart skip a few beats. "How can someone so big, be so quiet?" she grumbled, standing up and walking toward the staircase.

"We would have died long ago if not for our ability to move without detection," Barrack answered.

Pausing on the first step, she turned to look at him. "How old are you?" she curiously asked.

Barrack shrugged. "Age is irrelevant to us, and we stopped counting hundreds of years ago," he said. "Do you know your age?"

Delilah swallowed and nodded. "Twenty-nine. I'm only twenty-nine. You were serious, weren't you? You and Brogan.... You guys are like really old," she murmured.

"Yes, especially compared to you," he quietly replied.

Stunned, she nodded and lowered her gaze. She turned and slowly walked up the stairs, retracing her steps to her bedroom. She used the restroom, noticing the bucket of water next to the toilet. Brogan must have brought it up when she was drying off the dogs.

After washing and drying her hands, she returned to her bedroom. Walking to the window, she stared out at the storm and became lost in thought. She wrapped her arms around her waist. How could life change so much and so unexpectedly in such a short time? A sound behind her drew her attention back to the present.

Barrack's symbiot had followed her. She shook her head in disgust when it jumped up on the bed, turned in a circle and lay down—on her side. If that wasn't bad enough, it reached over with one paw and dragged her pillow closer, snuggling up with it before lying still. Walking over to the bed, she reached down and scratched the Werecat behind one golden ear before bending over and brushing her lips across its temple.

"This is my side of the damn bed. Don't get too comfortable," she murmured as warmth filled her.

Straightening, she walked out of the bedroom and back down the stairs. She would make lunch and then it would be time for some questions and answers. It was time to find out more about her unexpected guests and what they wanted.

"God, I hope it isn't world domination. That would totally suck," she muttered.

Twenty minutes later, she poured three bowls of soup and flipped the last grilled cheese sandwich out of the frying pan. She looked at the men through lowered eyelashes. They were quietly sitting and talking at the table in the dining room. She added an extra sandwich to each of their plates and decided it was a good thing she knew how to bake. She had a feeling she would be cooking a little more than she normally did.

This type of weather gave her a chance to refill her freezer. She had brought extra groceries for exactly that purpose. The house in town had an electric stove while this one had gas, so it didn't matter if the power was out. Of course, she was less likely to lose power for long in town. Still, if she had to choose between the two places, she would rather be here.

This house brought back fond memories of her grandmother and mom baking and canning while her granddad and dad worked on a variety of different projects ranging from tinkering with the old tractor, which was still in the barn, to being the official taste-testers for new recipes.

At this house, she could bake to her heart's content without worrying about heating it up, and she could store at least three months' worth or more of quick meals that she could pop into the microwave back in town.

"Lunch is ready," she called, looking over her shoulder with a smile when she heard footsteps behind her.

"It smells good. I did not realize how hungry I was until you started cooking," Barrack admitted.

"Here, if you don't mind carrying the plates in, I'll bring the soup. What would you guys like to drink? I have water, milk, iced tea, hot tea, or coffee—oh, and orange juice, but not a lot because it is too expensive," she added with an apologetic expression.

"Water is fine," Barrack said.

"I will take the soup," Brogan said, looking at the noodles with uncertainty.

"Thanks. I'll grab the drinks, then," she replied.

Pouring a cup of hot tea for herself, she grabbed two bottles of water from the refrigerator and stepped into the dining room. With a smile and a murmur of thanks, she slid into the seat that Brogan pulled out for her. Her gaze followed him until he sat down on her right. Barrack sat across from her. Both men looked down at their plates with expressions of resignation on their faces. She saw that their eyes kept moving to the bowl of noodles.

"Don't you like pasta?" she asked, picking up her fork and twirling it in her bowl.

"No, this is good," Barrack said, shooting his brother a look of warning that was impossible to miss.

Delilah stopped turning her fork and laid it against the edge of the bowl. She folded her hands under her chin and studied both of the men. A faint flush appeared on Brogan's cheeks, and he moved uncomfortably in his seat before he looked away.

"Okay, what is it? You don't like pasta? You don't like grilled cheese sandwiches? You are gluten free aliens?" she demanded.

"The meal is fine, Delilah. We will enjoy all of it, won't we, Brogan?" Barrack stated, picking up the toasted bread with orange-colored goo between it.

"I don't like Terrestris," he mumbled under his breath.

"You don't like what?" she asked, confused.

Brogan released a growl of frustration and looked up at her with an apologetic expression. "Terrestris. The Tiliqua like them, but they eat insects. Dragons don't like to eat insects if they can help it. At least not long ones like this. They are squishy inside," he muttered.

"You think.... I don't know what a Tiliqua or a Terrestris is, but you think the noodles are like worms?" she asked.

"We will eat whatever you prepare for us," Barrack insisted, shooting Brogan a fierce scowl.

Delilah looked down at her bowl. Picking up her fork, she studied the noodles. They did look like worms. In fact, that is what some of the kids at the dollar store called them. She looked up at the men and grinned.

"This is pasta. It is not worms or Terrestris or a Tiliqua, whatever that is. It is in a chicken broth and I added some bits of baked chicken to it to give it a little protein," she stated, lifting up her fork.

"It looks like Terrestris," Brogan insisted.

Delilah shook her head and took a bite. "Take a bite. If you don't like it, I'll make something else. What exactly do you normally eat?" she asked, tearing part of her sandwich off and dipping it in the broth. "As long as it isn't me or the dogs, I might have it on hand."

Both men watched her as she ate. She decided that if they saw her enjoying the meal that maybe they would at least taste it and see that she was telling the truth. She ate almost half of her soup and sandwich before Barrack reluctantly raised part of the sandwich to his mouth.

She smiled in satisfaction when his eyes widened in surprise, and he took several more bites. She watched Brogan frown at his brother before he tried the grilled cheese sandwich. He grunted and took a larger bite.

"So, what do you think?" she asked, licking her fingers before she wiped them on the paper towel next to her plate.

"This is good. This orange stuff, I remember something like it from our village," Barrack admitted.

She noticed that he had finished the first sandwich and was already working on the second. She looked at Brogan who had finished both sandwiches and was sniffing suspiciously at the noodles on his fork. He closed his eyes, opened his mouth, and took a bite. She grinned when his eyes opened wide, and he looked down at the bowl of soup with a different expression.

"This is not Terrestris," he exclaimed, twirling his fork in the bowl and lifting a large forkful to his mouth. "It is good."

Within minutes, both men were hungrily polishing off the rest of their lunch. Delilah stood up when they were almost finished, refilled her hot tea, and picked up the lemon-glazed pound cake she'd made and carried it into the dining room. She cut a generous slice and placed it on each plate.

"Now you can have your dessert," she teased.

A soft rumbling growl filled the room and both men stared at her with those strange little flames in their eyes. Blushing, she tapped her fork against her plate to let them know that it was the cake and not her that was being served. Shaking her head, she leaned back in her chair with a contented sigh.

"Okay, now that we all have full bellies, I want to know everything," she stated, picking up her hot tea and sipping it.

"Everything?" Brogan asked, his mouth full and his eyes wary.

"Everything," she repeated with a stern look. "Tell me where you're from, how you got here, why you're here, when are you leaving—heck, can you even leave? Did you guys crash here? How long did it take to get here?"

There was a moment of silence. She watched as they looked at each other. From the expressions flashing across their faces, she swore they were talking to each other without moving their lips. Finally, Brogan's expression turned stubborn and Barrack's turned to one of resignation. Turning her attention to Barrack, she listened as he began an incredible tale of a world that existed far, far away.

"Our story begins in a simple village...," he said.

CHAPTER FOURTEEN

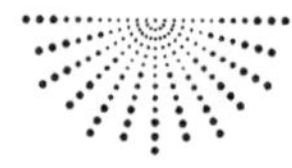

Brogan moodily stared out the window. The snow continued to fall with a thickness that made it virtually impossible to see more than a few feet from the house. He could hear the snap and the groan of the trees as the wind rushed through the forest.

"Are you going to stand there all day?" Barrack asked, leaning his shoulder against the doorframe to the kitchen.

Looking at Barrack over his shoulder, Brogan shook his head. No, he wouldn't stand here all day. He was waiting for the kettle to sing so he could make Delilah another cup of the tea that she enjoyed.

In the background, he could hear the music that she turned on. He walked past his brother into the kitchen when he heard the kettle start to boil. Glancing at his brother's face, he noted that Barrack wanted to talk.

"She will accept us," he murmured, pulling the covering off the loose tea and pouring it into the little gadget she used and dropped into a tall cup. "I thought she did well considering everything that you told her."

Barrack pushed off the doorframe and walked over to lean against the counter. "You could have helped a little," he complained.

Brogan shrugged. "You were doing fine," he quietly said.

He stiffened when his brother laid a hand on his shoulder. Turning his head to look into his twin's eyes, he grimaced. It was impossible to mask his feelings of doubt when he had such an intimate connection with his brother.

"She is confused and scared, but she listened and did not reject us," Barrack said.

Brogan tore his gaze away. "We can't let her die," he stated in a soft voice.

Barrack squeezed his shoulder. "We won't, brother. We won't," he swore.

Brogan's lips twitched. He picked up the cup of tea and turned to look at his brother. He felt better—more confident. His brother was right, she didn't reject them.

"She thinks we are crazy," he said.

Barrack chuckled. "Since when have we ever let that stop us?" he retorted.

Soft laughter filled the kitchen. Brogan felt a renewed determination as they walked toward the room to where Delilah had retreated. Everything was in their favor. They were all captive to the weather. They would take this time to show her what wonderful mates they were and court her using the techniques that Pearl and Asim taught them. They still had time.

"What is she building again?" Brogan asked.

"Something called moving bookcases. She said she read how to do it in a book called Popular Mechanics," Barrack replied.

"She really does read a lot," Brogan said, stepping into the room and almost having a heart attack. "What are you doing?"

"What...?! Oh!" Delilah's startled cry echoed through the room.

Brogan placed the cup of hot tea on the dark wood table. He stared at Delilah who was standing on a tall ladder measuring the wall. He silently cursed his having startled her. Barrack was already in motion by the time he placed her tea on the table.

Her cry changed to a gasp when Barrack caught her as she tumbled off the ladder. Barrack carefully lowered her feet to the floor, continuing to hold her when she leaned against him. Brogan strode over, turned her until she was facing him, and captured her face between his hands. He studied her frightened expression with a mixture of relief and worry.

"You…," he started to say before he shook his head.

Unable to express the fear he'd felt, Brogan leaned forward and captured her parted lips. She wrapped her arms around his neck. Barrack gently pressed against her from behind, sliding his hands down to her hips and pulling her closer to his long frame. The feel of her fingers threading through his hair and the touch of her tongue against his upper lip sent a burst of fire through Brogan.

Bite, bite, bite, bite. I bite, his dragon chanted in a contented voice inside his head.

We have to court her, Brogan groaned, his lips parting when she pressed her tongue against them and deepened the kiss.

Courting done. Time to bite, his dragon replied.

"So beautiful," Barrack murmured behind them.

Brogan felt Delilah's swift withdrawal at the sound of his brother's voice. He tried to reignite the flame inside her, but she had already broken the kiss and turned her face away from him. She breathed deeply before she slid her hands down to his chest and pushed against him.

"I… I… need…," she stuttered before she shook her head.

He studied her as she slipped out from between the two of them and started to leave the room. She paused and turned back to look at them, shook her head again, picked up her cup of tea, and hurried out of the room and up the stairs. He walked over to the door and watched her disappear down the long hallway to her bedroom. A moment later, he heard the sound of the door quietly closing and the distinct click of the key turning in the lock.

"She liked it," Barrack stated, crossing his arms across his chest.

A smile curved Brogan's lips. "Yes, she liked it a lot," he acknowledged, turning to look at his brother. "Where is that book she was looking at? I think it is time to step up our courting."

Ashville, North Carolina:

Olie 'Ray' Lister sat staring at the fire. He tapped his fingers on the arm of the elegant leather chair. His mind lost in thought. He ignored the quiet sound of the door to his office closing when his wife of twenty years walked by it. A moment later, he could hear their youngest son, Edison, complaining to her that the internet was slow.

Of course it was slow! More than half of the country was stuck inside for the storm of the century, but his son thought the universe revolved around his need for access to the internet. Ray was glad that he left the domestic responsibilities—especially those dealing with a disgruntled teenager—to Mabel.

His energies were better focused on the things he was good at, like making money. They had moved here from California because Mabel was concerned that the life in Los Angeles was too hectic for their three children, particularly Edison. Personally, he thought a good boarding school and time away from his mother would help their son more than anything else. Fortunately, the other two were away at college.

Dismissing his wife and son, he returned his focus to the current issue at hand, his newest planned community project that was on hold until he acquired the property he had his eye on. As a real estate developer in California, he had learned to give people what they wanted. In this case, fancy mountain retreats complete with a golf course, private air strip, and million dollar mountain views at non-L.A. prices.

He rose from his chair and walked over to the large display set up in the corner. He had carefully picked the area where he wanted to build his new planned community. The development would be close to National and State Parks, with easy access to the larger Eastern cities including those in Washington, D.C. and Virginia. The proposed site was not far from the ocean for those who would enjoy visiting the beaches but still worried about global warming. However, even the best laid plans could not be implemented if the pivotal acreage located at the center of the project belonged to someone else.

He had millions riding on this development. He'd already purchased the majority of the land he required. The local area attorney that he hired was very successful in convincing the locals to sign on the dotted line—all except the most crucial one.

Reaching for his cell phone, he dialed the attorney. He impatiently waited for DeWayne to answer. On the fourth ring, DeWayne finally responded in a distracted voice.

"This is D. Davis, Attorney at Law, can I help you?" DeWayne greeted.

"DeWayne, this is Ray Lister. I was calling to inquire about your progress with the purchase of the land on Saddle Mountain," Ray asked, turning to look out at the falling snow.

"Mr. Lister, I… I was going to call you but with the storm and all… I wasn't sure…." DeWayne responded, stuttering as he tried to gloss over the fact that he was lying. "She still refuses to sell."

"Have you checked all the tax and deed records?" Ray demanded.

The sound of DeWayne's heavy sigh blasted in his ear. "Yes, sir. She is paid up and there are no outstanding liens on the property," DeWayne replied. "Maybe if you offered her more money….?"

"Out of the question. Find a way to convince her or I will," Ray ordered.

"Yes, sir. I'll… I'll talk to Delilah again as soon as the weather clears," DeWayne promised.

"See that you do," Ray replied, ending the call.

He stood watching the snow accumulating on the ground. On rare occasions he called in his brother-in-law for assistance. Mabel's middle brother, Earl, was one of those guys who intensely disliked authority, following the rules, and being on the grid. These skill sets, if he could call them that, made Earl the perfect silent partner. Pay cash, no questions nor restrictions, and Earl would get the job done. Ray had the real estate in Los Angeles to prove how effective his brother-in-law could be at completing a difficult task.

He pressed the number programmed into his phone. "Ashley Gangs' Pawn," the deep, southern accent of an old man answered.

"Is Earl there?" Ray asked.

There was a moment of silence before the person on the other end answered. In the background, he could hear someone asking about an item. The old man answered the person in the shop before he responded to Ray's question.

"He's not here. Who's calling?" the old man asked.

"Ray," he replied.

"I'll tell him," the old man said, hanging up on him.

Less than a minute later, his phone vibrated. He looked down at the display. The caller ID showed it as coming from a private number. Pressing the button to connect the call, he lifted the phone to his ear again.

"Yes," he answered.

"How much?" Earl responded.

Ray smiled. Earl was very predictable. He wanted to know if it was even worth his time.

"Twenty," Ray said.

He knew he had taken his brother-in-law by surprise with his silence. The sound of a loud truck going by told him that wherever Earl was at the moment, his brother-in-law wasn't worrying about a major snowstorm. Once the truck passed, Earl spoke.

"What do you need done?" Earl asked.

Ray smiled. "I want you to convince someone to sell their property," he replied.

"Limits?" Earl demanded.

"None. I leave it up to you to get the job done," Ray replied.

"I want fifty. Leave it and the instructions at the usual place," Earl finally answered.

"It'll take me a couple of days. In case you haven't heard, there is a major snowstorm affecting our area," Ray dryly replied.

"I know. Wouldn't stop me," Earl retorted.

Earl's comment gave Ray an idea. Normally, he didn't suggest anything to his brother-in-law since it would be pointless, but the storm might be the perfect cover. There were always tragedies in the papers about an unexpected house fire or someone freezing to death after getting disoriented in a blizzard.

"Her name is Delilah Rosewater. She has two homes—one in town and one outside of town. The second is the one I'm interested in," Ray replied.

"That's all I need to know. Make sure the money is there, or she won't be the only one I pay a visit to," Earl warned, hanging up on him.

Ray lowered the phone in his hand. He turned when a tentative knock sounded on the door to his office. Irritation flashed through him when he saw Mabel's stressed expression.

"What is it?" he demanded.

Mabel looked at him with pleading eyes. "Can you please call the internet service provider and see if there is anything wrong with our service? Ed is beside himself because he keeps getting kicked out of his game," she said.

"Of course," he replied.

"Thank you, dear," Mabel said, her expression changing to one of relief despite the yelling coming from upstairs.

"I'll do it in just a few minutes," he promised, waving a hand for her to close the door.

The moment the door closed, he pocketed his phone and returned to his seat by the fire. He leaned back and closed his eyes. The sound of muted yelling filtered through the house.

Boarding school, he thought with a smile.

CHAPTER FIFTEEN

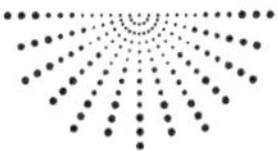

Delilah walked over to the bed and stared down at it with unblinking eyes. Her mind was still focused on that kiss. She blinked when Barrack's symbiot swiftly stood up and moved to the other side of the bed before lying down again.

Grabbing her pillow, she pulled it into her arms and hugged it against her chest as she twisted and fell across the bed. She lifted her hand when she felt something warm and soft under her head before it ever touched the mattress. Rolling onto her side, she saw that her head was cushioned on a golden pillow.

"I kissed him," she informed the symbiot, turning to look into its golden eyes.

The symbiot shimmered and sent her an array of images of itself excitedly dancing around in a circle. She groaned and flung her arm over her eyes. It didn't help—the image was still there. Dropping her arm, she leaned on her elbow and glared at the golden creature.

"Do you do this to them too?" she demanded.

The creature sniffed and grinned. If she didn't know better, she would be terrified of that mouth full of sharp teeth. Fortunately for her, she did know, and the look came off as anything but scary.

"What was even worse was it turned me on that Barrack was

watching—and that he liked watching us.I know they are twins, but come on! How can I be attracted to both of them? I mean—two guys at one time? How greedy is that?" she groaned, falling back against the pillow again and staring up at the ceiling.

Warmth spread around her wrists. Lifting her arms, she gasped when she saw the bracelets changing shape. Flipping onto her stomach, she pulled both of her sleeves up to watch the moving designs.

At first there was simply the form of a woman in gold. Delilah wondered who she was. All around the woman were stars and planets. The scene shifted, evolving until there was the woman with the stars, but the planet changed to a village scene.

Two images emerged out of the gold. She recognized Barrack and Brogan in their dragon form. Delilah could feel her heart skip when she saw Barrack's tortured expression as he was held by a mob of angry men. Brogan was lying nearby.

"No!" she whispered, horrified when she saw Brogan's lifeless body. "Please... It didn't happen. Not really. They are here. There is no way he could have died."

Her eyes moved to the woman. The golden figure waved her hand and the scene reversed itself. Delilah felt like she was seeing two different endings to the same movie—one that had happened and one that could happen.

One scene after another revealed itself to her on each of the bracelets. She saw the twin's journey to her world, her home, and finally the figure of a woman that had to be herself. Fascinated, she reached down and traced each of the designs.

On her right wrist, she saw herself standing between the two brothers. They were both touching her. Barrack had his body pressed to her back and his hands on her hips while Brogan held her hand, his body turned into hers. It reminded her of what had happened downstairs. All around them there were glittering stars as if they were either in space or outside on a world where the stars were close.

She looked at her left wrist. A soft gasp slipped from her when she saw three dragons wrapped around each other. There was no doubt that the two on the outside were Barrack and Brogan. It was the delicate female dragon between them that left her stunned. The dragon wore a necklace with a bird of prey on it—just like hers. Delilah raised her hand and touched the necklace around her neck.

"This is why I'm attracted to both of them. They were telling me the truth, weren't they? They really think I'm supposed to be with both of them," she said, her voice trembling as she looked at the symbiot watching her with wide, expressive eyes. "I'm not even sure I can handle one of them. How on Earth do they expect me to handle both?"

Dropping her head to the pillow, she shook it back and forth. She wasn't ready to deal with this. In less than twenty-four hours, she went from not having a boyfriend to having two aliens who thought she was their mate. None of the books she ever read had prepared her for this situation.

"I'm in so much trouble," she groaned, ignoring the snickering symbiot who was having way too much fun at her expense.

Two hours later, a soft knock on her bedroom door pulled her attention away from the book she was trying to read. Closing it with a snap, she placed it on the bed next to her before she leaned forward and wrapped her arms around her legs. She looked up when the door opened a crack.

"I brought some hot tea," Barrack said, waiting at the door. "May I enter?"

Delilah reached up and tucked a strand of her hair behind her ear. "Of course," she said with a shy smile. "What have you been doing down there? It sounded like you've both been pretty busy."

"Yes, we cannot read your language yet, but the book you have has many good illustrations and the process is not difficult to understand," he commented, placing the cup of hot tea on the nightstand.

He straightened and looked at the edge of the bed with hesitation. She patted the bed for him to sit down. It wasn't like this was anything new—though if she remembered that she had only met them yesterday it was, but it didn't feel like it.

And this is why my head is screwed up, she thought with a groan.

"What is wrong?" he asked in a gentle voice, cupping her cheek with his hand.

Delilah looked at him with wide confused eyes. The vivid image of his tortured face still haunted her. She reached up and touched his cheek, tracing the line of his beard.

"I want you to kiss me," she murmured, twisting so that she could lean closer to him. "I want to kiss you. Is that wrong?"

He frowned. "Why would it be wrong?" he asked, his voice deepening with emotion.

"I kissed Brogan," she pointed out with a rueful grin. "Which I happened to like—a lot, by the way."

Barrack turned his head and pressed his lips to her thumb which she was unconsciously rubbing near his mouth. She gasped with pleasure when he sucked her thumb into his mouth. Pulling her hand back, she twisted until she was on her knees.

"I know. I watched you. I found it very arousing," he acknowledged. "You were destined to be our mate, Delilah. We have waited centuries to find you. Why would we come to you if that bothered me? You hold...."

She cupped his cheeks and gazed into his eyes, searching for what caused the brief flash of grief. Every time she was around these men, she was beginning to realize they had many layers. She had a feeling it would take a lifetime to peel each one away.

But, oh, what fun it would be, she thought as she slid her hands over his broad shoulders.

"You said you wished to kiss me," he reminded her.

A shiver of awareness ran through her when he wrapped his warm hands around her waist and pulled her closer. Bending her head, she pressed her lips to his. They were as warm as the rest of him. Parting her lips, she touched the tip of her tongue to his upper lip before running it along the seam. His lips parted, and she deepened the kiss, wanting to taste him.

Threading her fingers through his hair, she clung to him when he lowered her back onto the bed. She felt the bed move when his symbiot jumped off, but even that slight distraction wasn't enough to deter her from doing more exploring.

She whimpered in protest when he started to pull away. She tightened her hands on his shoulders and pressed a series of kisses along his jaw. It took her a second to realize that he was giving her a chance to straighten her legs so he could cover her body with his own.

"I have dreamed of this moment for centuries," he told her in a voice filled with need and something else.

Delilah relaxed against the bed and looked up at him. She had spent the last two hours trying to read only to discover that she'd read the same page over and over again without comprehending a single word. Instead, the scenes from her bracelets played through her mind like a broken record—especially the one where Brogan lay dead and Barrack was captured.

"I saw you. I saw Brogan. Why would they hurt you like that?" she quietly asked.

Barrack had started to bend his head toward her when he paused. He looked down at her with a questioning expression. She could sense his withdrawal.

"What do you mean?" he cautiously asked.

She touched his cheek. "My bracelets—I saw things I didn't understand. Brogan was dead and you.... There was so much fear in their eyes. I know it can't be real. I don't understand what it meant," she confessed.

She was shocked when he suddenly rolled off the bed and stood up. Sitting up, she watched him run his hands through his hair. She didn't miss the heated look he shot his symbiot. The golden creature snorted and rose to its feet. With a toss of its massive head, it trotted out of the room.

Sliding off the bed, she walked over to stand next to him. His shoulders were stiff, and he appeared to be arguing with himself. She turned when she heard the sound of footsteps hurrying down the hall.

Puzzled, she looked toward the doorway and saw Brogan standing there, before she looked back at Barrack.

"You two can talk to each other," she suddenly realized with a sense of awe. "You can talk to each other, like, telepathically."

"Yes," Barrack replied in a stiff tone.

"You communicate with the gold things like that as well. They showed me images in my head. I didn't hear a voice, but I didn't need to. They talk with pictures," she murmured, trying to add this new information to the stuff they had already told her. "You didn't tell me everything."

Barrack turned from the window and waved his hand. "We told you enough," he defended.

Delilah knew her eyes reflected her feelings of frustration. They told her enough? How much was enough?

"Enough as in not telling me that Brogan died?" she snapped, pointing her finger at Brogan. "How is it that he is alive when I saw him dead? I want to know everything, Barrack! I don't want to know just enough. I want to know everything, so I can make an informed decision on the fact that you two seem to think I'm this mythical mate that you have been on a quest to find!"

"There is nothing mythical about it! You know that we are dragon-shifters and that we are aliens in your world. What does it matter other than we are your mate, and we have come to take you back with us? You will discover *everything* you need to know once we have claimed you," Barrack snarled.

Delilah fell back a step, shocked at Barrack's passionate response. The cool, calm brother was gone. In his place was a man with fire in his eyes and scales rippling across his skin.

He stood glaring at her for several seconds before he turned with a muttered curse and strode from the room, brushing off Brogan's restraining hand as he passed. A few seconds later, she heard the front door open and slam shut. Shocked, she started forward to go after him. The storm was intensifying. He could get lost, or worse, die out there. She stopped when Brogan reached out and touched her arm.

"What doesn't he want me to know? Why... Why do I feel like...?" her voice died as she tried to put her feelings into words.

"Like we are running out of time?" Brogan asked.

Delilah nodded and looked up at him. "I saw you...." Her eyes moved to his neck and a shudder ran through her.

"You saw me dead. Barrack would have died shortly thereafter," Brogan quietly finished for her.

She nodded. "What happened? How can you be alive?" she whispered, her voice thick with emotion.

Brogan looked around the room and stopped on the cup of tea that Barrack had brought up a short time ago. She watched as he picked it up. Reaching out, he tenderly grasped her hand with the other.

"You are right. You deserve to know everything," he replied.

"Do you promise?" she asked, resisting when he started to lead her out of the room.

He paused before he nodded. "Yes, everything—including our deaths," he stated.

~

Barrack took a deep breath of the frigid air. Blinding snow and howling winds buffeted him despite the fact that he was under a bridge. His dragon impatiently snapped at the snow and shook his head in irritation. He had shifted by the time he reached the bottom of the front steps and took to the air.

His body had been hard with desire from Delilah's kiss while his mind was overwhelmed with fear. His symbiot had tried to form around him, but he was still too furious with the creature for showing Delilah more than they were willing to share at this point and he had ordered it away from him. At the moment, it lay across from him, watching him with a combination of defiance and sadness.

We weren't ready for her to know, he growled, turning to shoot his symbiot a fierce look.

His symbiot shimmered in response and sneezed before turning its head away from his sharp, reproving gaze. Barrack wanted to snap at the creature, but even his dragon was ignoring his frustrations, siding with his symbiot. If it weren't so dangerous, he would have shifted and shoved his dragon so deep inside him that his primitive side would have spent a month trying to figure out a way out of his subconscious, and then he would have left his symbiot under the bridge to pout.

She deserve to know. Goddess said she must make choice, his dragon defended, melting a flurry of snowflakes with an impatient ball of dragon fire.

I know what the Goddess said, Barrack growled in response.

Barrack was about to make another retort when his symbiot surged to its feet and his dragon stiffened. He could feel the air around them changing. The change was unnatural. Something far more powerful was at work.

Barrack's dragon knelt and lowered his head in deference. He understood a fraction of a second later what was going on when the snowy scene in front of him faded, and he found himself staring into the vast, swirling blackness of space. Walking toward him was an ethereal figure of immense power.

"Aikaterina," he murmured.

His dragon trembled when she reached out and ran a gentle hand over his snout. She turned her gaze to his symbiot and silently beckoned it to come to her. Barrack sensed something different about the Goddess as she tenderly stroked his symbiot. She felt —fragile.

Come forward, warrior, she murmured, speaking directly to him.

Barrack shifted back into his two-legged form and started to kneel. He felt her hand against his cheek and looked up. Her smile was serene and her eyes compassionate. The last time she came to them, it was in the form of a Valdier maiden. This time, she kept her ethereal form.

"We need longer," he said, his gut twisting at the thought that she had come to take them back. "We have found our mate. She…. Please, we need more time."

Aikaterina stepped by him. She looked curiously from under the other side of the bridge before turning to look at him again. His symbiot followed her, pressing against her side.

"Time...," she murmured, looking back to the opening from which she had emerged. "A man from this world once said that time keeps us all a prisoner of the present, yet our life transitions from our past to an unknown future. This human sees what many don't. As for you, Delilah, and Brogan, your lives were preordained long ago."

"But you changed that when you stopped us from dying," Barrack protested, stepping closer to her. "We did not die, so our present now is intertwined with Delilah's whose path in life was also changed."

Aikaterina bowed her head in acknowledgment of his passionate words, but she did not agree with him. Fear rose inside him. What if she refused his request? How could he fight someone so powerful? She chuckled and looked at him with an amused expression.

"I did not come to battle with you, warrior. I came because I sensed your conflict. I merely thought you needed someone. Your brother is normally the one with the hot temper," she stated.

Barrack could feel his cheeks heat at her reply. It had never dawned on him that Aikaterina could see his distress and would come to his aid. Dragon's balls, he'd been upset enough times in the past and she never appeared.

"Your symbiot reached out to me. It worries about you," she informed him, looking down at his symbiot with an affectionate smile. "Do not forget that I have a connection to them as well."

"It showed Delilah what happened to us. We were not ready," he defended.

Aikaterina turned to look at him. "There may never be a good time, warrior. She is stronger than you realize. If you have doubts, ask your brother," she said, amusement shining from her golden eyes.

Barrack's lips twitched at the subtle reminder of Brogan's painful early encounters with Delilah. He released a deep sigh. He had overreacted.

"Yes. You also underestimate your true mate, warrior. Trust me when I say she is the perfect mate for you and your brother," Aikaterina encouraged before her gaze ran over the underside of the bridge and back out into the blizzard. "This world is almost as interesting as yours, warrior. Perhaps…."

Barrack watched as Aikaterina's expression changed from slightly pensive to serene again. She turned and slowly began to retrace her steps back through the dark portal. He took a step forward; then paused, his throat tight as he called after her.

"So, we have more time?" he asked.

"Watch your symbiot, warrior. When it fades, so too will the threads I have altered," she softly replied as the portal closed behind her.

"But… how long?" Barrack's throat tightened at the sadness in her voice.

He looked at his symbiot. He was shocked to see that it was in fact more transparent than he remembered. He'd been so preoccupied that he had failed to notice that he could now see through it.

"How long?" he demanded.

His soft hiss of dismay was lost in the howl of the wind. Calling forth his dragon, he shifted. He had to inform Brogan. More importantly, he needed to return to Delilah and reveal everything.

CHAPTER SIXTEEN

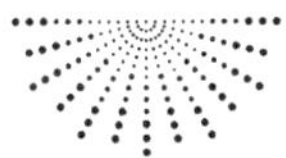

Delilah looked up from where she was dropping cookie dough onto the cookie sheet. She scowled when she saw Barrack quietly enter through the back door. The sharp remark on her lips died when she saw his expression, so worried and remorseful.

A rueful smile curved her lips as she placed the spoon back in the bowl. She grabbed the dishtowel and wiped the dough off her hands.

"Delilah, there is something we have to tell you," he began.

"I know," she interrupted, placing the dishtowel down on the counter and walking toward him. "Brogan and I had a long talk while you were gone."

His eyes turned to the doorway to the kitchen. Brogan leaned against the doorframe and returned his steady gaze. His brother nodded.

"I told her *everything*," Brogan said, emphasizing the last word.

Barrack nodded. "I apologize," he said, his voice filled with regret. "Sara warned us that you should be told. We should have listened to her."

Delilah could tell that Barrack's apology was for both herself and Brogan. She stepped forward and wrapped her arms around his waist. She'd had a lot to think about after her conversation with Brogan. She didn't know why she had been so shocked. Perhaps it was because she realized that her dreams about the two guys had been more than dreams, they had been memories of a previous life. It had also helped her that Brogan had told her more about Sara and Jaguin. Knowing more about Sara and Jaguin helped her accept the universe was a lot stranger than she ever imagined. She wasn't sure how all of this was possible, or if she was reliving some previous life over and over, like in a loop.

Well, not exactly previous, she thought. *More like parallel or alternate.*

"There are a few things that I should have mentioned to you two as well," she confessed, looking up at him.

"What things?" Barrack asked.

Brogan chuckled. "She had dreams of us before we arrived," he stated.

Delilah turned and glared at Brogan. He had given her a little bit of a hard time about that particular piece of information. Her excuse had been the fact that she knew nothing about aliens or Goddesses being real until she'd actually met them.

"It has only been a couple of days," she reminded him. "I have the right to wrap my head around the fact that you are real before admitting I had hot, sexy dreams about you two."

"Hot, sexy dreams?" both men exclaimed at the same time.

She'd known she had made a blunder the second the words had slipped from her lips. A furious blush rose up in her cheeks. A soft purr rumbled from Barrack's chest while Brogan straightened, the fire back in his eyes.

"How hot?" Barrack asked.

Brogan grinned. "How sexy?" he demanded.

Delilah swallowed. Brogan was closing the distance between her and Barrack. She could feel her body heat flaring up again. She swore it was like someone was dialing up a horny-switch inside her.

"Hot enough to melt snow and sexy enough to wet the sheets," she retorted.

Brogan reached out and ran his hands down along her hips before he pulled her against him. Her breath caught at the feel of his engorged cock. He had been pretty damn impressive in her dreams. Something told her that she needn't worry about being disappointed in real life.

"My cookies," she started to protest before she felt Barrack's hands sliding up to cup her breasts.

"After we wet the sheets," Brogan chuckled, pressing a hot kiss to her neck.

Delilah groaned, wrapping her arms around Barrack's neck when he lifted her into his arms. She buried her face against his neck. She might be crazy, but who the hell cared!

"I can't wait to see if this is going to be as good as my dreams have been," she mumbled against his neck.

Both men chuckled. "We will make sure it is even better," Brogan promised.

~

Bite, bite, bite, bite, bite....

Barrack gritted his teeth. He wanted to tell his dragon to shut up, but the damn thing wasn't having any of it. He'd never had so much trouble in his life controlling the beast!

Do not release.... Goddess! You are going to kill us all! he growled when he felt the first release of dragon fire in his blood.

"Barrack, you've got... How can they be so soft?" Delilah murmured, her fingertips caressing the scales running along his neck as he climbed the stairs with her in his arms.

"Delilah, my little fighter, I am close to losing control," Barrack admitted.

She tilted her head and looked at him with eyes filled with curiosity and desire. Her fingers paused before she began to stroke him again. He clenched his jaw when he felt his teeth starting to elongate.

"Are you losing control in a good way?" she asked, nipping at Barrack's neck before running her tongue over his skin. "Or a bad one?" she drawled suggestively.

Brogan chuckled over his shoulder at them. "In a very hot way, little book-reader. My brother wants you, but so does his dragon," he teased as his flaming eyes met his brother's strained ones.

Barrack was shocked that he was suddenly the more composed one out of the two of them. He'd honestly believed that when this time came, Brogan would be the one helping his brother keep from losing control, not the other way around. A harsh groan escaped him when Delilah leaned forward and ran the tip of her tongue along his neck. His dragon released a powerful wave of Dragon Fire.

"I don't see that happening," she laughed, her warm breath warming his already heated flesh even more.

She see, his dragon replied with confidence. *I bite. Mate come. I claim. We no die.*

No, no, no. Not until I tell you, Barrack growled, before he released a startled curse when Delilah tugged on his hair.

Delilah released his hair. "You can let me know if you don't want to do this," she replied, lifting her chin.

He could see the hurt in her eyes. Shaking his head, he slowed to a stop outside of her bedroom. Brogan turned and waited for them.

"Look inside me," he quietly requested.

Her eyes clouded with confusion. "How do I do that?" she asked.

"Close your eyes, Delilah. Our symbiots will show you," Brogan gently instructed.

Barrack watched as her eyelids fluttered before her lashes lowered to rest against her cheeks. Her lips parted on a startled gasp. He focused, conveying his feelings through the symbiot around her wrist and neck.

"Oh my! Oh! I… Oh, boy… Geez! Really?" Delilah exclaimed, her voice changing from shock, to more shock, to disbelief, back to shock again.

Her eyes popped open and she stared at him with her mouth partially agape. Her expression of doubt pulled a wry grin to his lips, but as he watched, wonder infused her countenance.

"Are you saying that I can…? That if we…? I'll be able to turn into a dragon?" she asked, her voice filled with awe and her heart skipping a beat at the thought.

"Yes," he quietly answered.

She shook her head in disbelief. "How cool would that be?" she breathed.

~

After months of dreaming about the two men, it was hard for her to wrap her head around the fact that the dreams were coming true. She didn't know if she was reliving another life or if some Goddess out in the great cosmos had been sending her a video message. The moment they touched her, she honestly didn't care. This was real and she wasn't about to tuck her tail between her legs and become a fainting damsel in distress. She also wasn't a scared virgin. A few boyfriends during college and a healthy appetite for experiencing life had taken care of that little membrane.

Barrack lowered her to her feet but kept his hands on her. She loved the power coursing through her at being able to ignite such a response in him with just a touch of her hands. Sliding them up his chest, she fingered the fastenings at the neck of his shirt.

One at a time, she released them, revealing more of his skin. Her breath hissed out when she felt Brogan sliding her sweater up and pulling it over her head. With agonizing slowness, they removed their clothes.

Brogan was driving her insane with his wandering hands. Her head tilted and she moaned softly. The twins rumbled their approval. Between Brogan's hands and Barrack's lips, her body was a trembling mass of need. They were a lethal combination.

"You two must have driven all your girlfriends crazy," she groaned when Brogan lifted her breasts so that Barrack could worship them.

"We've never shared loving together with a woman other than you," Brogan replied in a thick voice laden with desire. "Our dragons would not tolerate it."

"Well, cover me in chocolate, lick me clean, and call me one lucky bitch," she replied, feeling a sense of selfish glee at being the only woman to have enjoyed this with them.

~

Pleasure coursed through Brogan as his hands slid upward over Delilah's ribs to cup both of her breasts beneath her nipples. Barrack took advantage and bent to suck on first one taut, mocha-colored nipple before nipping at the other. A shuddering gasp sounded in the room. Delilah enjoyed having her nipples stimulated.

I enjoy doing the stimulating, Barrack replied to Brogan's silent observation. *I can smell her desire.*

I plan to taste her sweet nectar, Brogan replied.

For the first time in their lives, they were able to use their connection in a way they had never done before – with their true mate. They coordinated their caresses to maximize her pleasure. Each caress heated his blood until he was sure he had fire running through his veins. Her acceptance of them sent a piercing shaft of intense emotion through him.

"Whoa, I can feel someone is definitely hot!" Delilah moaned, rolling her hips against his crotch.

Brogan's lips parted to give her a teasing retort, but his dragon had a different idea. Before he realized what he was doing, his teeth had pierced the tender skin at the curve of her shoulder and neck and he began to breathe the Dragon's Fire into her blood. Her body stiffened and bowed, pressing her against Barrack.

His brother's dragon reacted to her thrust. Barrack's lips parted and his teeth grew. Still holding onto Delilah's breasts, he watched Barrack sink his teeth into the soft flesh near her right nipple. Their combined Dragon Fire swept through Delilah's body, beginning the changes that would bind them together as true mates.

His arms tightened under her breasts and he pulled her against his long form, holding her as the fire coursed through her veins. Her hands gripped Barrack's shoulders and she tilted back her head, pressing her cheek against his and releasing a loud cry as she came for the first time. Barrack supported her when her legs suddenly gave out from under her.

Barrack reluctantly released her, his eyes blazing with emotion. "We should not have breathed at the same time," he said, his voice thick with self-reproach.

Delilah's head rolled forward and she gave him a crooked grin. "Yes, you should have. Damn, that was.... Well, hot damn," she giggled before moaning again, her body moving in an erotic dance against both of them. "I swear I feel like my horny-bitch mode has kicked into overdrive."

"Horny-bitch mode?" Brogan asked, sliding his tongue over the mark he had left on her shoulder.

Delilah tilted her head again and gave him a goofy smile. "I read it in a book," she said, before undulating against him when the wave intensified. "Ahhh! I hope you guys know how to put out the fire in me because I swear I'm about to go into a major meltdown."

Brogan's hands slipped from around Delilah as his brother led her to the bed. A smile curved his lips when she looked over her shoulder and held her hand out to him. He grasped it, chuckling when she eagerly jerked him toward her.

Mate impatient, his dragon chuckled. *I like!*

I do too, my friend. I do too, Brogan replied, following them down onto the bed.

Barrack laid back on the bed as Delilah clambered up his body. Brogan's eyes flared when he saw her broad hips lift in invitation. He could see the effects of the Dragon Fire already working on her body. Brilliant, rose-colored scales appeared and disappeared along her back.

Barrack, I see her dragon, Brogan groaned, sliding his hands along her hips.

I do as well. Her eyes, they are beautiful, Barrack replied in a strained voice. *The fire is building.*

Wait for it, Brogan commanded, knowing that if they took her at the moment the Dragon's Fire peaked, it would spread faster, but also give her a better chance of surviving the changes already transforming her.

He held her hips, his fingers sliding along her buttock to her saturated core. He could see the sheen of moisture on the black curls covering her womanhood. He pressed into her, testing and stretching her.

"Oh, yes!" she groaned, pressing her lips against Barrack's chest as she tilted her hips, so Brogan could slide more deeply into her.

"She is ready," he said, gritting his teeth when she squeezed her vaginal muscles around his fingers.

"Yes... she is," Delilah panted, rocking her hips. "I need you both. The fire.... What is happening to me? I've never been so horny in my life!"

Brogan slid down along the bed when she pressed against him. Her lips were running down Barrack's body. He could see how close his brother was too losing control. Barrack's hands rose to thread through Delilah's hair when she suddenly wrapped her lips around his cock.

Grasping her hips again, he aligned his cock with her heated core. His bulbous head, slick with his own seed, slid deep inside her, impaling her on his long, hard cock. He watched as he buried himself in her as far as he could go. Her muffled cries echoed with Barrack's as she gripped his cock in her hand.

Connected with her now through the Dragon Fire and their symbiots, Brogan began moving with the waves of fire building inside her. He wanted to bite her again, to breathe more of the fire building inside himself, but was afraid to. The powerful waves building in him crashed against the fragile control he was trying to maintain.

He bowed his head, focusing on the sensations rushing through his body. The sounds of their heavy breathing, the slapping of their flesh as they connected, and the deeper caress of her vaginal walls against his cock sent him spiraling out of control. The primitive need of the male to claim his mate seized them both.

Her body tightened around his, swelling as the heat crested inside her.

Throwing his head back, his strangled shout joined with his brother's as she came around him. His eyes blazing with elation, he pulsed deep inside her. He could see her throat move as she swallowed Barrack's release.

Pride and pleasure coursed through him as he watched the scales of Delilah's dragon take shape, growing more visible, and rippling across her skin before fading. The change had begun. Before the night was over, he and his brother would have their true mate over and over and over again.

We have a lot of years to make up for, he thought.

"Our claim has just begun," Barrack said out loud, his eyes flashing with fire and his voice harsh with desire.

Brogan watched as Delilah slid her mouth from around Barrack and shuddered. "It's… coming… again…," she warned.

"Barrack, stretch out under her. This time, we both will take her at the same time," Brogan ordered with a wicked smile curving his lips as he ran his hand down over her ass.

Delilah hummed under her breath as she pulled the sheet of fresh baked cookies out of the oven. She placed them on the stove and turned the oven off, then leaned over, and sniffed the delicious smell of hot chocolate chip cookies baked to perfection.

These will taste almost as good as the guys, she thought with amusement.

She tilted her head and listened to the soft footsteps on the ceiling above her. Barrack was showering while Brogan had taken the dogs outside after he had come downstairs grumpy and growling that she had been missing when he'd come out of the bathroom. What could she say? She had woken up starving!

Now, the whole-house generator was running, she was freshly showered, was wearing some comfy sweats and a tattered sweater that had belonged to her father, and she had a batch of freshly baked cookies. Life was absolutely perfect. Of course, having two of the sexiest guys in the universe who had taken her to the stars and back last night might have been the real reason she felt so good.

She worried her bottom lip as she transferred the cookies to the wire rack to cool. As good as she felt about what had happened between herself and the two men upstairs, she wasn't oblivious to the complications that her new relationship with them caused. There was no doubt in her mind that the local residents would have a heart attack if they knew she was having a relationship with not one, but two guys. Throw into the mix that the brothers were aliens, add a dash of fire-breathing dragon, and a sprinkle of gold, shape-shifting creatures, and she could see the entire state of North Carolina being quarantined by the government.

She looked up when she heard Barrack talking to Brogan as they walked towards the kitchen and passed by Moonshine and Rum wrestling with Whiskey – Barrack's symbiot – and Gin – Brogan's symbiot. She had decided last night as she lay in bed between the two men that their symbiots needed names.

She had kept with the theme that she had started with the Rottweilers, and had grinned when both symbiots had sent vivid impressions of approval. She had come up with the name for the Rottweilers by accident a few days after she had brought them home when she'd discovered her granddad had had a little side business of making moonshine back behind the old smokehouse. She couldn't help but wonder if her grandmother had known about his illegal enterprise.

"Whatever you have made smells delicious," Brogan commented, running his hand over his hair to remove the last of the snow.

"Cookies," she grinned, holding up a plate.

Brogan grabbed several off the plate – ate one, then grabbed several more. Barrack grunted that Brogan needed to learn to share. She laughed and shook her head.

"I have plenty," she replied, leaning up to press a kiss to Barrack's lips. "You taste as good as the cookies."

"I find that hard to believe," Brogan teased. "These are delicious. They remind me of mother's sweets."

Delilah looked at them, startled. Why had she never thought of them as having a normal family with a mother and father? Hell, they could have a large extended family! The thought of them with a mom who had made cookies for them as a child made her chest feel tight. What must their parents have felt when they lost both of their children?

"I'll get some more," she said, noticing the plate that she was holding was already empty. "Just make sure you leave room for breakfast."

She started to turn back toward the kitchen when an intense pain hit her. The plate she was holding fell from her suddenly numb fingers. Her hand started to rise to her chest as the world began to tilt sideways. Deep inside her, she heard the faint but desperate cry for help. For a second, she wondered who the feminine voice belonged to before another wave of pain struck her hard enough to knock her knees out from under her.

The sound of Delilah's dragon in distress caused Brogan and Barrack to instantly reach for her. Belatedly Brogan realized the shattering sound was from the plate hitting the kitchen floor.

She was tilting toward him unnaturally, and he caught a glimpse of her eyes wide with pain, fear, and confusion, her hand beginning to rise to her chest before it fell limply to her side as her eyes rolled back in her head and she collapsed.

Help me! Pain. Help me.

He registered her soft, anguished moan seconds after she uttered it, and vaguely heard Barrack cry "Delilah!" Time felt displaced and disconnected as they caught her. The twin symbiots on her wrists and the one around her neck dissolved and slid beneath her skin.

The two larger symbiots burst into the room with such force that the dining room chairs and table tumbled like dominoes before stopping next to the window. Barrack's symbiot shifted and flowed over her while his became a floating bed. Brogan gently laid Delilah's unconscious body down.

Barrack reached out and ran his hand down over her face, trying to follow the information that their symbiots were conveying to them. Brogan paled when he saw the damage to Delilah's heart. The organ struggled to continue to beat.

"Her heart," he whispered, his hand trembling as he caressed her cheek.

Barrack's face was tight with tension. He was following the symbiot's progress. Brogan could see the strain on his brother's face. Neither of them had the knowledge of a healer, but Barrack knew more than he did. He could feel Delilah's frightened dragon connecting with her human half. The pulsing light of her dragon was the only thing keeping Delilah alive at the moment.

"Can they heal her?" Brogan asked, looking up at his brother.

Barrack's face became grim with determination. "If they can, it will take time," he answered.

That was not the 'yes' Brogan had been desperate to hear. Barrack's symbiot had threads of gold piercing Delilah's chest that were pulsing, sending tiny bursts of electricity to her heart.

But he no say no, his dragon insisted, feeling his mate's distress.

No, he did not say no, Brogan agreed, his hand tightening on Delilah's as the symbiot bed began to move through the room.

His fingers slipped from hers when the space became too narrow. Forced to follow, he slowly climbed the stairs. In the space of a few seconds, his world had gone from intense contentment with their true mate to spinning dangerously close to imploding.

She has to live, he thought, his heart slowing to beat in time with hers.

~

Show me the damage, Barrack instructed his symbiot.

Images of Delilah's heart appeared in his mind. He could see the muscle struggling to contract, but it couldn't. Sweat beaded on his brow when her heart slowed to the point it was barely beating. The symbiot sent small filaments into Delilah's heart and began sending pulses to keep it beating.

He walked beside Brogan's symbiot as the creature gently moved Delilah out of the dining room and up to her bedroom. Once upstairs, the symbiot moved over her bed and dissolved before reforming. Both creatures worked on Delilah while he and Brogan stood to the side, watching, waiting, and clinging to the small spark of life inside her. As the symbiots worked tirelessly on her, he was able to piece together what had happened.

We hurt mate, his dragon mourned.

No, her heart was weak. The Dragon Fire may have caused it to weaken further, but it is also what saved her life. She would have died if she did not have her dragon inside her, Barrack said.

Hear mate cry. She in pain, his dragon replied.

We will heal her. We did not come this far only to lose her, my friend. You will have your mate. She will fight to be with us, Barrack replied, his voice filled with determination.

She fight. She strong, his dragon said, growing quiet.

"Yes, she will fight," Barrack murmured, unable to believe anything else as he pulled the chair closer to the bed so he could hold Delilah's hand.

Brogan sat at the end of the bed. Neither man spoke. Their entire focus was on the beautiful, feisty, yet fragile woman fighting for her life – and theirs.

CHAPTER SEVENTEEN

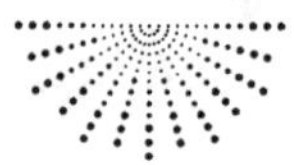

"How is she?" Brogan quietly asked, stepping into the room.

"Resting," Barrack replied, looking up from where he sat on the bed next to Delilah.

Brogan sat down on the edge of the bed and cupped her limp hand in his. Her fingers were warm. Lifting it to his lips, he pressed a kiss to her knuckles. Her expression was peaceful.

"Has she woken at all?" he asked, looking at his brother.

Barrack shook his head. "No," he replied.

Brogan bowed his head. It had been over twenty-four hours since Delilah had collapsed and stopped breathing. She would have died immediately if not for their symbiots' swift reactions.

At first, they believed her collapse was due to a delayed effect of the Dragon's Fire. The changes were hard on her body. Guilt plagued him most of the night. Maybe they had been too energetic with her. Their symbiots had worked on her throughout the night, repairing and healing each damaged muscle and checking each valve in her weakened heart.

The symbiots showed them that the damage was not caused by the change, but from a weak heart that had gone undetected since Delilah was born. He looked down at her chest. Lifting his other hand, he gently laid it over her heart.

"We came so close to losing her," he murmured, looking up at his brother with tortured eyes.

Barrack's gaze moved to Brogan's hand resting on Delilah's chest. "Our symbiots are checking everything. We are fortunate that they were able to reach her in time and repair the damage before it was too extensive. Once it is safe to leave, I want all of us to return to the ship and have the healer examine her," he said.

Brogan nodded in agreement. Pulling his hand away, he continued to hold her hand. He could feel his dragon reaching for her. A part of him had known he should prevent his dragon from touching his mate, but he also realized that most of Delilah's healing came from their connection. Delilah's dragon needed to know that the twin dragons were there for her as well.

Feel mate. She sleep, his dragon quietly said.

Let her heal, my friend, he gently murmured, understanding his dragon's desire to wake and call his mate.

Delilah drifted in and out of sleep. She could feel the changes going on inside her body but didn't understand them. Curious, she tried to focus. Her mind felt fuzzy, and thinking for long periods was difficult. Losing her train of thought, she was unable to pinpoint what felt different from before.

Waking again, she felt a small movement inside her that caused her body to twitch. It almost felt like something was sending tiny electrical shocks to her heart. She tried to move her hand to cover her chest but something was holding it and refused to let go. She couldn't understand why it was so difficult for her to wake up. Every time she tried, it felt like someone was pressing down on her chest with a heavy weight. She soon became too tired to fight against the relentless pressure, so she gave up. Sleep was so much easier.

Flashes of memory came and went as she slept. Sometimes she

barely caught a glimpse of them. At other times, the memories appeared to be playing in agonizing slow motion. Then, there were those that she reached for but couldn't quite grasp her.

As time crept by, the images became clearer and more organized. Her body bowed and a soft moan slipped from her as the weight holding her down rose and fell as if floating on a rough sea. She tried to turn her face into the warm hands that caressed her chilled skin. Finally, the sickening motion calmed, and the seas took on the characteristics more of a placid mirrored lake than the ocean of nausea and pain.

Delilah was finally able to relax. She felt—safe. The weight on her chest was beginning to lessen, and she could breathe more easily again. For a while, she was able to sink into a different, more restful sleep, one devoid of dreams.

She didn't know how much time passed before she surfaced again. This time, she could feel the panic inside her building as the crushing weight returned. Her lips parted, but she couldn't draw in a breath. Her starving lungs protested. At that moment, she knew she was dying.

No! I can't. We found each other. I'm not supposed to die. I have to live. If I die, they will be lost, she cried, fighting against the uneven beat of her heart. *Help me! Please! Please, help me. Don't let me... Don't let us die. Please.... Sara....*

Images of her friend promising never to leave her danced through her head. Her mother and father's harsh sobs and the doctor's quiet voice replayed as if it were happening right at that moment. She didn't understand. She had been fine. The kids in school were getting sick, but she had been okay until the night before.

The vision of her going to the cemetery to place flowers on her parent's graves started to replay before it changed. There were people gathered there. They were all in black. Standing off from the crowd, was Sara with her blond hair tucked into a messy ponytail.

"Sara," Delilah called.

Confusion struck her when Sara didn't acknowledge her. Turning to see what her friend was looking at, she was shocked when she saw her dad holding up her mother. Worried, she started toward them but the more she walked, the farther away they became.

Calling out to them to wait for her when she saw them turn to leave, she began to run. Her heart pounded in her chest, and she was gasping. She finally fell to her knees, frantically crying and trying to draw in a breath.

She was all alone. Leaning forward, she rocked back and forth and dug her hands into the ground. Her heart hurt, and she couldn't breathe again. Looking up with tears streaming down her face, she was shocked to see the headstone in front of her.

Delilah Amber Rosewater
Precious daughter
Died 10 years of age

"No! I'm not dead! I lived! Damn you, I lived. Barrack! Brogan! Help me! Help me!" she screamed, struggling to wake up from the nightmare that was suffocating her. "Please… help me. Don't… don't let me die. Please… I need you. I need you both."

We are here, elila. Rest. We will not let you go. I swear on our lives. We will hold you forever, Brogan murmured.

Sleep, Delilah. Let our symbiots heal your heart. You are very ill, little book warrior. They need you to remain calm, Barrack added.

Stay with me, she murmured, suddenly exhausted.

Always. Both men's voices blended as one.

Delilah forced herself to relax. She could feel the symbiots moving inside her, frantically repairing the damaged tissue and muscles of her heart. Releasing her last hold on awareness, her body and mind began to float.

Not float—fly, she corrected with a small smile. *I can fly like a dragon.*

~

Brogan woke from the dream with a soft hiss. He hadn't meant to fall asleep. He looked at the window and realized it was almost dawn. The snow was still falling, but it was a continuous gentle fall that looked more like someone was sprinkling powdered sugar from the sky.

"I love it when the snow falls like this," Delilah murmured.

Brogan slowly turned his head. He was afraid that he was still locked in the dream and only imagined Delilah's voice. His face softened when he saw her lying on her side looking at him.

"Good morning," she said, her lips curving in a shy smile.

Brogan's throat worked up and down but no sound came out. Rolling onto his side, he reached out a trembling hand and ran his fingers down her cheek. He took a shuddering breath when she turned her head and pressed a warm kiss to the center of his palm.

He looked at the door when he saw movement. Barrack stood in the opening, one hand holding the doorframe. He smiled at his brother.

"She's awake," he said.

Delilah rolled onto her back and frowned at Barrack. Brogan could tell from the confusion on her face that she didn't realize what had been happening. He sat up when she did. He could see the blush on her cheeks when the bedcovers pooled around her waist and she realized that she wasn't wearing anything.

Yanking up the covers, she held them up under her chin. He reached over and grasped one of her hands, holding it tenderly in his. She looked out of the window again, the frown on her face deepening.

"I dreamed I was dying," she confessed, not looking at either of them. "I don't like that dream."

Brogan watched his brother walk over to the bed. Barrack sank down on the edge and tenderly pulled Delilah into his arms. Brogan started to release her hand but she clung to him. Releasing the cover, she slid her other arm around Barrack and pressed her lips to his neck as he held her.

"You… We don't like that dream either," Barrack choked in a harsh voice.

She rubbed her nose against his skin. "Do I want to know what happened?" she asked with a sigh, pulling back to look at Barrack before turning to look at him.

"Your heart gave out," Brogan said, lifting her fingers to his lips. "There was a defect. You made it through the Dragon's Fire, but I fear the strain was too much."

"I… remember." Her eyes grew distant for a moment before they cleared, and she turned to look at him. "This is why I died before. My parents didn't know. I saw them at a funeral—my funeral. Is it…? Will I…?" her voice trailed off.

Brogan lifted his free hand. His brother did the same, and they each wiped away the tears from her cheeks. He shook his head and gave her a reassuring smile.

"Our symbiots repaired the damage," he said, cutting off her unspoken fear.

Concern swept through him when she closed her eyes and swayed. Barrack pulled her back into his arms and held her while Brogan ran a caressing hand down her bare back. Silent tears ran down her cheeks. They held her while she cried, knowing that she needed the tears to help her heal.

He was relieved when she sat back and took a deep, calming breath. With another sniff, she gave them both a watery smile. Brogan chuckled when her stomach rumbled.

"I want a hot shower and a huge meal," she announced.

"I will turn on the generator," Barrack replied, pressing a kiss to her forehead before releasing her and standing up. "I can prepare the meal as well."

Brogan grinned. "I will take a shower as well. Someone needs to keep an eye on you," he teased.

Barrack groaned. "I volunteered too fast," he muttered in disgusted exaggeration.

"You could always join us—after you turn on the generator, of course," Delilah suggested.

The hopeful look in her eyes sent a wave of relief through him. Her face glowed with a healthy sheen far different from the way it had looked yesterday morning when she collapsed. He chuckled when he saw the disappointed pout on her lips after Barrack shook his head and gave her a hard, brief kiss.

"Later. Let us take care of you," Barrack responded, glancing at him.

Brogan nodded in agreement. Until they were positive Delilah was completely healed, they would be cautious. Neither one of them wanted to go through what they already had in the past twenty-four hours.

"Oh, alright," she reluctantly agreed before she glanced out the window again. "I have some quiche in the freezer. If you turn the oven on to the number I marked on the wrapping and place it unwrapped on the middle rack, it would make a great breakfast. With the generator on, I can make some toast to go with it."

"We can make the toast to go with it while you instruct us," Brogan interjected.

"What does this quiche look like?" Barrack asked.

Delilah lifted her hands and formed a round circle. Brogan grinned when the covers that she was trying to keep tucked under arms sagged again, revealing her right breast. She released a huff and gave up on any attempt at modesty. From the wicked gleam in her eyes, she'd received exactly the type of response she was hoping for—their undivided attention.

"Oh, well, if you aren't interested in taking a shower while we have power you don't know what you are missing," she said, pushing the covers aside and rising to her feet. "The quiche is round. I have them on the top shelf of the big freezer. Any flavor is fine with me."

Brogan's eyes were glued to the enticing sway of Delilah's hips and ass as she walked to the bathroom. The men groaned when she lifted her foot and caught the bathroom door to close it. Shaking his head, he looked up at his brother with a rueful grin.

"She is feeling better," he said.

Brogan watched as his brother pulled his focus away from the door and scowled at him. He knew that they needed to give her time to heal, but that didn't mean they couldn't appreciate and admire their mate's delectable body. He shrugged when Barrack raised an eyebrow at him.

"You were admiring the view as much as I was. I'll behave—mostly," Brogan said, rolling off the other side of the bed, standing, and stretching his arms over his head. "You'd better put two of those round quiches into the oven. I'm hungry."

Barrack snorted and turned. "You are lucky I'm better in the kitchen than you are, otherwise you'd be the one downstairs," he retorted over his shoulder.

"I'm still better at repairing machines. Remember, we wouldn't be here if I hadn't repaired the engines on our ship," Brogan good-naturedly called behind his brother.

"That's what symbiots are for!" Barrack commented.

Brogan's laughter grew as he listened to his brother loudly stomp down the stairs. He waited until he heard the generator's faint hum when it came on. Turning toward the closed bathroom door, he began removing his clothes. The sound of the shower starting and Delilah's loud moan of pleasure made him undress even faster. Tossing his clothes on the chair by the window, he touched his symbiot.

Is she healed? he inquired, wanting reassurance before he stepped into the bathroom.

Warmth filled him, answering his question. His hand gripped the doorknob. He twisted it and pushed the door open. The bathroom was already filling up with steam from the hot water. Closing the door behind him, he stepped up to the clear shower doors and watched Delilah lift her arms to run her fingers through her hair. Through the fogged glass, he could see her profile.

I'm just going to help her, he silently swore.

All thoughts of behaving flew from his mind when he opened the shower door and she turned toward him. The look in her eyes held a promise that this was going to be a long and pleasurable shower. He stepped into the long stall and slid the door closed behind him.

"Would you mind helping me?" she asked, holding the liquid soap out to him. "I have an overwhelming need to feel your hands on me."

Brogan, remember what we agreed! Barrack's dire words of warning rang through his mind.

Either join us or go away, Barrack. Our mate asked for my help. I'm not about to tell her no, Brogan retorted,

He felt his brother connect with the symbiot on Delilah. The sounds of curses rang through his head until he muted them. Downstairs he heard the sound of the oven door slamming shut and seconds later the rapid ascent of footsteps on the stairs.

He had just begun to slide his soapy hands over Delilah's skin when the air pressure changed in the room as Barrack opened the bathroom door. Delilah's delighted giggle filled the air with joy around them when a naked Barrack opened the shower door and motioned for them to make room.

"Thank goodness I didn't listen to Bubba Joe and go with the fiberglass shower stall. All of us would have never fit if I had," she moaned, her breath speeding up when Barrack pressed up behind her.

What is the best prescription for making you feel better? Having not one, but two hunky, sexy, super-hot aliens soaping you down in a shower with unlimited hot water, Delilah thought with glee.

It was amazing how almost dying liberated a person of all their doubts and fears. Any misgivings she might have had quickly melted under the onslaught of their tender caresses. Their night together had been amazing, but she still had that tiny subconscious sliver of uncertainty haunting her.

All doubt was gone now. She wanted to live. She wanted to love. And she was not going to let anything get in her way, not even the two guys so determined to treat her like a fragile piece of glass.

Diamond, a voice whispered.

Delilah's hands paused on Brogan's chest. She had felt this strange pressure growing inside her shortly after she made love with them and the morning of her collapse. In fact, this strange voice was the one who had called out for help when she couldn't.

At first, she thought that it was the symbiots. They had always communicated with her before but in pictures, though, not words. Trying to focus while the men were running their hands over her made it difficult to determine what else was different about this voice. It actually felt like whoever was talking was inside her head.

I here now. We like diamond, not glass. We strong, the voice continued.

Who... are we? Are you my... dragon? Delilah thought, unsure if the voice could hear her.

You think, I hear. I think, you hear. We are one, the voice replied.

A mental image rose in Delilah's mind. The picture of a rose-colored dragon filled her mind. She was delicate with hazel eyes that danced with mischief. Her breath caught at the creature's beauty when she unfolded her wings and shook.

"Elila, are you feeling unwell?" Brogan asked, his hands coming up to capture hers.

"I knew it was too soon. We need to get her back to the ship and have the healer examine her," Barrack stated in a voice filled with worry.

Delilah frantically shook her head. She didn't want to lose the connection she had with her dragon, but she also didn't want the men to be worried about her health. She was fine. Hell, she was more than fine. She was a dragon-shifter!

"I see her," Delilah whispered in awe.

Barrack's hands tightened on her hips. "Who?"

She looked over her shoulder. "My dragon," she replied with a bemused smile. "She said we are like a diamond not glass."

She looked around when Brogan emitted a loud, muttered curse. Giggling, she saw a flash of green and white scales run along his body before disappearing. The giggles faded when she saw her arms.

"My dragon cannot wait for his mate," Barrack murmured, pressing his lips to her shoulder.

"I have scales," she whispered, her voice filled with awe. "I have scales. I have scales!"

Both men laughed. "Yes, you have very beautiful scales," Brogan agreed.

Delilah looked up at him. "Can I change? How do I change? Will it hurt? I mean, my bones will be like popping and snapping, won't they? It didn't look like it hurt when you did it, but I didn't see you actually change, but you both looked so awesome and.... Can I shift? Please?"

She gave Brogan her biggest and best puppy-dog eyes ever. The look had never failed to work on her dad or her grandfather. The doubt in his eyes wavered before fading to resignation. He glanced over her head at Barrack.

"No," Barrack said, his hand pulling her against him. "She is still recovering. We said we need to get her checked out by the healer before we did anything else."

"She's giving me the look," Brogan defended.

"Delilah, you almost died less than twenty-four hours ago," Barrack said, reaching behind him and turning off the shower before he turned her to face him. "No, no, no, no... yes!"

Delilah laughed and slid her arms around Barrack. She hugged him, loving the fact that she could do this. Being with them, holding them, felt natural and right to her now, and she was going to love every second of it.

"Where did that come from?" Brogan asked with a raised eyebrow.

Barrack made a face. "Shut up, my dragon slipped that one in," he muttered, lowering his head to rub his cheek against Delilah's wet hair. "But—there are some conditions."

"What kind of conditions?" she asked, tilting her head to look up at him.

"First, we need to get you dried off and dressed. I don't want you to freeze to death if you shift outside without your clothes on," he teased.

Delilah looked down between them. She couldn't keep the grin off her face when she saw the evidence of his not-so-frozen body. Her eyes twinkled with mirth when she looked up at him again.

"I know where I can warm my hands," she teased.

Barrack scowled at Brogan. "She is going to be trouble," he said with a shake of his head.

"She is listening," Delilah reminded him, reaching down and tugging on a part of his anatomy that definitely drew his attention back to her. "What is the second condition?"

"Food," Brogan chuckled, reaching over and pulling the shower door open. "Otherwise, we will be back in the bed until the snow melts."

Delilah released Barrack with a cheeky grin and took the towel Brogan was holding out. She jumped when Barrack smacked her on the ass. A soft, rumbling purr escaped her and her hand flew to her mouth in surprise. With wide eyes, she remained still as the two men dried her off before drying themselves.

I could get used to this, she thought in amusement.

Wait see what dragons do, her dragon chuckled. *Mates make me very happy. I make them very happy.*

How? Delilah curiously asked.

Her eyes widened even further, and her glance immediately moved down to Brogan's crotch. Her lips parted as her dragon continued to show her what dragons did when they were very happy. She didn't realize that she was lifting the towel higher and higher to hide her fiery cheeks until she felt the touch of Barrack's cool fingers against her heated skin.

"Are you alright?" he asked in concern.

Delilah nodded. "Yes," she squeaked, unable to say anything else without bursting into a fit of uncontrollable giggles

You are soooo bad, she told her dragon.

Yes, her dragon agreed, totally unapologetic.

CHAPTER EIGHTEEN

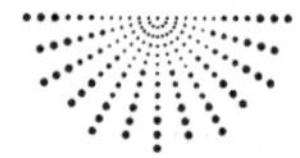

An hour later, Delilah stood on the back porch watching Brogan clear a section of ground in her backyard. Brogan's dragon grinned at her as he turned in a tight circle, sweeping his tail around. She giggled when Moonshine and Rum chased after his tail.

She couldn't believe how much snow there was! It wasn't until Brogan was several feet down that she finally realized how much there had actually been – and how much still continued to fall. On a bright note, it would keep any curious eyes away, so they wouldn't have to worry about being seen.

She was dressed from head to toe in her warmest clothes, and she had a full belly. If she hadn't been so excited about the idea of turning into a dragon, she would have retreated back upstairs to bed for a nap.

No sleep, other things to do. I show you, her dragon replied.

Did you just roll your eyes at me? How can dragons roll their eyes? Is that even conceivable? And I don't need you to 'show' me anything. I can handle this on my own, Delilah retorted with a roll of her own eyes.

Humph, her dragon snorted.

"Delilah, are you ready?" Barrack asked, stepping up onto the porch.

"Do you think it is safe?" she asked, worried about someone seeing them, despite her earlier thought that she didn't have to worry about that. She was giving herself a pass on some neuroticism, because how often did someone turn into a dragon for the first time?

"Our symbiots are patrolling the area. They will let us know if anyone approaches," he reassured her.

She reached out and took the hand he offered. Biting her lip, she was thankful for the path the two men had cleared. As it was, the snow on each side of her came nearly to her hip. She reached out and ran her glove-covered hand along the snow.

"I can see the crystals in it," she said, pausing to bend and look at the snow through new eyes.

"The eyes of a dragon can see very well," Barrack explained. "We can see in dim light as well."

"Well, that explains why you didn't use the flashlights I gave you," she said.

Barrack chuckled and nodded. "Yes, we did not need them," he responded, drawing her into the circle.

Delilah glanced nervously at the dogs before looking at Brogan, then back at Barrack. She rubbed her hands along her pant legs. Maybe this wasn't such a good idea. What if she became stuck as a dragon? Or worse! What if she became stuck with a dragon head and a human body or the other way around? While the idea of being a mermaid was really awesome, imagining half her own body as fishy had never excited her.

She winced when she felt her dragon roll in laughter. The damn thing sounded like it was stuck between her ears. A flash of irritation ran through her and she sent her dragon a mental poke in the butt.

"I'm not going to want to eat my dogs, will I?" she asked, tucking a lock of hair that had blown across her face back behind her ear.

Brogan's dragon snickered and looked at the dogs. She rolled her eyes when the dragon wiggled the area above his eyes and licked his lips with a long tongue. Of course, her dogs thought the look meant 'let's play', not 'I'm about to eat you'.

"Okay, I get it. I won't eat the dogs, but you have to admit that it could be a possibility" she pointed out.

Taking a deep breath, she lifted her head and nodded. *I can do this,* she thought. *I can be a dragon.* She pictured her dragon in her mind. The creature really was very beautiful.

The female dragon's head was much smaller than those of Brogan and Barrack. Her scales were a delicate rose pink color with highlights of dark red and bright, shimmering white. Her body wasn't as muscular as the twin dragons', but it was dainty and sleek. She looked like she was built for speed and capable of weaving in and out of tight spaces.

Mesmerized by her dragon's beauty, she reached out to touch her. The scales felt like how she imagined the finest silk would feel. Brilliant hazel eyes, the same color as her own, looked back at her with a soft glow of love and acceptance.

I wish I knew how to change into you, Delilah murmured, running her hand down along the long, slender neck.

You already have, her dragon replied.

Delilah blinked the world back into focus. Everything looked sharper, crisper, and clearer. She swung her head around when she felt a caress along her shoulder. Lifting her wing, she felt the thrill of being free.

"All those centuries waiting for you, we never saw you in your dragon form," Barrack quietly said, running his hands along the top of her outstretched wing. "But I knew you would be beautiful."

She looked at Barrack in silence, unsure of what do next, but less than a minute later, she was questioning why she had worried. Her dragon had her own agenda, and a big portion of it involved turning on the pair of twin dragons.

You slow, her dragon snorted.

Delilah knew her mouth would be hanging open if she were human again. Her dragon swung her tail around and slapped Brogan on his left rear hindquarter, surprising the male dragon. Brogan growled in warning, but her dragon wasn't done. She slowly moved her tail down along Brogan's side and circled around him before she turned her back to him and slid her tail between his legs, down his belly, and along a long slit.

What is that? Delilah asked before realization hit her between the eyes like a foul ball. *Well, color me red. You are about to bite off a lot of dragon,* she warned her own dragon.

Two dragons. They have to catch me first, her dragon retorted, snapping at Brogan when he rose up on his hind legs.

Delilah silently squealed when her dragon suddenly pushed off the ground and rose in the air. Knowledge, passed down from the first dragons, flooded her dragon, giving her the information she needed to be able to fly. Her wings stretched out, stroking the air for the first time. A wild, primitive urge to roar swept through her, and she didn't hold back. She released a long, lilting roar, and admired the sound.

Turning, Delilah could see Barrack in his two-legged form and Brogan in his dragon form watching her. Her wings stroked the air, keeping her aloft, and she twisted in the air with a flick of her tail, and swept over the tops of the trees.

The world had turned white for as far as she could see. This was the first time she had ever seen her grandparent's property from this vantage point above her acreage. The rugged beauty of the land took her breath away. A part of Delilah wished she could attach one of those little cameras to her dragon so she could record everything to look at later.

Gliding along just above the treetops, she could see the ghostly remains of the old smokehouse where she and the dogs had taken refuge just a few days before. A shudder ran through her when she thought of what could have happened to her and the dogs if not for Barrack and Brogan. She had little doubt in her mind that they would have perished.

Turning, she discovered a stream that she hadn't even known existed less than five hundred yards behind the remains of the shed. It wasn't very wide, maybe five feet across, and it twisted and turned before disappearing underground. Most of the stream was frozen except for the very center. Curious, her ears flickered back and forth when she heard the sound of trickling water.

She followed the sound to a small section a little farther down the mountain. Her sharp eyes spotted the tiny waterfall created where the water came out of a crevice in the rock to release the stream. She started to land, but decided the snow drifts were too deep. Twisting around, she was startled when a shadow covered her.

The beauty of the male dragon was undeniable. His thick muscular frame blended in with the wintry scene, which surprised her. It was as if the green and white coloring of his scales had captured the natural colors of the landscape surrounding them. Even his wings appeared almost translucent.

A sense of excitement built in her when she sensed Brogan's determination to capture her. Changing tactics, she surged through the trees under him. Her smaller, sleeker body made cutting through the virgin forest easy.

Look out! Delilah warned when another shadow appeared in front of them.

I see him long time ago. He try to sneak up on us, her dragon sniffed in derision.

Well, I didn't, Delilah mumbled.

That why you need dragon, her dragon chortled.

I get a dragon who is horny and a smart-aleck. How did I get so lucky? Delilah playfully huffed.

Personally, she couldn't have picked a better fit. The two guys needed someone who didn't put up with their attitudes and so did their dragons. Not only that, how could she not love a dragon who had a really cool sense of humor?

She giggled when her dragon rose up and shook a branch as she went over Barrack. A huge glob of snow fell on top of the male's head, coating him in the white fluffy powder. Brogan didn't help matters when he almost ran into a tree. Poor Barrack ended up with a double dose of the cold stuff. Barrack's loud sneeze, followed by the sound of sizzling water, sent Delilah into a fit of laughter.

They played and chased each other for over an hour before the two males decided they had had enough and captured her in a field filled with the Christmas trees her father had planted the year before he died. Her mother hadn't had the heart to cut any of them down.

Brogan caught her first, wrapping his long tail around hers and gripping her neck in a gentle bite that kept her from moving as he mounted her from behind. Her dragon roared when she felt the male pull her tail to the side and enter her with one long thrust. Locked together, Brogan folded his wings down along her sides and began to rock in an ancient rhythm that gave birth to her Dragon Fire.

Fire licked through her, building with each thrust. Her dragon groaned and arched her hips when Brogan's teeth pierced the skin of her neck and he breathed out the Dragon's Fire. Her body responded instantly with a desire so intense, she felt like she was going crazy. Brogan's larger body held her down as she strained against him, snapping her jaws and trying to free her tail.

They came together, the fire burning hot enough in them that the snow sizzled and steam rose around them. A shudder ran through Brogan's dragon before he slid out of her and released her neck. Delilah gasped when her dragon swung around and snapped at the larger male. She watched with curiosity as her dragon advanced on Brogan.

What's wrong? You felt like you enjoyed that to me, Delilah muttered.

Barrack here. I show males I alpha, her dragon stated.

Why? I mean – the three of us – we didn't have any issues, Delilah awkwardly tried to explain.

Dragons different. Males fight. They kill each other, her dragon warned.

Fear blossomed inside Delilah. She hadn't thought of the fact that the guys might not be as agreeable to being a threesome in their dragon form. There was a wild look in the eyes of Brogan's dragon as he lifted his head and snarled. Fury twisted his features when Barrack landed a short distance away.

In horror, she saw Barrack crouch and bare his own teeth at his brother. These were two alpha males, born to rule, born to fight, born to kill. A cry of frustration rose inside her.

Let me out, Delilah begged, fighting against her dragon's control when the two males charged each other.

Not yet. They face off, I get in middle, her dragon said, watching and waiting for the right moment to intervene.

The sound of snapping jaws and loud roars had to have been heard for miles. Residents probably thought it was an avalanche, because, really, who would guess that two dragons were the reason for the earthshaking rumble?

Another cry was torn from Delilah when Barrack caught Brogan around the neck with his tail and flipped his brother as if he were as light as a feather. Brogan flew through the air, striking the large Christmas Trees and snapping them like toothpicks. Brogan skidded to a stop and dug his claws into the snow. Bending, he grasped one of the broken trees and threw it at Barrack.

Barrack barely ducked the flying branches that snapped the tops off of a half dozen nearby trees. Fear changed to anger as she watched the two brothers fight. They were destroying something that had great sentimental value to her. This was the last thing she had of her father that would live and grow, and they were ruining it.

Furious, she stomped forward when the two males collided again. They were locked in battle. Their wings fought to wrap around each other even as their teeth and claws raked to draw blood. Picking up one of the broken trees with her tail, she swung it like a baseball bat.

The two males parted as the tree whizzed by their heads. Jabbing the tree at Brogan, she snapped at Barrack. Both males warily watched her as she snapped, growled, and ranted.

You broke trees! her dragon roared, swiping at both of them with the broken tree trunks. *You not break trees! These Delilah's father's trees. Bad mates. Bad mates!*

Mine, Brogan growled, snapping at the tree when the female dragon tried to hit him with it. He stepped forward. *I claim my mate.*

I claim you, her dragon snapped. *I no claim no more if fight.*

She mine! Barrack snarled, stepping forward.

In fury, the female dragon slammed the tree into Barrack's chest and lifted off. She snapped her tail at Brogan, catching him in the ear as she flew by. Delilah wasn't sure what was going on, but it had the attention of the two males.

What now? Delilah asked.

Now I claim my mates, my way, her dragon informed her.

Do you see her? Barrack demanded, his eyes scanning the forest below them.

No, Brogan replied in a blunt tone.

She comes first, Brogan, Barrack gently reminded him. *We have to control our dragons better. If we kill each other, we all die.*

She's mine, Brogan growled, his eyes flashing with fire.

Control your dragon, brother, Barrack demanded.

I'm trying, Barrack. He... He refuses to share, Brogan replied.

He has to, or we are all doomed, Barrack repeated.

We have to find her. You go left, I'll go right, Brogan stated.

Barrack bowed his head. They were flying low through the forest, looking for tracks in the snow left by Delilah's dragon. They had followed her, but she had vanished over a rise. Fear began to build in both of them.

Barrack's eyes continued to search the ground. When he sensed an impending attack, he quickly glanced at Brogan. Brogan was flying beside him, so it wasn't him. Twisting, he released a roar and folded his wings toward his attacker and reached out with his claws. He was stunned when delicate, rose-colored claws locked with his.

They fell the short distance to the snow, slowed by her wings and cushioned by the thick layer of white flakes. Her tail wrapped around his and she slid her underbelly up along the long, narrow slit that protected his genitals. The sweet musk of her desire filled his nostrils and his dragon reacted to the chemical seduction.

His aroused dragon swiftly hardened. The female dragon lowered her head and rubbed her neck against his lips. The blatant invitation was obvious – the female wanted to mate and she had chosen him. He bit down on her neck, holding her and breathing in his Dragon Fire at the same time as he penetrated her narrow slit, impaling her and locking her to him with a growing desire that stretched her sensitive core.

As the last breath of the Dragon's Fire left him, he released the female dragon's neck. His wings rose to hold her trapped against his body as she rocked. Desire scorched both of them, pulling loud grunts and cries as they came together.

His head turned when he heard the soft crunch of snow. Locking eyes with his brother, he saw that Brogan's gaze was on where the female dragon had her snout tucked under his wing. She raised her head and called to Brogan. Barrack's body, still locked with the female, stiffened when Brogan stepped closer. In this position, he was defenseless.

Brogan cautiously stretched his head toward them as the female continued to call. When his brother was close enough, he saw the female dragon rub her cheek against his. It took a moment for him to realize exactly what their mate had done. She had not only brought Brogan close to them, but she had created a situation where they were both vulnerable. His eyes locked on his brother's exposed neck. With one powerful bite, he could severe the main artery in Brogan's neck.

Relaxing against the snow, he watched as the female dragon licked and caressed Brogan while remaining wrapped in his wings. She was theirs and they were hers. He reached up and rubbed his nose against Delilah's neck. They had truly found the one mate who could love a set of twin dragons.

CHAPTER NINETEEN

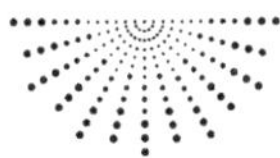

Today was the first day that the weather forecast had called for light snow showers instead of the blizzard conditions they'd had for most of the last four days. Comparatively, it was a beautiful day, but the dogs hovered at the edge of the porch, elated to be out and be able to see, yet hesitant to step on the path that had been cleared for them. Delilah shook her head at them.

Brogan, on the other hand, was staring intently up at the mountain.

What is it? Barrack asked, stepping out onto the porch with the two symbiots.

My dragon senses danger, Brogan replied.

Do you know what kind? Barrack asked, wrapping his hands around Delilah's waist and pulling her into the protective shadows of the porch. He ignored her startled squeak and wrapped his arms around her to keep her still.

No, Brogan replied. *Keep her safe. My symbiot and I will explore.*

Barrack inclined his head. His gaze scanned the area, and his dragon woke – alert to the tension running through both men.

"Where are you going?" Delilah asked in surprise.

"I wish to check out the area. I will return shortly," Brogan said, lifting his hand to run the backs of his fingers down along her cheek.

"Oh," she replied, unable to keep the disappointment out of her voice. "I was hoping we could go flying in a bit after the dogs have had some time outside."

"When I return," Brogan promised.

"Okay, well, be careful. The trees are pretty heavy with snow and they can snap at any time."

Brogan chuckled. "I will be careful, *elila*. Make sure Barrack keeps you warm while I am gone," he teased, sliding his leg over the skimmer his symbiot had formed.

They watched from the porch as he sped away. Delilah leaned back against Barrack and he rubbed his cheek against her knitted cap-covered head. His arms tightened around her when she placed her hands over his. Pleasure washed through him at her affectionate embrace of his touch.

She had been very quiet the last few days. Brogan and he had been very sensitive to her moods since her transformation. They were trying to be patient and give her time to come to terms with the changes in her life.

"I swear those symbiots can do the most incredible things," she sighed, her eyes following Brogan as he disappeared through the trees.

Barrack chuckled. "Would you like to see what else they can do?" he teased.

Delilah heard the suggestive nuances in his voice. Shaking her head, she laughed and pulled out of his arms. Stepping onto the path they had cleared for the dogs, she grinned up at him.

"Later. The poor dogs need some exercise. Between this weather and me neglecting them because I've been captured between two sexy hot bodies, they are about to go crazy," she said. "Besides, I need to check on my truck. The engine heater only works if we have electricity and since it has been off, I need to make sure my only mode of transportation hasn't frozen up."

"The doors have snow in front of them. We can wait until it melts to check your truck and I can have my symbiot watch the dogs," Barrack countered with another suggestive grin.

She chuckled and shook her head. "I guess I'll need a dragon to help me melt the snow," she said, ignoring the pout on his lips at her teasing rejection.

A rumble of approval slipped from him when Delilah shifted into her dragon and promptly flipped her tail up at him. When she did it a second time, he saw more of her soft underbelly and the protected slit. He knew she was teasing him and trying to get him to shift with her.

She sniffed inelegantly when he chuckled and folded his arms. His dragon was growling at him in frustration and straining to take his mate up on her invitation. He would love to, but it would leave them too vulnerable. Until he knew what danger Brogan had sensed, his first priority was the protection of their mate.

He released a quiet chuckle when she blew a thin line of fire at the snow. She was still learning how to control the flames of her dragon. While flying came naturally, controlling their flames was a little trickier. The natural flow was full-on incineration of anything they wanted to get rid of, not a finely wielded stream of fire.

He descended the steps, and had taken almost a dozen steps toward the garage to show her how to control her flame when he heard an unfamiliar sound. His head turned toward the front of the house. Delilah was focused on melting the snow and hadn't heard the approaching vehicle.

"Delilah, *little fighter,* I need you to shift back immediately. Someone is coming," Barrack quietly called.

~

Delilah turned her head at Barrack's soft warning and focused on what she could hear. A couple of engines were headed their way. She murmured to her dragon. The female dragon shimmered and grunted in frustration. She didn't like having to remain hidden.

A moment later, Delilah stood near the door to the shed when a pair of snowmobiles came up the driveway. It took her a minute to realize that the man on the first snowmobile was Bubba Joe.

Amusement coursed through her. She had honestly never thought of Bubba Joe as being a motorcycle – or in this case snowmobile – kind of guy. The only thing she had ever seen him in was a pickup truck that had to be older than hers.

He slowed to a stop and pulled off his helmet. He gave her an easy grin before his eyes moved to Barrack and the grin turned to a frown. Delilah decided it might be better to keep the attention on herself.

"Hey, Bubba Joe! What are you doing here?" Delilah asked, curious about who else was with him.

"Hi, Delilah. I went by your place in town to see if you made it through the storm okay, but it was empty. Mr. Clausen said he saw you packing up the dogs in the truck. I figured you must'a come up here," Bubba Joe said, glancing over at Barrack again.

She warily watched as Bubba Joe placed his helmet on the front of the snowmobile and climbed off. He pulled down the flaps of his hat to protect his ears. A smile curved her lips when his face softened as Moonshine and Rum came bouncing over to him. The man loved animals, there was no denying that. For a brief second, her heart hurt for Bubba Joe. She knew he liked her – a lot. She liked him too, but not in the same way.

She cleared her throat. "Yeah, my furnace decided to take a dump at the last minute. This house is in better shape thanks to the new windows and doors you helped install," she said, tucking her hands in her jacket pockets.

"Glad to hear that. Hey, guys, how are you two doing? Cold, I bet. I see your momma has you in nice sweaters," Bubba Joe said, squatting and rubbing the Rottweilers' heads before he straightened and shoved his hands in the pockets of his heavy coat. "You could have come to stay at my place. You still can. I can take you down on the back of my snowmobile."

Delilah's sensitive ears heard the soft growl of disapproval. The dogs must have heard it as well because they both whined and looked back at Barrack with their heads lowered. She shot Barrack an easy grin paired with a hard glare before turning back to smile at Bubba Joe.

"That's alright, but thanks for the offer. I have this place and the dogs. It isn't fair to burden anyone else with them," she replied in a light, cheerful tone before turning her attention to the other two people sitting silently on the snowmobile. "I… Would you like to come inside for some hot chocolate, tea, or coffee? I've got some freshly made cookies and lemon cake, too," she politely asked, remembering her parents' rule of offering refreshments to guests – even the uninvited ones.

"That sounds great. Rudy, do you and DeWayne want some?" Bubba Joe asked.

"DeWayne? What are you doing here?" Delilah demanded as a dark scowl swept across her face.

DeWayne reluctantly removed his helmet and held onto it. His wary gaze swept over to where the dogs were now digging in the snow. Delilah could just imagine him wondering if she was going to bury his body in the hole.

"Now, Delilah, you know Rudy is my cousin. I stayed with him and Aunt Lavern through the storm. I didn't know that Rudy and Bubba Joe were coming here," DeWayne muttered.

"You're lucky my momma taught me to be nice – sometimes," she retorted, pursing her lips. "Come on in and I'll make some hot chocolate. I know you don't drink coffee, Bubba Joe."

Delilah turned and looked toward the house. Barrack was standing on the corner of the front porch waiting for them. From this angle, it was hard to see his expression, even with her new dragon super-eyes.

She had only taken a few steps when a surprising growl escaped her as Bubba Joe reached out to grab her arm. Her hand flew to her mouth and she stumbled. She felt another growl rise up in her throat and she covered it with a cough. Her dragon was pissed about something.

What are you doing? she demanded in an incredulous tone.

He no touch you! Only mates touch us, her dragon snarled.

This is Bubba Joe, for crying out loud! I've known him since we exchanged bruises in kindergarten. He is my friend, Delilah huffed. *I won't let you or anyone else, including Brogan and Barrack, tell me who I can and can't be around,* she added in warning.

"Are you okay, Delilah?" Bubba Joe asked, bending down to look into her face.

She sighed and nodded. "I'm okay, Bubba Joe," she replied in a quiet voice. "How's your mom doing?"

She listened as Bubba Joe shared all the stuff going on in town. Her eyes scanned the porch, noting that Barrack must have taken the dogs in. She hoped that Whiskey was keeping a low profile.

My symbiot is keeping an eye on things from afar, Barrack informed her.

Delilah bent her head and smiled. She had forgotten that they could communicate this way. Looking up, she could see him standing near the front door.

"Who's that?" Bubba Joe asked.

Delilah picked up the slight sound of resentment in Bubba Joe's voice. They climbed the stairs. Rudy and DeWayne's voice faded and they froze on the second step. Delilah cleared her throat as the silence grew.

"Ah, Barrack, this is Bubba Joe. He is a childhood friend from town and has been helping me out with the renovations. That's Rudy and DeWayne," she introduced. "I'm going to make some hot chocolate, would you care for some?"

She gave him a pointed look when he remained standing in front of the door. He reached down and opened the screen, standing to the side in silence. Delilah rolled her eyes at the steely glare he gave Bubba Joe as they walked through the door.

"Who's that?" DeWayne asked, practically shoving Rudy out of the way so he wouldn't be the last one in. "I didn't know you had a boyfriend. If I had known, I wouldn't have asked… you out."

Bubba Joe's head turned at that and he added his heated glare to Barrack's. Delilah decided she had enough male testosterone for the moment. Peeling off her jacket, she hung it up on the hall tree and toed off her boots.

"Hang up your coats and your guns, boys. I'll be in the kitchen making hot chocolate. Barrack, why don't you come help me? The rest of you know where the sitting room is," she stated, not wanting any of them any closer.

"Thanks, Delilah," Bubba Joe said, peeling off his outer jacket.

She decided from the freezer suits and other clothes the men were wearing, it would take them a little while to get undressed anyway. She strode down the hallway to the kitchen with Barrack silently following behind her. The moment they rounded the corner of the kitchen, she swung around and grabbed the front of his jacket. A wicked grin curved her lips and she rose up on her tip toes to press a hot kiss to his lips.

"What was that for?" Barrack asked, his eyes flaming at the almost defiant caress.

"Because I wanted to and because I can," she chuckled. "You have nothing to worry about. I like Bubba Joe, but he's not my boyfriend. I like Rudy but have probably only said a dozen words to him in my entire life. I can't stand DeWayne. The guy grates on my nerves worse than fingernails on a chalkboard. He is the same age as me and has the backbone of a jellyfish – which don't have one, by the way."

"Yet, he wishes to court you," Barrack said, placing the pot she handed him on the stove.

"In his worst dream," she muttered under her breath. "If I knew how to load my granddad's old shotgun, he'd still be picking buckshot out of his ass with a pair of tweezers and a handheld mirror."

Barrack grunted as he stirred the mixture that she was pouring into the pot. "Brogan and I should be grateful for that small favor as well or we would have been doing the same," he reminded her.

"Yes, you would have," Delilah agreed, crumbling up a touch of fresh mint and dropping it in the pot. "If you can stir that, I'll cut up some cake."

"Perhaps if you do not offer them the sweets, they will leave sooner," he suggested.

Delilah shook her head. "I have been taught by my parents to feed any guest – even the unwanted ones. Why do you think you and Brogan ended up back in the house?" she said with a sweet smile.

"Your parents did a good job raising you," Barrack called after her as she carried the desserts into the dining room.

"Yes, they did," she quipped over her shoulder.

She grinned as she placed the plates and desserts on the table. Her gaze lifted when she felt eyes on her. Bubba Joe was staring at her like he had never seen her before. Her face flushed and she wondered briefly if she was flashing any rose-colored scales. If she was, that might be a little difficult to explain.

"Do you need any help?" Bubba Joe asked, walking into the dining room.

"If you can set the plates out while I set the silverware, that would be great," she said, finishing cutting the lemon cake.

She picked up the plates and started to turn toward Bubba Joe. He reached for them and froze, his eyes locked over her head. She saw his throat move slowly up and down as he swallowed. She wanted to close her eyes in exasperation. Instead, she put a bright smile on her face and looked over her shoulder.

"Yay, you're back just in time for some hot chocolate and cake... and as you can see, we have guests," she added with a subtle warning.

CHAPTER TWENTY

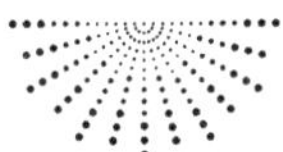

Half an hour later:

Far off in the distance, Brogan heard the faint sound of a transport leaving. He rose to his feet and scanned the area. This was the third spot he had found where someone had been. He turned and looked in the direction the man had obviously been observing. Once again, he saw Delilah's home.

Have you found anything? Barrack asked.

Someone was watching Delilah's home. I have found the spot where I believe he was when I first sensed him, Brogan replied.

Do you know who it is? Could it be Jaguin or Adalard? Barrack asked. *I half expect them to come once the weather is clear.*

No, this is human. I will see if I can track him, Brogan replied, turning to follow the tracks he had seen heading to the bottom of the mountain.

Be warned: Delilah has company, Barrack told him dryly.

What do you mean? Brogan demanded, his eyes searching the house.

He cursed when he saw the two transports in the front yard. A growl of frustration tore through him. If there were humans there, that meant they knew about him and Barrack – or at least, they knew about Barrack. His gaze moved from the tracks in the snow to the house and back again.

See if you can find anything. I am here, Barrack said.

Who are they? Brogan demanded. Barrack didn't immediately answer him, and his gaze moved back to the house.

Men who wish to court our mate, Barrack finally admitted. *She is going to serve them hot chocolate and sweets.*

And you let her?! Brogan demanded.

It is called Pearl's Rule Number 1. I am using my brain. Go find the danger to us, Brogan, and leave our mate to me, Barrack muttered.

You know, I have really tried to forget that woman and her rules, Brogan stated with a slight shudder at the memory of Pearl and her small torture device. *Keep those males away from our mate or I will.*

Brogan pulled away from his connection with his brother. He needed to focus on the tracks. Motioning for his symbiot, he mounted the hovering gold skimmer, and they wove through the trees, following the narrow double lines in the snow. The tracks led down to the road and Brogan could see where a transport had been. A wide path leading down the road showed that the vehicle was equipped with a deflector to clear the snow from its path.

Wary of traveling along the road, he tried to follow the tracks of the transport from the edge of the forest. He had to cross the road several times to keep sight of where the vehicle had gone. A wave of frustration ran through him when he reached the main road. It appeared the vehicle had traveled both ways and he couldn't tell which was newer with the falling snow covering up the tracks.

He scanned the sky. Dark, heavy clouds were filling in the brief patch of blue. He could feel the temperature dropping again.

Tired of snow. Go to mate. She make chocolate, his dragon said.

Brogan's lips twitched when his symbiot sent him the same visual image of a huge cup of steaming chocolate. He knew they both wanted to return to the house because of the men. Neither creature was bothered by the cold.

On the other hand, he could feel it seeping into his bones and he wouldn't mind something sweet and delicious to warm him up. He chuckled when both his dragon and his symbiot pulled up a very vivid image of Delilah last night spread out on the bed with bands of gold wrapped around her wrists and ankles – before switching to an image of a strange man smiling down at her. He shook his head and scowled.

You both did that on purpose! Brogan muttered, shifting uncomfortably on the symbiot skimmer.

The sound of his dragon snickering in his head had him wishing at times that they were two separate entities. At least that way he could tell his irritating other half to shut up and go away. Of course, he would probably be as successful with that as he was with his symbiot.

You miss me if I go away, his dragon retorted with a low rumble.

For maybe a nanosecond, Brogan replied.

A wave of warmth and pleasure coursed through him at the easy banter. He hadn't felt this relaxed – since forever. The tension and anger that had continuously consumed him since he was a youngling wasn't completely gone, but the need to rip someone's head off had disappeared.

It didn't take him long to return to Delilah's house. They silently slid to a stop on the backside of the large shed. His symbiot shifted into a Werecat. He debated what he should do before he sent his symbiot an order to search the woods for any other traces of the human they had been tracking.

"This is the one time when having Jaguin here would have been helpful," he mused to his symbiot.

His symbiot shook off the snow accumulating on its back before releasing an annoyed sigh when more snow took its place. Brogan patted the symbiot, sending a burst of warmth and affection to it before turning his attention toward the house. His eyes narrowed when he saw Delilah and a human male standing in the dining room.

His eyes flared with a savage emotion when he saw the man lean into her. From this angle, it looked like the man was going to drape his body over Delilah right there on the dining room table. He started forward across the yard.

What you going to do? his dragon demanded, fire building in his throat.

"I'm going to rip his head off," Brogan savagely replied.

Striding through the deep troughs in the snow that he and Barrack had created for the dogs and Delilah, he sprang up the stairs to the porch. He pulled open the back screen door and pushed open the door to the mudroom. The door behind him had barely shut before he did the same to the kitchen door.

He saw Barrack look up as he came in. The look of warning on his brother's face changed to resignation when he swept past him. He heard Barrack's faint warning to not kill the man, but his eyes were glued on the face smiling down at Delilah.

The human looked up and saw him. Brogan didn't bother hiding the flames in his eyes or deadly intent in them. The human's face paled and a sheen of sweat appeared on the man's forehead.

Delilah's body stiffened and she straightened. When she turned her head to look at him, the message was clear – we have guests and your dragon is showing.

"Yay, you're back just in time for some hot chocolate and cake… and as you can see, we have guests," she greeted with a forced cheerfulness.

Brogan didn't care that his dragon was showing. He did care that the man was too close to Delilah. Wrapping his arm around her waist, he pulled her against his body and stepped back, taking her with him.

"Brogan…," she began, placing her hands over his.

"I thought you said his name was Barrack?" the man replied in confusion.

"I am Barrack. This is my twin, Brogan," Barrack dryly replied.

The man swallowed again. "There are two of you? I mean, there are two of you. Which one…?" a confused expression crossed the man's face as he stared back and forth between the two of them.

Brogan realized what the man was talking about when the human's gaze settled on Delilah. He tightened his arm around her waist when she tried to push them away. He wanted the human to know that Delilah was off limits.

"She is ours," Brogan said, his voice deep and rough from his dragon being so close to the surface.

"Yours? As in... both?" the man stuttered.

"Alright! I do believe the hot chocolate is ready. Brogan, why don't *you* help me carry the drinks in? Bubba Joe, can you let the other guys know to come into the dining room?" Delilah asked in a sweet but firm tone.

Brogan winced when he felt her elbow him in the stomach. She twisted in his arms and grabbed him by his shirt, pulling him behind her. The moment they were in the kitchen, she looked to make sure that none of the others could hear her.

"Do *not* act like a Neanderthal in my home. Do *not* embarrass me in front of my friends. But most of all, DO NOT LET THEM KNOW YOU ARE AN ALIEN!" she hissed.

"He was practically draped over you on the table," Brogan growled, pointing back at the dining room.

"I don't care if he had an apple in my mouth and had me laid out on a silver platter. Barrack and you would be in danger if anyone knew you were aliens. My world...." She paused and took in a deep breath. "My world would freak out if they knew about you two. They would hunt you down and do mean, stupid, horrible things to you... and me," she explained in a quiet voice. "I also happen to like the men in there – save one who I only tolerate because it is fun to watch him run from the dogs. I live here, Brogan. This is my home. I don't want people... I don't want Bubba Joe or Rudy or even DeWayne to think of me as some sort of slut."

Brogan could feel the hurt in her through his symbiot. He looked over her shoulder as the other men shuffled in, warily looking into the kitchen at him. Barrack had remained at the entrance to the two rooms, making sure that the men didn't come any farther, while still being able to hear what Delilah was saying.

"Forgive me, Delilah," he murmured, realizing that he had let his jealousy endanger them all.

Delilah gave him a rueful smile. "I'm not ashamed of my feelings for you or Barrack. We just have to be careful. Come on, the sooner they eat and drink, the sooner I can kick all of them out," she sighed.

"I like that," Brogan admitted with a sly grin. "I will pour the drinks."

CHAPTER TWENTY-ONE

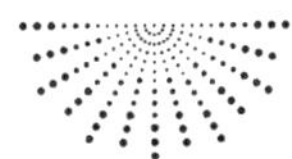

Exactly one hour later, Delilah stood on the porch watching the three men leave. She wrapped her arms around her waist and shivered. Almost immediately, she felt two warm bodies on each side of her.

"You were supposed to wait in the house until they were gone," she said, not looking at either man.

"They are gone – enough," Barrack quipped.

She shook her head and turned back toward the house. "You two are bad," she retorted.

Delilah stepped into the house when Brogan pulled the screen door open. The two Rottweilers darted past her and up the stairs. She knew exactly where they were going – her bedroom. Thank goodness she had spread a thin blanket across the bed to protect the comforter. She shook her head when she heard the sound of the door closing when one of them – probably Moonshine – hit it too hard, causing it to swing closed. She'd have to remember to go rescue them in a bit.

"Bad in a very good way," Brogan replied, deepening his voice.

She felt her body react to the tenor of his voice. "I swear you two have a one-track mind!"

"Yes!" they both agreed with a grin.

Shaking her head, she walked down the hall and into the kitchen. She filled the sink with warm, soapy water and began piling the dirty dishes into it. They had turned on the whole house generator while the guys were here so they could use the restrooms and she could have water. She wanted to get everything cleaned up before she turned it back off. She didn't want to think of what her next fuel bill would be.

"Can you get the rest of the dishes off the table?" she asked.

"Yes," Brogan replied.

He returned to the dining room and gathered the rest of the dishes while she started washing them. Barrack was rinsing them and placing them on the drainer. They were almost done when Brogan stiffened and turned his head. A moment later, Delilah heard a knock on the door.

She looked at the men and shrugged. "I wasn't expecting anyone. The storm is picking up again; no one should be out," she said, drying her hands on a dish towel.

She handed the towel to Brogan and walked down the hall to the front door. Peering out, she frowned when she saw two men standing on the front porch. Opening the door, she sighed when she saw one of the men was DeWayne.

"What do you want?" she demanded.

"Can… can… we… come… in, Delilah? I'm freezing!" DeWayne asked, his teeth chattering. "Rudy's… snowmobile broke down. He… and Bubba Joe… have gone to get… to get Bubba's uncle's big truck. We couldn't fit three of us… on it.

Delilah's eyes went to the other man standing quietly next to DeWayne. Her gaze went to his truck and she saw the logo for the local power company. She couldn't believe the power company would send someone out in this weather, but then again, she realized that was exactly what they would do.

"Come on in. DeWayne, you can defrost in the sitting room. I'll turn the fire up," she said.

She stepped to the side to let DeWayne pass her. She was in the process of turning back to the power guy when a startled squeak escaped her. The man wrapped one arm around her neck and lifted a gun in the other hand. Her eyes widened in horror when she heard the muffled sound of a thud and DeWayne stumbled forward a step before he collapsed, a large red stain spreading from the small, black hole in the back of his jacket.

The cry on her lips died when the man turned the gun to her head. He caught the door with his foot and slammed it shut. Delilah stumbled when he took a step to the side.

"Tell the other man to come out," the man quietly ordered.

Fear choked Delilah. Her dragon roared, wanting to shift, but she was afraid that any sudden movement would endanger her. The symbiots could heal a lot of wounds, but not a direct shot to the head.

"I don't...," she started to say before her voice faded in a strangle gasp when he tightened his arm around her neck.

"I saw him, sweetheart," the man whispered in her ear. "Don't make me put a bullet in your pretty body too soon. We can make this as easy or as difficult as you want. Now... call him."

Delilah nodded. "Barrack...," she called in a trembling voice. "Barrack... I...," her voice faded once again when she saw Barrack step into the hallway.

Remain calm, little fighter. This human thinks there is just one of us. Brogan is moving into a better position. We will not allow him to hurt you, Barrack reassured her.

Delilah heard the generator stutter and cut off. The light in the hallway went out. It was still light outside, but growing dimmer thanks to the storm. She could see Barrack's glare move to the man holding her.

DeWayne needs help. He isn't dead. I can hear his heart beating, but he is hurt really bad, Delilah said.

She looked down to where DeWayne lay on the floor partially in the front foyer and partially in the sitting room. Biting her lip, she focused on one of the symbiot bracelets on her wrists. It resisted her instructions at first. The creature didn't want to leave her and didn't want to touch DeWayne.

Please... Please help him... for me, she begged.

It took several pleas before the symbiot bracelet dissolved, flowed under her clothing and pooled on the floor. Out of the corner of her eye, she could see it slip inside DeWayne's clothing. Warmth from the other bracelet filled her and she looked up to see Barrack watching her. He knew what she had done.

Where are the other symbiots? she asked.

They have arrived, he replied.

"What do you want? I mean, if you came here to rob me, you made a huge mistake. I'm just a librarian. We don't make a lot of money. I also don't have much of value here except some of the antiques, and I don't see you carting those away in this weather," Delilah said.

She knew she was babbling, but she hoped that if she could distract the man, Brogan and the symbiots would have the time they needed to rescue her.

"Shut up," the man said.

Delilah frowned. That was not the reaction she was expecting. Her lips pressed together when he nodded his head at Barrack.

"Get down on the floor, hands out. One false move and I put a bullet in her brain," the man stated.

Barrack's mouth tightened into a straight line before he slowly lowered himself to his knees and slid forward so that he was lying on his stomach. Her heart hammered in her chest. The man tightened his hold around her neck before dropping his arm and firing two shots directly into the center of Barrack's back – there was no warning, no threats, nothing but the two consecutive shots.

Delilah screamed and began fighting. Horror and pain shot through her. Her dragon howled with anguish and rage. She frantically tried to remove the symbiot on her wrist, so she could give it to Barrack.

Harsh sobs choked her more than the arm threatening to cut off her oxygen. She didn't care. Her only concern was to help Barrack.

"No!! No! Let me go. How could you? Why?" she sobbed.

He shot Barrack. Oh, God! Please, Brogan. He shot Barrack in the back, she cried, out of her mind in grief.

She fell to her knees when the man suddenly released her with a thrust between her shoulder blades. Scrambling on all fours, she bent over Barrack's still body. The symbiot on her wrist melted and disappeared into the two holes. Afraid the man would attack again before the symbiot could heal Barrack, Delilah draped herself over his body to shield him. Turning her head toward the man, she looked up at him with tears streaming down her cheeks.

"Why? Who are you? What do you want?" she whispered in a barely audible voice.

The man shrugged. "You should have signed the papers when you were asked to do so, Ms. Rosewater," he replied, reaching into his pocket and pulling out a thick bundle of papers. He tossed them on the floor next to her along with a black pen. "Sign the paper where it is highlighted."

Delilah stared at the bundle of white papers in confusion. Her eyes moved to where DeWayne was lying flat on the floor. Had DeWayne been a part of this?

"DeWayne...," she began to say in an uneven voice.

"Mr. Davis is nothing more than a small town attorney who failed to deliver. Now, sign the papers," the man instructed.

Delilah shook her head. "What good would it do? I'd contest anything that was signed under duress."

"Oh, there won't be any contesting. Now, sign the papers or I'll start putting bullets in you," the man warned.

Delilah's hands shook as she picked up the bundle papers and unfolded it. A quick skim of the pages told her everything she needed to know. That bastard, Olie Ray Lister, was behind this. Fury ignited within her. Her fingers curled around the papers and she looked up at the man with eyes that held the flames of her dragon in them.

"What the fuck?!" the man hissed.

A creak on the stairs and a menacing snarl filled the air. The man looked up at the stairs and fired several shots, his eyes panicked and disbelieving. The shots hit Barrack's symbiot, Whiskey, but the golden creature merely opened its mouth and coughed up the bullets. The man stumbled to the front door.

"What is that thing?" he hissed.

Delilah watched his gaze moved to her as she stood up. She knew that Brogan was on the other side of the door waiting for the man. Brogan's symbiot, Gin, stepped out from the sitting room to stand between her and the man at the door.

"Your shit-out-of-luck card," she informed him as her features partially began to shift into her dragon. "Whiskey, heal Barrack."

"What are you?" Earl choked out in shock when Delilah Rosewater's face began to transform.

He watched as swirls of what looked like scales began to appear along both of her cheeks and down her neck. Her hazel eyes had a strange flame in them and her pupils looked elongated. The gold creature on the stairs lost its form and passed through the spindles of the railing, then flowed over the man he had shot in the back.

He swallowed when another golden creature in the shape of a huge cat stepped out of the sitting room and snarled at him. Twelve inches or longer fangs caught the dwindling light from outside. He turned his gun on the creature and emptied the last few rounds into the monster before reaching under his coat and pulling out another gun.

This one he aimed at Delilah. He started to empty his gun into her, but the fanged creature rose up and absorbed the bullets before they reached her. Twisting the doorknob, he yanked open the door and turned to flee. He made it as far as the third step before he looked at where his burning truck was parked.

He started to turn and retrace his steps, but froze when the gold creature walked out of the door. Stumbling on the steps, he lost his balance and fell heavily to the ground. He rolled onto his stomach and started to push up when dread washed through him. Looking up, he stared into the flaming eyes of his worst nightmare and death.

His lips opened in a scream that never came. Instead, an eerie blue flame surrounded him. In the briefest fraction of a second, his brain registered the fact that his outstretched arm with the pistol in it was disintegrating before his eyes. All other thought was gone as nothing, but the fine ash of his remains blew across the snow-covered ground, mingling with the new falling snow from the sky.

CHAPTER TWENTY-TWO

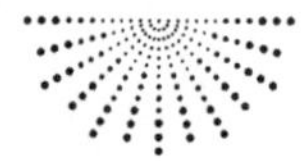

Delilah sank down onto the floor next to where Barrack was still face-down on the floor. She released a startled cry when he groaned and tried to push up into a sitting position. Her arms shot out to steady him when he trembled, and he ended up lying on his back. He shook his head as if to clear it and looked up into her eyes.

"Brogan?" he muttered in a harsh voice.

Delilah looked out of the open front door. She could see Brogan sweeping his tail over the area where he had toasted the man. Brogan turned his head and his eyes locked on her face. She gave him a wan smile, knowing that her lip was trembling. Her eyes filled with tears and she began to shake uncontrollably.

She pulled her gaze away. Lifting her hands to cup Barrack's cheeks, she studied his face, then leaned forward, and pressed her lips to his. She couldn't hold in the sound of her sob.

"I thought you were dead. Oh, God, I thought you were dead," she whispered, breaking down and burying her face against his throat.

She felt him shift positions, twisting until he was sitting on the floor and pulling her onto his lap. He held her as she cried. No book could ever have prepared her for what had happened this time.

The sound of a muffled moan finally broke through her crying. She turned her head and looked over at DeWayne. He groaned and rolled over onto his side.

"What'd I do this time, Delilah? Damn, but you know how to hit," DeWayne moaned before he shook his head and sat up, blinking as he looked out of the front door. "Do you know you have the door open?"

"Yes," Delilah answered with a sniff.

"Do you know that it is snowing again?" DeWayne muttered, rubbing at his eyes.

"Yes, DeWayne, I know that it is snowing again," she replied with a sigh.

DeWayne rubbed his eyes and blinked again. "Do you know that you have a dragon in your front yard?" he asked in a voice that was barely audible.

Delilah giggled. "Yes, DeWayne. I know I have a dragon in my front yard," she replied before she looked down at the papers on the floor. "DeWayne, I need to ask you something and tell you something. If I'm your client, you have to keep it quiet, no matter what, right?"

"Uh-huh," DeWayne answered, scooting back when the dragon suddenly changed into a man and walked toward them. "I… I don't think I'd want to tell anyone this."

Delilah reached up when Brogan held his hands out. Rising to her feet, she wrapped her arms around Brogan's waist while Barrack rose to his feet to stand next to them. The two symbiots reformed into large Werecats and sat down. Delilah turned and looked at the burning remains of the truck before catching the door behind Brogan and shutting it. With a deep sigh, she turned and looked at DeWayne.

"Why don't I prepare some tea and we'll explain what happened?" she said in a voice that still trembled with emotion.

"Can I have another hot chocolate – with a shot of Whiskey?" DeWayne mumbled, rising to his feet and running his hands down over his chest.

"Yes," she said, reluctantly pulling away from Brogan and bending to pick up the papers.

"You sit down. I will make the drinks," Brogan said.

Barrack shook his head. "No, I will. Remember, you are terrible even with the replicator on our ship," he said.

Brogan chuckled and slapped Barrack on the shoulder. "If you insist," he said.

Barrack winced and rotated his shoulders. "The next time, you get to be the decoy. That hurt!" he grumbled, walking down the hall to the kitchen.

"I did not know he would shoot you without warning. I thought all humans talked as much as Pearl," Brogan defended.

"Ship.... Replicator.... All... humans?" DeWayne repeated faintly.

"They're aliens," she said with a smile.

DeWayne's eyes widened, and he swallowed hard. Delilah could feel his eyes on her back as she made her way through the sitting room to the dining room. She paused by the small cabinet mounted to the wall. Opening it, she pulled out a brand new bottle of Jack Daniels. She unscrewed the top and took a deep swig before wiping across her mouth with the back of her hand that was holding the papers.

"I want to know why Ray Lister sent someone to kill me," she said, placing the bottle on the dining room table and sitting down. "Start talking, DeWayne, or my granddad's shotgun is going to be the least of your concerns."

Delilah's dragon was more than happy to share what she meant with DeWayne. The pale, shaking lawyer slid into the chair across from her. He reached over and grabbed the bottle of whiskey in front of her, opened it, and drank half before he put it back down with a resounding thud.

"Sometimes I hate being a lawyer," he muttered.

~

Several hours later, Delilah watched Bubba Joe drive the heavy truck his uncle owned back down her driveway with a very quiet DeWayne in the passenger seat.

Brogan and the symbiots had removed the burnt remains of the mystery man's truck. She didn't ask them where they had put it or how they did it. At this point, she didn't honestly care. She was still too shaken by what had happened.

Delilah had been impressed with how professional DeWayne had become once he went into his lawyer mode. After several hours of discussion, Delilah had finally accepted that there was no way that she could stay here. DeWayne had been the calm voice of reason. While Brogan and Barrack had made good points, they had both been more emotional.

The decision to leave was hard. The things in this house – and the house itself – had so much sentimental value for her. They had finally worked out what would become of her property and all her belongings. She had been shocked when DeWayne offered to purchase the property with the intent of living here.

"My grandparents left me pretty well off," he admitted. "I've always wanted to move back to this area. I'm honestly ready for a change and I like what you've done to the house," he admitted with a sheepish grin. "I've been thinking about opening a Bed and Breakfast. The next question would be – what do you want to do with the money from the sale of the house?"

"Give it to the library," Delilah automatically replied. "In my mother and father's name," she added.

"I'll set up a trust so it lasts. I… Are you sure about this, Delilah?" DeWayne asked, studying her face.

"Yes," Delilah replied, smiling at DeWayne and reaching out her hands to grip both Brogan and Barrack's.

A short time later, the sound of a pickup truck drew their attention. Rising, she looked fearfully at the door. DeWayne peered out the window. He looked back at her with a smile.

"It's Bubba Joe," he said.

She nodded and released the breath she was holding. Barrack had wrapped his arm around her while Brogan had followed DeWayne to the sitting room to look outside. She gripped Barrack's arm, feeling the fear slowly fade.

Half an hour later, she had retreated upstairs. She opened the door to find her two beloved Rottweiler protectors were passed out on her bed. Once again, she was thankful that they had been locked in her bedroom during the incident earlier. She had no doubt in her mind that the man who attacked them would have killed the two dogs.

"Oh, *hell* no! I told you, that is *my* side of the bed. Get your mangy, totally worthless asses over," she growled.

After pushing and shoving them, Moonshine finally got up and walked over to the other side of the bed while Rum rolled so he was mostly off of her side. Twisting as she fell onto the bed, Delilah stretched her arms over her head and blindly stared up at the ceiling.

"I'm going to another world," she murmured. "I'm leaving Earth and going far, far away where there are aliens and spaceships."

"And a place where our dragons can soar," Brogan said from the doorway.

Delilah turned her head and stared up at him. She could imagine her eyes held both excitement and pure terror. The men and her dogs would be the only familiar comforts that she would know on the new world she was traveling to – and perhaps Sara, if she could find her friend.

"Are you sure that humans can live there?" she asked, her voice trembling with uncertainty.

"We are very sure. Our king and the princes have human mates... and younglings. There is another set of twins from our village who also have a human mate and a child," Brogan said, walking over to the bed and sitting down.

She held her hands out to him, and her gaze softened when she saw a look of uncertainty flash across his face. He looked down at their joined hands.

"...And your friend Sara will also be there. Everything will be well, Delilah. We will do everything we can to make you happy," Barrack vowed.

"I know. It is just a lot to take in," she said, looking up at him with tears shimmering in her eyes. "I know I can't stay here now, but this isn't like packing up to move to a new town or even a new state. What if things don't work out? What if...?"

Her voice faded as all kinds of fears suddenly rose and swamped her mind. Barrack walked around the bed and motioned for the dogs to get down. She sighed when the two Rottweilers jumped down and happily trotted out the door.

"At least they listen to you," she muttered with a piqued sniff.

Brogan twisted around and laid down next to her. "They know that this is our side of the bed," he teased.

Delilah giggled. "Thank you," she murmured, snuggling up between the two men. "I realized I could have lost everything I loved today. When I saw you on the floor...." She looked at Barrack, her eyes dark with memories. "When that man...."

Barrack rolled over and captured her lips. Delilah opened for him. She needed this connection to help push away the memories of Barrack lying on the floor. She poured all of her love into the kiss she gave him in return. Her body heated when he deepened the kiss.

Her fingers worked frantically at the buttons of his shirt. Tonight would be about erasing the fear – her fear of losing them and her fear of what her new life would be like on a world far, far away. He ended the kiss and she tilted her head back when he brushed a series of small kisses down along her throat.

"Barrack," she gasped. He slid his hands under her shirt and the feeling of his fingers against her heated flesh was incredible.

"You have too many clothes on, Delilah," he muttered, rolling off of her.

She looked over at Brogan. He had already removed his clothes. A smile curved her lips. She could look at both men 24/7 and never get tired of the view. Her fingers moved to her pants. She had barely unfastened them before Brogan was pulling them and her panties off. Her shirt and bra quickly followed suit.

Her breath caught when she suddenly found her arms pinned above her head and her legs spread wide. Delilah's body immediately went into meltdown when Barrack bent his head. The first touch of his tongue against her sensitive nub left her panting and straining to break free.

"Tonight we will love you until you remember nothing but our touch," Brogan promised, bending to capture one of her taut nipples in his mouth.

Closing her eyes, she believed him. Her body hummed as they whispered impassioned words of love and adoration, promising her a life that she'd thought only existed in fairy tales, a life filled with two loving men in a house in the woods near a village where instead of being scorned, they would be welcomed.

"Bite me," she gasped, coming hard against Barrack's lips. "Let me feel the heat."

Her loud cry filled the room as both men eagerly fulfilled her every desire before finding their own pleasure. The Dragon's Fire burned through them with the same intensity as that of their first night together.

Delilah lay draped over Brogan, her body relaxed as the darkness gave way to the light of day. She didn't move when Barrack returned from the bathroom and gently stroked her body with a warm, damp cloth, but she sleepily smiled down at Brogan when he gently rolled her over. Her fingers slid from his when he rose.

"Where are you going?" she murmured.

"The dogs need to go out," he said, bending to press a kiss to her tender, swollen lips. "I will return."

"Love you," she murmured, her eyes slowly closing in exhaustion. "Love you, both."

"Not as much as we love you, *elila*," Brogan replied before brushing another kiss across her lips. "Sleep."

She nodded and turned into Barrack's arms when he returned to the bed. Snuggling close to him, she released a contented sigh. If life was about the adventures, then this was one she was happy to sign onto it for the rest of her life.

"Sleep, my little fighter," Barrack murmured, rubbing his cheek against her hair. "We will have many more adventures to come."

EPILOGUE

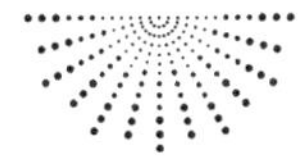

Delilah looked at herself in the bathroom mirror and grinned. She was glowing. There was no other way to describe her shining eyes and the stupid grin she couldn't keep off her face. She was happy. Her nose twitched and she drew in a deep breath.

Breakfast! her dragon growled in delight. *Hungry!*

Me, too! she giggled.

Of course, they would both be hungry since they were the same person, but she couldn't help but think of them as being separate. Having a voice in her head was weird, yet not weird at the same time. Delilah thought of her dragon more like an extension of herself.

Because I am, her dragon replied.

She was still trying to sort out the complex relationship in her head as she descended the stairs. She paused halfway down when she heard a knock at the front door. Her heart skipped a beat as memories of the day before rushed through her.

Her gaze turned to Brogan as he paused at the foot of the stairs in the hallway. He looked up at her, then stepped forward to open the door when the knock sounded again.

"You found us," he greeted.

"Yes," a male voice replied.

"Is... is Delilah here?" a woman asked.

Delilah couldn't see who was at the door, but she immediately recognized the woman's voice. Her hand lifted to her mouth and she bit down on her knuckles when Brogan opened the door all the way to reveal a tall woman with long blonde hair standing in the doorway next to an even taller man.

"Sara," Delilah choked out, tears filling her eyes. "Oh, Sara."

She rushed down the stairs, meeting Sara at the bottom. They wrapped their arms around each other and held on as if afraid that one or the other would disappear. Trembling with emotion, Delilah leaned back far enough to gaze into her friend's eyes.

"You...." they both said at the same time.

"I missed you," Delilah said, struggling to talk over the emotions cascading through her.

"Me, too," Sara replied, before turning to the man quietly standing in the doorway. "Jaguin, this is my friend, Delilah. Delilah, this is my true mate, Jaguin. He.... I love him."

Delilah wiped the tears from her cheeks with one hand and held out her other to Jaguin. "It's a pleasure to meet you. Come in! I.... We were just about to have breakfast. Have you eaten?" she asked, reaching for Sara's hand as she talked. "I want to know everything."

"Everything?" Sara repeated, looking at Brogan and Barrack with a worried frown.

"She knows about us – and her," Barrack said.

Sara nodded in relief, turning to look at Delilah. "I have so much to share with you. I'd love some breakfast and you can tell me how you met these two," she said with a grin, looping her arm through Delilah's. "By the way, the house looks fabulous. It looks a lot like when your grandparents were alive."

"Yeah, but a fat lot of good all that hard work will do me now," Delilah laughed.

~

"I see you were successful," Jaguin replied, stepping inside so Brogan could shut the door.

"Yes," Brogan replied.

Jaguin raised an eyebrow. "We brought a transport. It is out front. It looks like the weather here got as bad as what we experienced at Paul's ranch," he observed. "What did you burn up?"

Barrack chuckled. "We'll tell you at breakfast," he said. "Delilah loves hot chocolate. Would you care for some?"

"As long as it is not like that bitter black stuff that Sara enjoys drinking," Jaguin said with a shudder.

"This is much better," Brogan promised.

"I think those were the last boxes," Sara said, looking around the room.

Delilah nodded. A bittersweet smile curved her lips as Jaguin and Barrack carried out the last of what she wanted to take with her. It hadn't taken long to pack up. She had been in the process of moving everything up to this house and hadn't unpacked yet because she was still working on the renovations. She frowned as she looked out of the window for the hundredth time. The snow had stopped falling and the sun was actually out.

"What's wrong?" Sara asked, coming up to wind her arm around Delilah's.

"Brogan left hours ago and still hasn't returned," Delilah murmured, worried.

"What does his symbiot show you?" Sara asked.

Delilah pulled her arm free of Sara's and lifted the left wrist. She ran her fingers over the smooth surface. She focused on Brogan.

Are you okay? she asked.

A flash of warmth immediately filled her. *I am on my way back, elila. All is well. I love you,* he replied.

I love you, too, Delilah answered.

"That he is enjoying himself and will be back soon. I guess the prospect of being back in space for months again has him needing to spread his wings, one last time," she admitted in a rueful tone. "What is it like? Traveling in space?"

"Fantastic, fun, and thankfully not as long as expected," Sara admitted with a laugh. "I think I hear the dogs barking. They may want to enjoy some outdoor time as well. Let's go make a snowman."

"I have some carrots," Delilah laughed, following Sara out of the sitting room to the front foyer to bundle up.

Brogan slipped into the home office of Ray Lister. His gaze scanned through the room. A fire burned in the gas fireplace. Two chairs were in front of it. There was an empty glass on the end table between the chairs and the fireplace. The room had a masculine feel, as if the human male spent a lot of time in it.

Turning to the right, he walked over to where a large square table with a contoured relief map was displayed. Brogan immediately recognized the overview of Delilah's property. In the background, he could hear a woman trying to calm an agitated young male. A moment later, he heard an older human male yelling at the boy.

"You are registered and start on Monday. This is the finest Military academy in Virginia. You need some discipline. You are going," the man shouted.

"I hate you! You don't care about this family. All you ever do is see how many people you can screw out of their property so you can make more money," the boy yelled. "Now you're going to ruin my life, too!"

"You've done a good enough job of that without my help. The money you turn up your nose at is what gives you all these unappreciated comforts and luxuries that you have. Maybe it is time you learned to appreciate what it takes to make it," the man retorted. "Mabel, make sure he is packed and ready to leave tomorrow morning. The school is sending a van for him."

Brogan heard a door slamming and a woman softly crying. A

moment later, heavy footsteps on the tile floor warned him that Ray Lister was heading for his sanctuary. Brogan's eyes narrowed when Ray paused outside of the door.

"Damn it, Earl. Where are you? You should have returned those papers to me by now," Ray muttered to himself.

The doorknob rattled before it turned, as if the man opening it was distracted. Brogan saw Ray's head was bent and he was looking at the device he was holding in his hand as he entered before he closed and locked the door behind himself. Ray walked over and picked up the empty glass before he moved to a small bar set up against the wall near the fireplace. The man poured himself another drink, drank it, and then swiftly poured another one before he turned and froze when his gaze swept over the display table and finally caught sight of Brogan.

"What the…?!" Ray exclaimed in shock. "Who the hell are you and what are you doing in my house?"

Brogan didn't reply at first. A sardonic smile curved his lips and he dragged the nails of his left hand along the elaborate display board. Ray paled when his eyes followed the movement of Brogan's claw tipped hand. Brogan had partially shifted to his dragon.

"Is this… Is this some kind of joke? Are you a friend of Edison's?" Ray demanded, placing his full glass on the end table.

"No," Brogan softly replied.

He held up the bundle of papers that the man – 'Earl' – had ordered Delilah to sign. Ray looked at the papers, bewildered, and started to reach for them. He appeared to have second thoughts when he looked at Brogan's hard expression.

"You sent someone to my mate's home," Brogan said.

Ray's eyes narrowed. "I don't know what you are talking about," he retorted.

Brogan didn't miss how Ray's eyes swept over the blood splattered on the outermost sheet of the papers. He could hear the man's heartbeat beginning to speed up. Fear had a distinct scent and Ray was very afraid.

"Delilah Rosewater," Brogan prompted.

Ray's lips pursed. "You sound foreign. Are you here illegally? If you can get the Rosewater woman to sign those papers, I can help you with that," he said.

"The man you sent shot my brother and another man. He would have killed Delilah," Brogan stated in a calm tone.

Indecision flashed across the other man's face before he turned to study the display board once again. A look of desperation came into Ray's eyes. His gaze returned to Brogan and the papers he was holding.

"I didn't tell Earl to kill anyone. He was supposed to get Ms. Rosewater's signature on that piece of paper. Obviously, he failed. I'll offer you the same deal I offered Earl – two thousand dollars to get her signature. That's a lot of money where you come from," Ray said with a phony smile that didn't reach his eyes.

"I don't use money where I come from," Brogan replied.

Impatience crossed Ray's face. "I need those papers signed. I don't care how you get the signature, but I'll make it worth your while. If you are already fucking the bitch, that should make it easier. This is a business deal. Either you take it, or I can find someone else who will," he stated.

A soft snarl echoed in the room. Ray's eyes widened as Brogan began to slowly shift. He wanted to see the terror blossoming in the other man's eyes.

"I am voiding your business deal," Brogan replied in a guttural tone.

He reached out and grabbed Ray by the throat with one claw and lifted the man off the floor. Turning his head, he shifted completely into his dragon. The claw around Ray's throat tightened, cutting off the man's terrified scream.

Holding up the papers, he exhaled a thin burst of dragon fire. The papers ignited before they disintegrated into a pile of ash on the polished floor. He returned his attention to Ray who was staring at Brogan's empty hand. The man's fingers froze on his claw.

"Ple… Please…," Ray gasped.

Brogan shifted back into his two-legged form. He continued to hold Ray up by the throat. His nose wrinkled at the smell of urine when Ray pissed himself.

"The only thing keeping you alive is the boy upstairs and your mate. If you come anywhere near Delilah's property again, I will be back, and nothing will save you," Brogan warned.

"Yes...," Ray replied, his voice weak and trembling.

Brogan lowered Ray to the carpeted floor and shoved him backwards. Shifting once more, he turned and released a long stream of fire at the display board. The superheated flame turned the display board and the table to ash without leaving a mark anywhere else. With a final menacing look at Ray, Brogan surged forward, shattering the large plate-glass window.

His large wings lifted him higher. His symbiot, in the shape of a fighter, shimmered into view for a brief moment before closing around him and disappearing again. It had all happened in the blink of an eye.

Brogan rolled his shoulders as he settled onto the seat that his symbiot formed around him. With grim satisfaction, he fingered the recording device Jaguin had given him earlier. DeWayne could use the recording against Ray if the man tried anything else.

"Let us return to our mate, my friend. I'm ready to leave this cold world and return to where we can all fly free," he said.

~

Valdier home world:

Delilah stared in fascination down at the world below her. After being on board a space ship for months, she could appreciate how much she missed natural sunshine and wide open spaces. Thank goodness there were places on the ship that could replicate areas to make her feel like she was still on Earth. She would have to remember to thank Jaguin for the thousandth time for programming places that she was familiar with into the computer's simulation program.

The journey had been fascinating overall. The technology alone had made her head hurt trying to figure out how half of the stuff worked. Brogan and Barrack had been extremely patient and Sara – well, there was a reason Sara was her best friend.

She turned when the door opened behind her. A smile curved her lips when she saw Sara's excited, smiling face and Brogan and Barrack's tender gazes on her. She smoothed her hands down over the new blouse and skirt she was wearing.

"Are you ready?" Brogan asked.

"As ready as I'll ever be," she said with a weak smile. "How long will it take to get to your village?"

"An hour," Barrack replied. "We would like to stop at our old home first."

"Asim and Pearl have been overseeing the rebuilding of our home for us," Brogan said.

"We'll have a home?" Delilah asked, her eyes widening in pleasure and relief. "I was afraid.... I mean, I thought we would have to stay with your parents or somewhere else for a while."

Barrack laughed and shook his head. "No, we are selfish enough to want you for ourselves," he teased with a wicked grin.

"If you do not like it, we can build you a new home," Brogan promised.

Delilah laughed, rushing forward and throwing herself in Brogan's arms. She rose up on her toes to kiss him before pulling free to do the same to Barrack. She sighed when Barrack deepened the kiss. He didn't break the kiss until Jaguin pointedly cleared his throat.

"I thought you were in a hurry to get off this damn ship?" he reminded Barrack.

Barrack chuckled. "Let's take our mate home, brother," he said, reluctantly releasing Delilah enough so that she could fall into step between them.

"With pleasure," Brogan said, grasping Delilah's hand in his.

~

Several hours later, Barrack stood on the other side of the bridge, looking across at the village where he and Brogan had grown up. It was larger than he remembered. He could hear people talking and laughing as they went about their daily lives.

"Do you think they will remember us?" Brogan asked, standing beside him.

"Of course they will remember you. You guys are too awesome to forget," Delilah retorted, her eyes gleaming with determination while her hands nervously played with the hem of her shirt. "What if your parents don't like me?"

"Of course they will like you," a woman's serene voice said behind them.

Barrack stiffened and slowly turned. Aikaterina walked toward them. Her eyes glimmered with power. He swore he could see the very center of the universe in their depths. He blinked when she paused in front of Delilah.

"Thank you," Aikaterina said, lifting her hand and tracing it down along Delilah's cheek. "You are indeed strong enough to handle these twin dragons."

Delilah shrugged and gave Aikaterina a shy smile. "It wasn't that hard. A snow shovel and a kick in the.... Well, you know what I mean. They are pretty easy to love, too," she joked.

"I believe your words were 'two very hot, sexy and extremely horny guys'," Aikaterina replied.

Delilah flushed and shot the snickering twins a reproving glare. Barrack grinned. He planned on proving every word was true to Delilah. His gaze returned to Aikaterina and he frowned. A moment ago she'd looked incredibly powerful, but now she looked almost fragile.

"All life must come to an end eventually, warrior," she said.

"Will we...?" Brogan asked, his gaze turning to the village.

"No, you have changed your past. The present will remain locked, but the future is for you to unveil," Aikaterina replied. "I must say goodbye. Do not fear, warriors, your village will accept you.'

Barrack watched as Aikaterina rose and faded. He turned in a circle, searching the sky, but there was nothing. The sound of a shout drew his attention. Turning back to face the village again, he saw that an older man had noticed them and stopped in mid-stride to stare at the three of them.

"Barrack…?" the man's strangled voice called out uncertainly.

Barrack wrapped his arm around Delilah's waist. She clung to Brogan with her other hand. Together the three of them started across the bridge. The man met them as they reached the end of it.

"Brogan," the man's voice trembled and he reached out. His gaze moved to Delilah. "Who…?"

"Hello, Father," Barrack greeted.

"Father, this is Delilah. She is our true mate," Brogan replied, his eyes searching the growing crowd of people. "Mother…."

"Brogan," Lesann called, pushing forward. "My sons."

Delilah watched as Barrack and Brogan were embraced by their parents. She smiled back at Lesann as the woman wiped at the tears on her face. A startled laugh escaped her when she was lifted up off her feet by a tall young man. She shook her head at Brogan and Barrack when they turned and growled at him.

"You can't kill me; Father and Mother would be mad at you," the young warrior said with a grin.

"…You must be Merck…our brother," Barrack said, his eyes running over the younger warrior.

"I heard you got your ass kicked," Brogan added.

Merck flushed and shrugged. "Yes, and I deserved it," he admitted, looking at Delilah. "I'm glad they found you."

"Me, too," she said, curious about the sadness she could see in Merck's eyes.

"Come, there is so much you must tell us," Bane said. "My sons have returned with their true mate!" he shouted to the onlookers.

A loud cheer rang through the village. Delilah gazed about at everything in wonder. Their original plan was to travel to the village after a brief stop. Instead, they had stayed the night in the new home that Barrack and Brogan had asked Asim and Pearl to oversee the construction of before traveling to the village this morning. She knew the men delayed their return to give her more time to adjust to being on their planet. She could also feel the tension in both men at the thought of returning to the place of their birth.

"I dreamed that they would return one day. It broke my heart the day they left, but I understood why. They have never truly had a welcoming home – until now. Thank you," Lesann said with a tearful smile. "Thank you for changing their destiny and giving them a chance at life."

"I think you have a very compassionate Goddess to thank for that," Delilah murmured.

She smiled and looked over her shoulder at where Aikaterina stood on the bridge watching them. The Goddess returned her smile before fading again. The sadness she'd felt about the twins' necessary seclusion turned to laughter when several small dragons bounded up to her with flowers in their mouths.

"Well, so this is what a dragonling is," she laughed. "I can't wait to have a few of my own."

Twin rumbling growls drew silence before laughter as everyone realized that the twin dragons had their eyes on their mate and very devilish grins on their faces. Delilah laughed and shook her head.

Yep, she thought with satisfaction as Brogan wrapped his arms around her and Barrack brushed a kiss across her lips. *I've found me two very hot, sexy, and extremely horny guys from Planet Hornywood. This life is definitely better than my first one!*

To be continued: Waking a Golden Goddess

READ ON FOR SAMPLES!

MAGIC, NEW WORLDS, AND EPIC LOVE IN THE MANY SERIES OF S.E. SMITH…

SAMPLE OF DESTIN'S HOLD

Synopsis

Destin Parks will do whatever it takes to rebuild the city he calls home, even if it means working with another alien ambassador. The Councils hope Jersula 'Sula' Ikera's logical mind and calm demeanor will resolve the upheaval caused by the previous ambassador, but no one could have anticipated Sula's reaction to the hardheaded human male she has been assigned to work with. His ability to get under her skin and ignite a flame inside her is quite alarming, mystifying, and leaves her questioning her own sanity.

Together, Destin and Sula must race to stop an alien cartel before anyone is taken off-planet, but the traffickers are not the only ones they will be fighting against – a battle is coming, bigger than anything they've yet seen...

Read on for the first two chapters of Destin's Hold!

Chapter 1

"No!" a low, tortured hiss escaped Destin as he fought against the paralyzing memories holding him prisoner.

He struggled to free his mind, caught between the realm of nightmares and consciousness, but couldn't break free. After several long seconds that felt like an eternity, he jolted awake with a shudder and drew a deep breath into his starving lungs before slowly releasing it. Pushing up into a sitting position, he noticed he was tangled in the bed sheets.

Destin ran a hand over his sweat-dampened face before reaching to turn on the lamp next to the bed. It was missing. It took him a second to remember where he was and that the lighting system was still alien to him.

With a groan, he fell back against the pillows and drew in a series of deep, calming breaths, holding each one for several seconds before releasing the air in a slow, controlled rhythm. It was a meditation technique he read about years ago. He continued until he felt his pulse settle down to a normal rate.

A glance out the door told him it was still dark. He groaned and laid his arm across his eyes. He was up way too late last night or should he say this morning. Unfortunately, it didn't matter the amount of sleep he got, his body was programmed to wake early.

Destin dropped his arm back to his side and stared up at the ceiling. It was smooth and undamaged. There were no patched places, no cracks, and no bare metal beams. The architects and engineers back home were slowly making progress, but home was nowhere near as nice as Rathon, the Trivator home world.

Throwing aside the twisted sheets, he rolled out of bed. The jogging pants he slept in hung low on his slender hips. He ran a hand over his flat stomach and curled his toes into the soft, plush mat under his feet before he began his daily stretching exercises.

The taut muscles in his neck, back, and shoulders bulged as he tried to work the tension out of them. He might not be as tall as his Trivator brother-in-law, but years of hard work and targeted training had made his body the perfect fighting machine. Scars crisscrossed his flesh, each one a testament to the challenges he had faced over the past seven years.

His arms rose and he stretched, enjoying the cool breeze blowing in from the open doors and caressing his bare back. He could smell the fragrant aroma from the flowers blooming in the garden just outside and the tangy scent of salt from the nearby ocean. The weather here was a balmy seventy degrees if he had to guess.

He turned toward the doors and closed his eyes, blocking out the view of the garden and its high protective walls designed to keep out the wildlife. He tilted his head and listened to the sound of waves crashing against the shore. It was soothing last night, luring him to sleep, but now it felt relentless and violent, an echo of the adrenaline he woke up with.

Destin ran a hand down over his hard, flat abdomen again. His fingers traced a barely visible three-inch scar. It was a new one. He got it when a skittish street urchin fought to return to a building that was slowly collapsing.

Two years ago, he would have died from such a wound. He owed a huge thanks to Patch, the Trivator healer back on Earth. Patch had doctored him up, and after a few weeks of rest, Destin had been ready to travel off the planet.

He shook his head and opened his eyes. His travel through space to a distant world was unimaginable seven years before. It was hard to believe that Earth had received their first contact with aliens almost a decade ago. It was even harder for him to believe he was on an alien planet at the moment – at least until he looked around at the buildings and landscape. Twin moons, thick forests, flying transports, and bizarre creatures made him feel like he woke up in some alternate reality.

Destin turned and quietly made the bed. He grabbed a black T-shirt out of the drawer and pulled it over his head. He didn't bother with shoes; he wouldn't need them where he was going. Within minutes, he silently exited the house that belonged to his sister, Kali, and her *Amate*, Razor.

He crossed through the garden to the far gate. Punching the security code into the panel, Destin waited while the lock disengaged before he quietly slipped through. He made sure the gate was closed and the security system engaged before he turned along the path that led down to the beach. Both Razor and Kali had warned him to stay on the marked paths. He understood why after his arrival. From the air he got a brief glimpse of one of the wild animals that inhabited the planet. Destin was very glad the paths were secured against creatures like that.

The Trivators believed in living in harmony with the other creatures on the planet. They used only the areas they needed to live and kept large sections of green space. Most of the creatures were fairly harmless, but there were a few that were extremely dangerous – to both thc Trivators and their enemies. Invaders would first face the dangers of the forests if they landed outside the protected cities.

The roads and walkways were kept safe by specially placed security markers embedded into the paths. The markers were programmed with the animals' DNA. The embedded sensors detected when an animal approached the marked areas and a shield formed to stop the creatures from entering the path.

Destin didn't understand all the specifics; he just knew that he didn't want to tangle with that creature he had glimpsed from the air. The long tusks, six legs, and massive scaly body were formidable enough from a distance. He really did not want a closer look and was very happy that most travel on the planet was done by air.

The city he saw upon his arrival was magnificent. Large spiraling towers glittered with muted lights while transports moved along the ground and flew through the air. The tower on the far end spilled water from the top of the building in a dazzling waterfall into the Trivator-created reflection pond. Several of the transports disappeared under the reflection pool and reappeared on the other side. The more he saw, the more his excitement grew at the possibilities for Earth.

He paused at the top of the stone steps carved into the side of the cliff and looked out over the vast ocean. The sun wasn't up yet, but there was enough light on the horizon to see the waves break on the outer reef. He stood still, appreciating the beauty and peacefulness of his surroundings.

Destin couldn't remember the last time he had stopped to appreciate the beauty of anything. Death, destruction, fear, and responsibility had been his constant companion for as long as he could remember. He drew in a deep breath and released it.

No longer would that kind of destruction dominate his life. The Trivators' first contact had plunged the Earth into a panicked chaos, but in the past two years, he began to see a change. Progress was being made to heal the wounds. For him, the most important indication that life was getting better was seeing his sister Kali's glowing face and the living proof that there was hope for the future in his beautiful niece.

Originally, he had been reluctant to come, but Kali's quiet plea and Tim's, his second-in-command, assurance that the work Destin had done to restore a new Chicago would be carefully monitored by the team he had built convinced him that he needed the break. That reassurance, combined with his recent brush with death, reminded him of what was important – family. He felt like if he ever wanted a chance to see Kali again, and meet his niece, he had better rearrange his priorities. Until last night, he was convinced he had made the right decision. Now, he wasn't so sure after hearing what happened on another alien world called Dises V.

Destin shook his head at his musings. No, even with what he knew now, he was still glad he came to visit. Seeing Kali again and meeting Ami gave him a renewed purpose to return to Earth and fight for a better life for others.

Focusing on the stone path in front of him, he started down the stairs. He needed a good run to help clear his mind. He might as well enjoy the last few days he had here while he could. Once he returned to Earth, there was a city to rebuild and a lot of fires to put out, among other possible threats.

At the bottom, his feet sunk into the powdered, snow-white sand. He took off at a brisk pace down the long narrow beach beside the looming cliffs. For a brief moment, he was able to lose himself in the enjoyment of his surroundings and replace thoughts of his nightmares with dreams of something better – dreams of rebuilding his city and maybe, just maybe, finding someone to share it with.

~

An hour later, Destin walked back along the beach. Sweat soaked his shirt and he pulled it off. There was a secluded cove farther down the beach that he discovered on his second day on the planet. He would take a quick swim before heading back to Kali and Razor's house.

If he was lucky, Ami would be awake and waiting for him. His fourteen-month-old niece had taken a shine to him. It might have been all the toys he brought that put the hero worship in her eyes, but Destin didn't care. He had planned a new gift for each day of his stay. Mabel, one of the grandmotherly women that was with the rebellion from the beginning, suggested it.

Destin crossed the empty beach and entered a hole amidst the rocks that had been carved by centuries of wind and water. The narrow gap glistened with natural crystals found in the rocks. Lifting his hand, he ran the tips of his fingers along the rocks. The crystals lit up under his touch. He would love to take some back to Earth with him so he could study them.

His hand fell to his side when he reached the opening leading to the small cove. Out of habit, he glanced around to make sure the area was secure, then walked over to a large boulder protruding from the sand. He tossed his sweat-dampened shirt onto it and pushed his jogging pants down. He stepped out of his pants and shook the loose sand off before he placed them on the boulder next to his shirt. Afraid he might lose the medallion he wore, he slipped it over his head and slid it into the pocket of his pants. His hand ran along the waistband of the jockey shorts he wore, but he kept them on. Life had taught him to never get caught with his pants down. You never knew when you might have to fight, and doing it in the buff could be a little distracting.

Destin walked to the edge of the water and stood looking outward.

The gentle waves rolled over his feet and he curled his toes into the wet sand. A smile curved his lips and he slowly walked forward until he was waist deep. Drawing in a deep breath, he dove under the incoming wave, enjoying the refreshing feel of the water as it washed the sweat from his skin and cooled his heated flesh.

His arms swept out in front of him and his legs moved in strong, powerful kicks. The water was crystal clear and he could see the ripples in the white sand along the bottom. He swam as far as he could before his lungs burned and he was forced to surface for a breath of air. He turned onto his back and floated, lost in thought. The peacefulness of the moment, combined with the beauty and freedom of just watching the clouds, pulled the last of the tension he had woken up with out of his body. For a little while, he was alone in the universe with nothing else to worry about.

Jersula Ikera stomped across the soft sand in a foul mood. The thin, dark blue silk cover she wore clung to her lithe body and floated behind her. If anyone saw her from a distance, she would look like she was floating across the powdery white crystals that made up the sandy beach.

Her long white hair was unbound and blew around her. Her icy blue eyes flashed with an uncharacteristic fire and her pale blue lips were pressed into a firm line of irritation. She had come down to the beach to escape for a while, at least until she could find her center and restore the calm mask she relied on to interact with others.

A swift glance up and down the beach showed it was deserted. Jersula – Sula to her family and her few close friends – breathed a sigh of relief. She could mull over the orders she received early this morning in private. They were distressing, but she knew she needed to release some of the anger she was feeling if she wanted to get through the day without making a mistake that could devastate her career.

"Why? Why are they sending me to that horrible place again?

Wasn't once enough? Who could I have angered so much that they would send me there again?" she muttered under her breath.

Her mind flashed to the dozens of people that could be responsible. She knew her icy reserve and sometimes blunt attitude had angered certain members of the Usoleum Council, but she was always right in her assessments! It wasn't her fault that most of the political members of the council were sweet, confused people who couldn't think their way out of a wormhole.

Sula glanced back at her transport to see how far she walked along the beach. Not far; it seemed that stomping wasn't the fastest way to travel.

The small transport glinted in the sunlight. It was given to her when she arrived on Rathon six weeks ago. She had hoped to be appointed the new ambassador between her people and the Trivators. That hope was brutally crushed when her new orders arrived this morning before dawn.

"No, I have to return to that horrible, war-torn excuse for a planet brimming with savages! Those uncultured, hostile, brutal beasts who were ignorant of *any* life forms outside of Earth until a few years ago! They haven't even mastered space travel," she snarled under her breath in frustration before her footsteps slowed and she blinked back tears of annoyance. "That is what they are... ignorant beasts!"

Her anger boiled when she thought of her previous visit. The last time she had been to the primitive planet called Earth, her assignment was to assess the situation left by the previous ambassador who was killed, and it had been impossible to do anything when she received no support from the Trivators or the humans.

At the time, she was forced to wait two weeks before the Trivators would even allow her access to Councilor Badrick's starship. By the time she was finally allowed to board, the previous crew had been recalled, a new crew assigned, and all of Councilor Badrick's reports and personal files had vanished. The only things Sula was left with were a clueless crew, a Trivator named Cutter who had regarded her with suspicion, and a human male who had dismissed her with a look of contempt during their one and only meeting! It wasn't until much later that she unraveled the reasons behind the Trivator and human's animosity. Unable to blink back the tears of frustration this time, she lifted an impatient hand and brushed them away.

Sula had reported her initial findings on Badrick to the Council and her father, and within weeks of arriving on Earth, she was recalled to her home world, Usoleum. Believing she was being groomed to take over the Ambassador's position at the Alliance Headquarters, she had worked day and night on a variety of issues, but it had all been for naught. She had discovered a hidden cache of Badrick's files, and shortly after reporting the discovery, she was reassigned to Rathon. Here, she was to work with the Trivators to wring every bit of information possible from those files and to strengthen Usoleum's relationship with the Trivators after the damage wrought by Badrick's unconscionable behavior – a behavior that had mortified her family.

There were a large number of files to sift through, and in the meantime, she adhered to her assignment to grovel at the Trivators' feet for the past six weeks. It should have shown the Usoleum Council that she would make an excellent Ambassador to the Trivator Council here on their planet. But once again, her hopes were crushed. Sula was the only living Usoleum with experience on Earth, and she was now reassigned there to finish her original task, which is to clean up the mess Badrick left behind – almost two Earth years later! Her only hope for any kind of real success with the humans lay in parsing useful information from those files. To get even the slightest bit of trust and good will on Earth, she needed to be able to answer the question preying on everyone's mind: where were the rest of the missing human women?

Sula still had a couple of days left on Rathon, however, and part of reassuring the Trivators and the Alliance that everything was under control included attending some ceremony between a member of Chancellor Razor's family and a Trivator warrior. It would begin in a couple of hours, and if she was not able to gain control of her emotions before the ceremony, her career would be in even worse shape than it already was.

"This is an insult!" Sula hissed, discarding her maudlin misery in favor of the more empowering anger she felt earlier. "If Father thinks my brothers are so much better at diplomacy than I am, then one of them should be the one to attend the ceremony, not me! When they need a problem solved, they send me in to fix it. Father knows I am more than qualified for the ambassador position. Yet he gives the position to Sirius, the progeny who is least qualified. All Sirius wants to do is chase women that he couldn't do anything with and play at the gaming tables! He isn't even fit to be – to be – to care for the racers in the stables, much less be the Ambassador to the Trivators," Sula muttered with a slashing wave of her hand in the air.

Sula released a long sigh and stepped through the narrow chasm in the rocks. She gazed out at the water protected by the small cove for several seconds before she walked toward it, drawn to the soothing waves. She missed her world. It was mostly water and her people were born within its beautiful seas. They live on land, but the water is where they find solace.

Sula's hand moved to the tie of the gown and she released it. The garment fell to the sand around her feet. Her body was covered in a form-fitting dark blue suit made for the water. She spread her fingers and the fine membranes between them spread like small webs. Stepping forward, she relished the first touch of the water against her skin. Pleasure coursed through her, cooling her fury and soothing her despair.

Her gaze scanned the water. The waves broke against the reef almost two hundred meters offshore. It would be a short swim for her, but she could do it several times before she had to return to her temporary lodging to prepare for the ceremony. Sula slowly walked forward until she was deep enough to sink down below the surface.

The two almost invisible slits along her neck opened and she drew water into her gills. The refreshing liquid filled the second set of lungs with life-giving fluid, extracting the oxygen trapped in the water into her blood when she exhaled. She loved living and working near an ocean. A shudder went through her when she thought of her next assignment. It was so far from the large oceans that covered most of

Earth. There was a long, narrow lake, but it wasn't the same. She would have to make periodic trips to the coast to satisfy her body's craving for the salty water.

And I'll need to swim frequently to keep from killing that arrogant human male if he is still there, Sula thought. *Perhaps I will be lucky and he will already be dead, and a more reasonable human will have replaced him.*

Remorse swept through her at her hateful thoughts. It was so unlike her. She hated the idea of hurting anything or anyone. Her six older brothers teased her, saying that was why it was ridiculous that she would even consider becoming a member of the Alliance Council.

Sula pushed the negative thoughts away. She would lose herself in the pleasures of the ocean around her. Pushing off the bottom, her body cut through the crystal-clear liquid like a laser cutter through steel. All around her, colorful fish and plant life flourished in a world few could appreciate.

The cove was protected from the larger marine life that lived on the other side of the reef. She had researched Rathon's oceanographic environment and decided it would be best to stay within the protected barriers that sheltered the coast line. 'Nature's unique fencing' is the way Sula liked to think of it.

She was starting to feel more herself, more collected, but a wave of longing swept through her to just let go, to be wild for a few unadulterated minutes – not the frazzled, bitter release from the beach, but something… untouchable. To hell with her father's belief that she wasn't capable of dealing with the stress of being a leading member of the Usoleum Council or an integral part of the Alliance. She knew she could if she was given the opportunity.

Closing her eyes, she twisted until she was facing upward and allowed her body to slowly sink to the bottom. She relaxed her arms and a serene smile curved her lips. Maybe she would just forget about the ceremony and stay here all day. It wasn't as if it really mattered if she attended. No one, especially the Trivator male and his human mate, would even miss her.

Finally, the peace that Sula was searching for settled over her. Her body floated above the soft white sand. The light from the rising sun created shafts of glittering beams that reflected off the silver threads in her bodysuit and made them sparkle like diamonds. She was unaware of how ethereal she looked against the satin bottom of the ocean, or the fact that she wasn't alone.

Chapter 2

Destin dove beneath the waves and began swimming toward shore. As much as he hated it, he needed to get back to the house. He had promised Ami that he would make her some mouse-shaped pancakes this morning just like he used to do for her mommy.

He swam only a short distance when he caught a glimpse of something sparkling under the water. Surfacing, he glanced around with a frown before he took a deep breath and dove back down. He blinked when he saw the body of a young woman floating along the bottom. His heart thundered in dismay. He had seen enough death in his lifetime. The beautiful woman floating serenely near the bottom was too young to face such a fate.

Kicking downward with hard, powerful strokes, he reached for her. His eyes burned from the salt water, but he refused to close them. He grabbed her arm and quickly pulled her against his hard length, then changed his grip to hold her more securely around the waist as his feet pushed off the bottom.

Her slender hands clutched his bare shoulders, and her brilliant, light blue eyes snapped open. Destin and the woman locked gazes in mutual shock. Her delicate, pale blue lips parted, and Destin was afraid she would instinctively draw in a mouthful of water. Unsure of what else to do, he covered her lips with his. The moment his lips touched hers, a wave of heat swept through him and he couldn't help but wonder if he had captured a real, live siren.

Destin knew he should release her – or at least her lips – when they surfaced, but the fire that had ignited when he had pressed his lips to hers appeared to have short-circuited that part of his brain. She was not helping his resolve, either. Her hands tightened on his shoulders, but she didn't push him away and her soft lips trembled slightly as her breath mingled with his. It took several seconds before he finally forced his body to obey his command to stop. He reluctantly lifted his head, but still kept her firmly pressed against him.

"Are you okay?" he asked, blinking to clear his eyes of the salt water.

"I… You… Of course, I'm… You!" the woman sputtered before her eyes widened in recognition. "You aren't supposed to be here!"

Destin's lips curved up at the corners. "Where am I supposed to be?" he asked with a raised eyebrow, studying her face with a growing sense of dismay. "I know you…," he started to say.

"You should be back on that horrid, barbaric world," the woman snapped, pushing against his shoulders. "Release me!"

Recognition hit Destin hard. His arms slackened enough that the woman – Jersula Ikera – was able to pull away from him. She pushed at the water to put some space between them, her light blue eyes flashing with fire. This was a much different woman than the one he had briefly met back on Earth. This one was…. The sudden image of a siren flashed through his mind.

Trouble, he thought with a grimace, twisting around and striking out for the shore. The moment he was in shallow enough water to put his feet down, he did. He wanted to put as much distance as possible between him and the Usoleum Councilor he met back on Earth.

He ran the back of his hand across his heated lips. He could still taste her. It was a good thing his back was to her, otherwise she would notice the physical evidence of his reaction to her. It suddenly occurred to him that she would have been aware of it when she was pressed against him.

Damn it! Well, he wasn't going to remind her by giving her a second look. He was sure that would thrill her even more – not.

Destin muttered a string of expletives under his breath as he exited the water. He strode across the beach, passing the film of dark blue material lying against the white sand. He kept his back to her while he grabbed his jogging pants and pulled them on with stiff fingers. He ran his fingers through his soaked hair. The dark brown strands were cut into a short, military style and would dry soon enough.

Destin grabbed his T-shirt off the boulder. It was still damp from his run and he decided it wasn't worth pulling it on. He drew in a deep, calming breath and slowly released it before turning around to make sure Jersula had made it back to shore. He would feel pretty rotten if she drowned while he was trying to hide the major hard-on he had. He could just see himself trying to explain that to Razor and the Trivator council!

A frustrated groan escaped him when he saw her emerge from the water in the form-fitting blue material that left very little to the imagination. Destin's gaze froze on the twin peaks of her nipples pressing against the fabric, and he swallowed hard. They were hard pebbles, perfect for….

"It has been too damn long since I've been with a woman," he muttered under his breath.

He forced his eyes back to her face. His lips quirked up at the corners when he saw her eyes were still shooting indignant sparks. She looked a hell of a lot different than she did when he first met her. He found her fascinating then, too, which hadn't helped his temper during their one and only meeting.

Her long silky white hair, glacier blue eyes, and unusual blue lips had made it difficult to look away. She was an ethereal ice queen. At the time, he was furious with himself for reacting like that to an alien. He had thought she must have been cast in the same mold as Badrick, but the woman angrily snatching up the silky fabric off the sand was anything but icy. He remembered her heated breaths and the softness of her lips.

She clutched the fabric in front of her and her long legs cut across the loose crystals, quickly closing the distance between them. He couldn't help but notice that her hair was the same color as the sparkling sand. Her cheeks were a slightly darker blue than before and matched the deep color of her eyes. He would have to remember that when she was angry, her eyes changed to the color of the ocean back home.

She was breathing heavily by the time she stopped in front of him.

His gaze swept over her face, noticing the strand of hair stuck to her cheek. Without thinking, he tenderly brushed it back.

"I'm glad you are alright. When I first saw you floating along the bottom, I feared you were dead," he murmured.

Sula's lips parted in surprise. She swallowed and lifted her hand to touch her cheek, pausing when she felt his hand hovering near it.

"Why... Why did you kiss me?" she asked softly.

Destin dropped his hand to his side and he glanced over her shoulder to the ocean behind her. In his mind, the countless faces of those he had to bury over the years superimposed over her face as she lay so still under the water. He didn't look at her when he replied.

"I thought you had drowned. When I touched you, you opened your eyes and I saw your lips part. I was afraid that you would inhale water and choke. It was the only way I could think of to protect you," he replied with a shrug. "Anyway, I'm glad you are okay. I apologize if I offended you. It wasn't intentional. I've got to go," he said in a stiff tone.

"I...," Sula started to say, but her voice faded when he turned and started to walk away. "Human... Destin!"

Sula's soft voice called out behind him before he had gone more than a few strides. Destin slowed to a stop and partially turned to look back at the alien ice queen who had captured his attention over a year ago. He waited for her to speak again. She swallowed and lifted her chin.

"Thank you," she said. "... for trying to save me, even though it was not necessary."

Destin bowed his head in acknowledgement and turned away. As ghosts from his past rose up to choke him, he knew he needed to put some space between them. Sula was alive, not dead like so many others he had been responsible for. Over the past year, he had worked hard on learning to control the haunting thoughts that often tried to drown him. There were too many would've, could've, should've moments over the last seven years that could never be changed. Dwelling on those memories did nothing but pull him into a deep abyss that threatened to suffocate him.

Sula was in no danger at all and that should be the end of it. There was no reason to keep touching her. It threw him off balance that he had this aching need to feel her lithe body against his again, regardless of whether he had a reason or not.

This reaction was much more intense than the first time he saw her. At that time, he was still reeling from everything that had happened – Colbert's death, Kali being wounded and leaving the planet, the loss of the men who had fought beside him, and the realization that he now had what he wanted – Chicago to rebuild. That, on top of discovering how many women and young girls were kidnapped from Earth for the Usoleum Councilor's greed, made his physical attraction to the new Councilor too much to deal with at the time.

Destin focused on the narrow gap in the rocks in front of him. The moment he was on the other side, he broke into a fast jog. He didn't stop until he reached the back gate to Kali and Razor's home.

When Sula had called out to him, her gaze was focused on the maze of scars across his back. When he half turned, she noticed more on his thick arms and chest, but it was the one on his left cheek that had briefly frozen the words on her lips. Her fingers had ached to trace it. What happened to him back on the planet he called home?

She didn't move until he had disappeared. Glancing down, she shook out the silk cover and slipped it back on. A frown creased her brow when she saw a necklace in the sand near the boulder where Destin Parks had retrieved his clothes.

She walked over to it and picked it up. Her fingers brushed the sand from the small oval disk. Strange symbols, written in the language of the humans, were engraved on the front of it. The medallion appeared to be able to slide apart. Unsure if she should try to see what was inside or not, Sula bit her lip and looked back in the direction Destin had disappeared.

"What harm can it do?" she murmured with a shrug.

It took her a moment to figure out how to work the slide. A tiny catch held it closed. Once the catch was released, the rectangular metal piece slid open. On the side facing her was the image of a young, dark-haired little girl smiling back at her. Frowning, she turned the piece over and saw another image, this one slightly faded. It was of an older woman. She had the same dark hair and shining eyes of the little girl – and of Destin. A series of numbers were etched into the back of the medallion.

Sula knew this must be Destin's family. She carefully closed the piece and pushed the catch back into place. The long, leather cord had a clasp at the end. Destin must have taken it off before he went for a swim.

Her gaze moved back out to the water. For a moment, she could feel his lips against hers and his strong hands on her waist. Her eyelashes fluttered down and a soft moan escaped her when she remembered his body against hers. She had never felt such a reaction to a male before and it shocked her. Especially given who he was and how he had reacted to her when they first met. It was surreal.

Sula lifted the necklace and fastened it around her neck. She had no pockets and didn't want to take a chance of losing it. She would find out where Destin was staying and have a courier deliver it to him. She went through the gap in the rocks and retraced her earlier steps, this time at a slower pace. Her fingers trembled slightly when she lifted them to touch the medallion.

"Well, now I know that Destin Parks did not die back on his planet. What I would like to know is why he is here on Rathon," she whispered, staring down the long beach. "And will he be staying here or returning to his world?"

A growing sense of urgency filled her the closer she got to her transport. She needed answers. It might take her a while to find them, but she was very tenacious. She wouldn't stop until she found out what she wanted to know about a certain human male.

Destin's Hold

SAMPLE OF TOUCHING RUNE

Synopsis

Rune August has lived again and again through many different time periods, but has never found tranquility until she walked into St. Agnes Home for Orphans in New York City in 1894. When her new home is endangered, she doesn't hesitate to fight back – and win. But that win comes at a terrible price.

Refusing to leave the children unprotected, she watches over and protects them in a different form... as the beloved statue in their center garden. But eventually the orphanage is renovated, and Rune finds herself packed away and sold.

Sergei Vasiliev and his best friend and bodyguard, Dimitri Mihailov, run one of the most powerful computer software development companies in the world. Both men carry deep scars from their life on the streets and from living in the world of the ultra-rich. Sergei knows men want him for his power and women want him for his money. Dimitri knows that some people would do anything to gain the secrets their company is developing.

Sergei purchases the statue for their home outside of Moscow because there is something… enthralling about it. He knows Dimitri will see it, too.

Read on for the just over three chapters of Touching Rune!

Chapter 1

New York City, St. Agnes Orphanage 1894

"Rune, look at me!" Mary Katherine cried out as she twirled around in the new dress that Sister Helen had made for her. "Don't I look beautiful? Do you think the Wrights will choose me?"

Rune grinned as the excited six-year-old twirled around in a circle so her dress would fly out around her. Sister Mary stood to the side, smiling serenely. Neither one of them let on that the faded dress had seen better days or had been passed down time and time again. To both of them, Mary Katherine looked beautiful with her shiny brown curls and rosy cheeks.

"I think the last thing you need is a bouquet of flowers to give Mrs. Wright," Rune said as she pulled out the leftover flowers she had tucked away for just this occasion. "I bet she would love them as much as she'll love you."

Mary Katherine gasped and ran over to give Rune a huge hug before she carefully took the small offering. Her eyes shone with excitement as she stared into Rune's warm brown eyes. A small dimple formed as she smiled up at Rune.

"Oh thank you, Rune," Mary Katherine whispered. "I'll take very good care of them until they come."

"It is a good thing they won't be long," Sister Anna said sternly from behind Mary Katherine. "Come along, Mary Katherine. The Wrights are here to see you now."

Rune leaned down and hugged the delicate little girl. "Remember to smile and be polite," she whispered. "They are going to love you as much as I do."

"I love you too, Rune," Mary Katherine whispered before she gave Rune a quick kiss on her cheek.

"Go shine for them, rosebud," Rune whispered back as she watched Mary Katherine follow Sister Anna into the orphanage.

Sister Mary walked over to where Rune stood watching the departing figures. She brushed a strand of long dark brown hair back behind Rune's ear that had fallen loose. She studied the face of the young woman who had appeared out of nowhere five years before when they desperately needed help.

A serious outbreak of Whooping Cough had struck the orphanage. The four Sisters of St. Agnes had been unable to handle the almost thirty children who contracted it. Rune had walked in and taken over when Sister Helen and Mother Magdalene came down sick as well. She had been a part of their small family ever since.

"Do you think they'll adopt her?" Rune asked in a soft, worried voice.

"Only God knows, child," Sister Mary said. "My goodness, what happened to your wrist?"

Rune looked down at her wrist in surprise. She started to pull the sleeve of her blouse back over it, but Sister Mary reached down and gently gripped her hand so she could take a closer look at the dark bruises that marred the delicate skin.

"It's nothing," Rune started to say, but Sister Mary refused to release her right wrist.

"Who did this to you?" Sister Mary asked in concern. "Was it that dreadful Mr. Randolph?"

"Sister Mary," Rune sighed. "He came to see me over in the market. I took care of him. There is nothing to worry about."

"What did he want?" Sister Mary demanded. "Was it about the orphanage again? The church will not sell him the property. We have a written agreement from the Archbishop himself that as long as there are children living here, it will remain open."

"I told him that," Rune replied, looking around the garden that she had created for the children. "He… wanted me to convince you that you needed to change the Archbishop's mind or he would have to take matters into his own hands."

"You need to tell Mother Magdalene. She needs to know he threatened you," Sister Mary insisted. "What else did he say?"

Rune blushed and lowered her head. She couldn't tell the Sisters what else Walter Randolph said. She had become livid at his crude comments and she had let him know she would not let him talk to her in such a manner. She brushed her long braid over her shoulder and shrugged instead of answering Sister Mary.

"He just wanted me to convince Mother Magdalene to talk to the Archbishop," she mumbled.

Sister Mary's lips tightened as she looked at the lovely young woman standing in front of her. She could see the flush on her cheeks and the anger in her eyes as she looked at the ground. She reached out and touched Rune's cheek and smiled in understanding.

"You are a very lovely young woman, Rune," Sister Mary said. "You have a heart of gold and you have given that gold to not only the children who live here but to the Sisters of St. Agnes. I just want you to know that we are here for you as well."

Rune lifted her head and gazed at Sister Mary with a look of determination in her eyes. "You… all of you… are the family I lost," Rune whispered. "I won't let anything happen to you. I'll protect you and the children, no matter what Randolph threatens to do."

"You are part of our family as well, Rune," Sister Mary said. "Never doubt that."

Rune smiled and was about to reply when suddenly the center courtyard garden was overflowing with excited children. Mary Katherine came running as fast as her legs could move. She had a huge grin on her face.

"Rune! I've got a family," she called out as she threw herself into Rune's open arms. "I have a mommy and daddy."

"And they have a beautiful daughter," Rune laughed as she swung Mary Katherine around in a circle before setting her down and smiling at the young couple walking toward her.

"I believe these came from you," the young woman said with a smile as she lifted the small bouquet of flowers. "Thank you."

Rune smiled back. "No, thank you," she responded as the other children gathered around to wish Mary Katherine goodbye.

Rune watched with a combination of happiness and sadness. She had dreamed a long time ago about having a family, but it was not meant to be. Instead, she accepted the children and Sisters into her heart and let them fill her life with joy.

She looked around the cheerful garden that she had worked hard on. Brilliant flowers bloomed everywhere. They reminded her of the children; each different, delicate yet colorful.

Yes, I will do everything in my power to protect them, she thought as love swelled inside her. *This is what I was meant to do.*

Chapter 2

Rune turned the corner and held her breath as she pressed her back against the cold brick and mortar building. Walter Randolph and his men were looking for her. She cursed under her breath. Ruby had warned her as she gathered the last of her flowers that had not sold for the day. Ruby, who sold scented soap beside her, had told her that she would take care of everything and have her brother drop it off at the orphanage later that evening.

Rune had barely had time to whisper her thanks before one of Randolph's men spotted her. Hiking her long skirt up, she had run as fast as she could. She heard Randolph yell out behind her but she wasn't about to wait.

He's probably mad about the black eye I gave him yesterday, Rune thought as she dodged between two horse-drawn wagons filled with barrels of fresh fish from the docks. *I'll give him another one today if he tries to touch me again.*

She groaned when another one of Randolph's men spotted her. She was two blocks from the orphanage. She knew the horrid man wouldn't try anything there. She was fed up with him and his demands. She had to vary her times and the spots where she sold her flowers three times in the last two weeks because of him.

Rune pushed off the wall as the man started down the alley toward her. She turned the corner and ran headfirst into a tall, lanky form. Hard hands grabbed her arms to keep her from falling. With a silent moan, she looked up into the twinkling eyes of Officer Olson Myers.

"Why, Miss August," he said in his cheerful, deep voice. "Where is the fire?"

Rune pushed her long hair back behind her ear and smiled nervously up at the officer who often came by to see the children. Sister Mary and Sister Helen liked to hint that he really came by to see Rune, but Rune refused to rise to their baiting. She knew better than to encourage the young officer to believe there could ever be more than friendship between them.

"I was just on my way back to the orphanage," Rune replied, glancing behind her. She turned back with a smile and touched Officer Myers arm. "Would you be so kind as to escort me? I know the children would love to see you."

Olson grinned down at Rune, his thin mustache curving upwards. "I would be honored, Miss August. How are you doing on this fine evening? Did you sell all of your lovely flowers today?"

Rune mumbled an answer. She knew that they were being followed as they walked slowly back to the orphanage. She fought the urge to just turn and yell at the man to tell Randolph to leave her and the Sisters alone. She didn't, though. Walter Randolph might be a slimy weasel, but he was a very wealthy and powerful one.

It took almost an hour before Rune was able to peel herself away from the friendly officer once they reached the orphanage. Sister Helen had to offer him a cup of tea. Sister Mary had to give him a piece of cake. Mother Magdalene asked him how his day was and if he was courting anyone.

Rune had rolled her eyes at that obvious attempt to feel out his intentions. She had finally taken pity on the poor, blushing man and exclaimed that it was time to get the children ready for their nightly bedtime ritual. She grimaced as the Sisters all stood up and looked expectantly at her.

"Let me get your hat for you," Rune grunted out.

Rune led Olson out of the sitting room and into the small foyer. The soft giggles coming from the stairwell had her raising her eyes in warning to the line of children looking down at them. She winked at two of the youngest ones, pulling more muffled giggles from her audience.

"Yes, well, it was very nice of you to have me for tea and refreshments," Olson said, nervously rotating his hat in his hands. "I was wondering if perhaps, after church this Sunday..."

"I don't attend church, Mr. Myers," Rune said shortly.

"You don't... but you live...," Olson said, confused as he looked around at the home filled with religious artifacts.

"No, I don't, and yes, I do," Rune said firmly as she opened the door. "I hope you have a very pleasant evening. Please be careful of the last step. It has a slight dip in the center and can be slippery."

Rune stood in the door as Olson gave his stammered goodbyes. She knew she had taken him by surprise with her comment, but she didn't care. She didn't answer to anyone... not anymore. She had made her decision long ago and she accepted the consequences. She didn't feel like she had to explain or answer to anyone why she felt the way she did. They would never understand anyway.

How did you explain that you had lived and died a hundred times to someone who believed that you went to heaven or hell after you died? she thought as she watched him hurry down the road.

Her eyes narrowed on a dark shadow across the street. The figure stepped out into the dim light of the lamp post. The scarred face of the man who had followed her earlier stared back at her.

Rune lifted her chin and gave the man a cold smile. She had met men like him many times before. She had fought with a man just like him the first time she had died. She had sworn as she lay dying on the cold, muddy ground centuries before that she would never bow to a tyrant.

She closed the door and leaned back against it. Her eyes went to the single pair of eyes staring down in silence at her. Eyes so much like… Rune forced her mind to close on the distant memory that haunted her still. She smiled and walked over to the stairs leading to the children's dorm. She didn't say a word as she held out her hand to the small boy who stood up as she approached. Together, they walked in silence down the long corridor.

"The local lawman left just a few minutes ago," the scar-faced man said as he spit on the pitted dirt road next to the carriage that pulled up next to him. "I wasn't sure he was ever going to leave."

"And the young woman?" the dark figure sitting in the back of the carriage asked. "She is still inside?"

"Yes. She looked right at me," the man replied, shifting from one foot to the other in unease. "She didn't look like she was scared either."

A chilling silence met his response. "Did you get the items I asked for?" the man in the carriage finally asked.

"Yes," the man replied. "But I don't feel good about burning down a holy place. I can kill a man or that young woman if you want, but burning down some Sisters and a bunch of kids just don't sit right with me."

Walter Randolph sat forward in the carriage just enough for the man to see the cold brutality glittering in his eyes. He didn't care how the man felt. It wouldn't matter. Sam Weston was nothing more than a cutthroat he had hired down at the docks. His body would be found in the burnt remains of the building. Weston would be blamed for an arson gone wrong.

Randolph only needed the man to gather the items that were to be used and to be there. He would kill him after Weston and he used those items to set fire to the orphanage. But first… first he had a certain female that he wanted removed. Rune August had been a thorn in his side for the last two years. She had petitioned the mayor and several wealthy philanthropists to support the orphanage. His arguments that the property was too valuable to be wasted on a bunch of indigent children had fallen on deaf ears. He soon discovered that the more vocal he became, the cooler his reception among his peers had become, thanks to her interference.

He had come to the conclusion that he needed to take care of the situation himself. Time after time, his meetings with the stubborn but beautiful Miss August had led to nothing but frustration, both physically and financially. She had rebuffed his attentions just as she had refused to take his money.

"You are not being paid to feel things, Mr. Weston," Randolph said coolly. "Have the items in the back alley behind the orphanage after midnight. I want to personally oversee this… task."

"Yes, Mr. Randolph," Sam muttered before he stepped back. "I'll be there."

"You'd better be, Mr. Weston," Randolph said before he tapped on the roof of the carriage. "You'd better be."

Randolph looked out the window of the carriage as it pulled away from the curb. His eyes rose to the figure silhouetted in the upper window. A cruel smile formed as he saw the figure disappear as the light inside was blown out. Tonight he would not only make the property available for his future plans, but he would have the beautiful Miss August under his control.

~

"Rune, where are you going?" Timmy asked.

Rune turned and pulled her dressing gown closed. Timmy had come to the orphanage a couple of months before. He was a soft-spoken boy of eight whose eyes held too much sorrow. His father had died when he was just a babe and his mother of tuberculosis two months ago.

"You should be asleep," Rune whispered sternly. "What are you doing up?"

Timmy looked down at his hands and didn't reply at first. Rune sighed and knelt down in front of him. She gently tilted his trembling chin up so he could see she wasn't mad.

"How about some warm milk and a small piece of cake?" she asked softly. "It always helps me when I have a sad dream."

Timmy looked into her eyes with a serious expression. "Do you have sad dreams too?" he asked, raising his hand to touch her cheek as she nodded. "I dreamed about my mom. She was coughing again and couldn't stop."

"It is hard when someone we love dies," Rune said sadly. "Just remember, as long as you keep them in your heart, they are never really gone."

"Do you keep your family in your heart?" Timmy asked innocently.

Rune schooled her face not to show the pain she still felt at times. She often wondered if anything would ever heal the grief she kept locked away deep inside her. Being around the children and watching them grow helped.

"Yes, Timmy," Rune replied as she stood up. "I keep them locked inside my heart so I never forget them. Come on. Let's go see if Mother Magdalene saved us any of Sister Mary's pound cake. You know she loves it."

Timmy giggled and slipped his hand into Rune's. They snuck down the stairs and through the corridor. Rune decided to cut through the garden. She loved going into the garden on a clear night.

Timmy giggled again when Rune teased him about being quiet as a mouse. She was about to remark that maybe they should be stealing some bread and cheese when a movement on the other side of the garden caught her attention. There was a flash and brilliant orange flames flared up, silhouetting a form that Rune was only too familiar with along with the scarred face of the man who had been watching her earlier.

"Timmy, wake the others," Rune said, pushing the boy behind her. "Run! Tell them fire! Wake the others now!"

Timmy's eyes were huge as he briefly looked over his shoulder at the two men. One stared back at them in surprise while the other glared at them in fury. He stumbled as he turned, his hand searching desperately for the handle to the door.

"Get him!" The man with the furious expression ordered. "Don't let him alert the others."

"Run, Timmy," Rune ordered as she moved to stand in front of the door. "Save them, Timmy. It is up to you now."

~

Rune knew deep down that her time here had come to an end. She never understood how she knew, she just did. Fury built deep inside her as the pain of losing her new family swept through her. She had sworn that she would protect the children and the Sisters with every fiber of her being, and she would do so.

She heard the door slam behind her as Timmy finally raced inside. She could hear his frightened voice rising as he ran back to the dorms and the rooms belonging to the Sisters and Mother Magdalene. She ignored it as the scar-faced man ran toward her.

Hoping to surprise him, she raced forward and grabbed his arm. She let her slender weight hit him head-on. He grunted and stumbled sideways when she refused to let go of his arm.

"Get the boy!" Randolph growled out harshly as he wrapped his arm around Rune's waist and ripped her away from the scar-faced man. "Kill him."

"No!" Rune screamed.

Fury unlike anything she had ever felt swept through her. She slammed her head back into Randolph's face, breaking his nose from the sound of the crunch. She turned as his arm fell away from around her and swung her fist.

"You bitch!" Randolph snarled out as he slapped Rune across the face, knocking her down. "You've ruined everything."

Flames were crawling up the wall behind them as the wooden frame of the kitchen area caught. Rune's eyes moved from the flames back to the man standing over her. She waited until he bent to grab her again before she threw the dirt that she had gathered in her hand into his eyes.

Randolph cursed loudly and stumbled backwards. Rune's eyes narrowed in determination when she realized he was in front of the burning door. Pushing up off the ground, she charged him, wrapping her arms around his waist and pushing him through the flames. They both landed on the floor of the kitchen as the door gave way. Randolph lost his balance and fell on his back with Rune on top of him.

Rune gasped as he rolled so that she was trapped under him. She barely had time to raise her hands to protect her face when he raised his hand to strike her again. He cursed in frustration and rolled off her, coughing as the smoke thickened the air.

Rune rolled away from him and crawled onto her hands and knees. She looked at him with watery eyes. Flames were beginning to roll along the ceiling of the kitchen now and the wall where the door leading to the garden was engulfed. She pulled herself up using the table. Seeing the knife that they had used earlier to cut the pound cake, she reached out and wrapped her fingers around it.

"You stupid bitch," Randolph cursed as he wrapped his fingers around the wrist holding the knife. "You could have had everything money could buy."

Rune jerked, trying to break his grip. She cried out when he squeezed hard enough to almost break the delicate bones in her wrist. He reached over and grabbed the knife in his free hand.

"Money could never buy my loyalty or make me care about a self-centered bastard like you," Rune choked out as sweat from the heat of the fire threatened to scorch her skin. "You are through," she whispered. "Not even your money can save you from this."

Rune could hear the bells of alarm and the yells of voices as people gathered to form a water bucket brigade. She could hear the sharp whistle of a policeman and the bells on the team of horses pulling the water wagon. A large beam cracked and fell behind Randolph. Rune reacted the moment his attention was distracted. She pushed as hard as she could against him. Pain exploded through her even as she watched as he lost his balance and fell back onto the burning beam. A second beam collapsed, trapping him between the two.

His screams followed Rune as she turned back toward the empty space where the door leading to the garden now stood. She walked forward, ignoring the flames. They could do nothing to her. She was already dead. She could feel the blood draining from her even as the pain from the knife that Randolph had stuck into her as he fell threatened to overwhelm her. She wanted to reach the garden. The garden that she loved. The garden with the flowers that she grew to sell for the children. The garden where their laughter echoed.

Rune fell to her knees near the center. Mother Magdalene, who was standing in the doorway leading into the dorm area, rushed forward. She gently helped Rune down before rolling her over onto her back. Rune stared up into the night sky as the familiar peacefulness of death swept through her. The stars glittered despite the thick smoke and the red haze of the flames.

"Please," Rune whispered, looking blindly up at the stars. "Please, let me stay this time. Let me watch over and protect them. Please don't take me away again. I'm so tired of wandering. Please..." her voice broke.

"Oh, child," Mother Magdalene whispered as she brushed Rune's sweat dampened hair back from her face. "What have you done?"

Rune turned her face into the withered hand and sighed. "I promised to protect you," Rune whispered with a serene smile. "Don't cry for me, Mother Magdalene. I'll be alright. I won't... leave you... or the... children," she forced out softly before she faded away.

Tears coursed down Mother Magdalene's cheeks. She touched the still face of the young girl who had appeared out of nowhere and captured the hearts of everyone she touched. She brushed the damp hair back, holding Rune tightly for a moment. She gently closed Rune's eyes with trembling fingers.

"Mother Magdalene!" Sister Mary whispered in shock as she rushed up to where Mother Magdalene was holding Rune's lifeless body. "Oh no! Oh, poor child," she cried as she bowed her head to pray.

Mother Magdalene looked up at the stars and whispered her own prayer. She prayed that Rune would finally find the peace and happiness that she deserved. Her only regret was that she had never learned what put the shadows in the young girl's beautiful brown eyes.

"Please help her find happiness," Mother Magdalene prayed. "Please give her a second chance to find someone who will love her enough to chase the shadows from her eyes."

Chapter 3

Present Day New York City

"You know it helps if you tell me when you plan to deviate from your plans before you do, don't you?" Dimitri Mihailov told the man sitting across from him in exasperation. "As head of your security, I need to know this so I can plan accordingly."

Sergei Vasiliev didn't look up from the tablet he held in his hand. His brow was creased and the scar that ran from the corner of his left eye across his cheek pulled as his lips tightened in displeasure.

Dimitri sighed and waited. He had known Sergei long enough to recognize when his friend was upset. They had grown up together on the streets of Moscow. Dimitri had been the brawn during that time while Sergei had been the brains.

A lot of things had changed since their youth. Their combination of brute force and brains had worked in their favor. Both of the men's assets were in the billions, though few realized that Dimitri was the second part of the Vasiliev-Mihailov dynasty. He kept a lower profile which allowed him to move unnoticed behind the scenes. A fact that had helped in their acquisitions over the years. Neither one of them would ever forget the poverty of their youth. It was a distant shadow to them now, but the scars left behind were a powerful reminder.

Time had changed them both. Sergei was no longer a scrawny boy. The tight fit of the black cashmere sweater he wore emphasized the thick muscles under it. He had filled out as he grew older until he was almost as powerful as Dimitri. A long scar marred the left side of

Sergei's face, a constant reminder that even having wealth did not guarantee safety. Guilt pulled at Dimitri. He had almost been too late to save the one man he knew trusted him.

"Knock it off, Dimitri," Sergei growled out in Russian. "I can feel your guilt radiating off you. For the last time, it was not your fault."

"I should have increased the security around you," Dimitri grunted out. "I knew there was a threat. I should have done more."

"I knew there was a threat as well," Sergei said with a deep sigh. He turned off the tablet and looked at Dimitri's face that was partially hidden in the shadows as he sat back against the limousine's rich leather. "You warned me. I was the one who chose to ignore the warning. Do not blame yourself for my own stupidity, Dimitri."

Dimitri snorted. The thought that anyone, including Sergei, could ever use the word stupid and his friend's name in the same sentence was ludicrous. Sergei was constantly referred to as one of the smartest men in the world in the major business magazines.

Dimitri gazed out the window at all the holiday decorations and the crowd of pedestrians bundled up against the chill in the air outside. He didn't say any more on the topic. It was an old argument that neither one of them won. Dimitri continued to feel guilty and Sergei became more cynical about the world.

Sergei could feel the frustration coming off his friend. In truth, Dimitri was the only human on the planet that Sergei trusted and he knew his friend felt the same. A lifetime of danger, first on the streets of an unforgiving city, then in the cutthroat world of the super-powerful, was enough to make anyone jaded about humanity.

He set the tablet he had been working on aside and folded his arms across his broad chest. Something else was bothering his friend and it wasn't the scar on his face. Dimitri looked... apprehensive.

"I was invited at the last minute to attend a charity event to raise money. Simone and Petre invited me. I could hardly turn them down," Sergei said. "We are leaving as soon as it is over."

Dimitri's head turned and he scowled darkly at Sergei. "You could have told me," he said. "What is the charity for this time?"

Sergei shrugged. "I don't know. Probably another hospital or orphanage benefit."

"Will Ms. Ferguson be attending as well?" Dimitri asked in a voice devoid of emotion.

Sergei's lips curved, pulling on the scar on his cheek. "No. It was time for us to part ways," he responded in a hard voice. "She was making demands. It became necessary to end our acquaintance."

Dimitri's eyebrow raised in surprise. Sergei's latest lover had been the beautiful but shallow Eloise Ferguson, a top model and a horrible actress, at least in Dimitri's opinion. She had tried to hide her greed for Sergei's wealth behind a fake smile and a camouflage of innocence. There was absolutely nothing innocent about the former beauty queen who had lost her virginity at a very young age.

Dimitri had made it his business to know everything about the beautiful actress who came from an upper middle class family. She liked beautiful things and had a tendency to live beyond her own financial means.

"What demands?" Dimitri asked.

"She claimed she was pregnant," Sergei responded.

Dimitri grimaced. Several other women had tried that same trick before. There were advantages to being a cold, cynical bastard. One was to make sure that each of their lovers was on some form of birth control and checked regularly. The second was neither of them ever let the woman they were with supply or touch the condoms that were used.

Sergei had caught one of his previous lovers purposely damaging a condom in an attempt to snare a lifetime of support from him. Dimitri had never given any of his lovers a chance in the first place. He had seen things even Sergei had not and had learned to be cautious at a very young age. Of course, none of his lovers were aware that he was as wealthy as Sergei. They all thought he was the lowly bodyguard, fit only to amuse them if they couldn't draw Sergei's attention.

"Is she?" Dimitri asked carefully. "Has she been seen by a doctor?"

"Two," Sergei replied, picking up the tablet. "The first was her choice; the second mine. I want Dr. Umberto Angelo's medical license. He took a bribe and lied about the results. It is not the only thing he has done. I will send you the information about his tax evasion and hidden accounts so you can hand it over to the authorities. Also check what he has been doing on his frequent trips to the Philippines. I think you will find he has been indulging in other unlawful activities."

"Done," Dimitri said, reaching into his jacket pocket to pull out a small notepad.

Sergei shook his head. "When are you going to come into the twenty-first century and use a computer to help you take notes?" he asked in amusement.

Dimitri scowled at the softly glowing tablet. "You know I always break the damn things," he grumbled. "They don't like me."

"Yet, you are a master at setting up security programming." Sergei looked at Dimitri again and frowned. "What is bothering you, my friend? You seem distracted tonight."

"Do you think you will ever find a woman you could trust? One that you would want to spend the rest of your life with?" Dimitri asked, glancing at Sergei before looking back out at the colorful lights decorating the streets.

"Do you mean like we used to talk about finding or just one that I can trust enough to breed an heir?" Sergei asked before a sudden ugly thought crossed his mind. "Have you… found someone?" he asked tersely.

"No," Dimitri snorted out. "I don't think there is a woman alive that I would be interested in being tied to for the rest of my life."

Sergei released the breath he was holding. They had talked about finding their perfect woman when they were younger. As they had grown older, they often compared the women they were dating with the one they wished for so long ago.

She would be strong. Dimitri insisted she would have to be to live with them, but in a good way. In their adolescent minds, she would fit perfectly between them. She would be the one to complete them and make them the family they never had.

She would also be intelligent, compassionate, loving, and Dimitri added this trait as well, a little bit stubborn. Sergei had asked why he wanted their woman to be stubborn. Dimitri had replied she would need to be stubborn if she was expected to put up with both of them at the same time. Not to be outdone, Sergei had added that if she was stubborn, then she also needed to be passionate enough to handle all the loving they would give her.

They had laughed as they wished upon the stars that night so long ago. They still talked about it on occasion, usually when they retreated to their 'lair' to regroup from the world of humanity.

Sergei looked out the window as they passed a large group of colorfully dressed women who were eyeing the limousine. His lips curled in distaste as one of the women opened her coat to reveal the minuscule dress she was wearing. He had seen the same type of women when he was poor. He had no more use for them now than he did when he was younger.

"Then I guess that answers your question," Sergei replied. "I haven't found a woman either."

Dimitri breathed out a sigh. "I have to admit I was worried you would present Ms. Ferguson as a candidate. I don't think I could have faked a hard-on with her," he admitted in distaste.

"What about Stella?" Sergei asked, referring to Dimitri's latest lover. "Are you still seeing her?"

"No," Dimitri said without any other explanation. "How long do you plan to stay at the mansion? I need to make sure the new system I installed last month is working."

"I'm not sure," Sergei frowned and thought for several long moments before he answered. "At least until after the first of the year. I have no desire to join in the festivities or attend the 'required' parties."

Sergei knew that Dimitri worried about him when they secluded themselves at their home outside of Moscow. They had bought the huge mansion together, transforming it into their primary development lab/home shortly after they became millionaires. Dimitri took over the lower floors while Sergei transformed the upper floors. Each also had homes around the world, but preferred to stay at the Moscow residence together. It reminded them of their roots and gave them time to work on some of their new software designs in privacy.

Since the kidnapping attempt, Sergei was spending more time locked away from the world. In truth, he found little to like about the world around him and preferred the isolation. He emerged on occasion to visit a new lover or attend meetings that needed his specialized attention.

Neither he nor Dimitri ever brought a woman to their home there. It was an unspoken pact that that home would be reserved for their 'wish' woman. He set the tablet down again and focused his attention on his friend.

"That should give me enough time to test out some of the new systems I have been working on," Dimitri replied. "It is not good to bury yourself there for too long," he started to add before clamping his lips together when Sergei's eyes flashed in warning. "I know... if you wanted my advice you would ask for it."

Sergei smiled darkly. "Some things are best left alone, my friend, even with you. I will be fine, Dimitri. You have enough security there to protect every leader in the world. You saw the report that we may have a possible security issue at our headquarters in Los Angeles. Someone is leaking details of the new defense programming. I want you to find out who it is and take care of it."

"Is that what has put you in a bad mood?" Dimitri asked, accepting the sudden change in topic.

"Yes," Sergei said. "You know how I feel about anyone who lies or steals from us."

"Do you want whoever it is alive or dead?" Dimitri responded cynically.

"Alive," Sergei replied with a cold grin. "I want them to wish they were dead by the time we get done with them."

"Done," Dimitri said with a dark smile of his own and jotted down a note in the notepad.

Both men turned as the limousine pulled to the curb outside of Sotheby's. Dimitri slid out of the back seat first. He looked around carefully before he nodded to Sergei.

"Make sure the jet is ready to leave," Sergei murmured to Dimitri. "This shouldn't take long."

"Of course," Dimitri replied as he and three of his men surrounded Sergei as several photographers approached from the sides.

Sergei ignored them. He knew that Dimitri had some of the best and most deadly men in the world protecting him. Nothing could get through his friend's security, nothing.

Two hours later, Sergei and Dimitri were seated on one of the Vasiliev-Mihailov private jets heading to their secluded home outside Moscow. The auction had taken a little longer than they expected. Ms. Ferguson had shown up outside to give a dramatic performance for the paparazzi. Dimitri had two of his men escort Sergei's former lover away while he shielded Sergei.

He glanced over at Sergei. He studied his friend with a puzzled expression. Something strange had happened at the auction. Dimitri had no desire to attend so he asked Sergei to make an anonymous donation for him while he started on the Los Angeles issue.

Dimitri knew something unusual had happened when Sergei emerged from the auction room so distracted that he hadn't even noticed his former lover trying to gain his attention. Dimitri had waited patiently for Sergei to explain what happened, but phone calls from several of his men in California had prevented him from asking when Sergei remained silent. By the time he got off the phone, they had reached the airport.

"What happened?" Dimitri demanded after the stewardess left them alone again. "Did Simone or Petre ask you to build them a new hospital or something? I've never seen you so distracted. You didn't even notice Ms. Ferguson's little performance," he added dryly.

"What?" Sergei asked, looking up at Dimitri with a frown. "No, not a hospital."

"Sergei," Dimitri said, handing his friend a drink. "You are acting stranger than usual. Either you tell me what happened or we return to New York and I find Petre and Simone."

"I bought something," Sergei replied after several long seconds. "A statue."

Dimitri frowned. "You bought a statue? What for?"

"For the atrium," Sergei replied with a frown. "It should go in the atrium."

Dimitri sighed in exasperation and took a sip of the aged brandy he was holding. He didn't understand why in the hell Sergei suddenly decided he wanted a statue for an atrium that hadn't been touched in almost a century. Hell, Dimitri wasn't even sure he remembered where it was! The mansion they had purchased was actually a former palace during Russia's more prosperous age. It contained over a hundred rooms, many still in the same shape as they were when it was built.

"Why would you buy a statue for an atrium that we never even go into?" Dimitri asked.

"I don't know," Sergei replied. "I just knew we had to have it."

"What is it a statue of and where did it come from?" Dimitri asked in exasperation. "How much did you pay for it?" he asked suspiciously.

"It is a statue of a young woman," Sergei answered before he took a deep drink of his own brandy. "And we each donated a million US dollars for it."

Dimitri choked on the sip he had just taken. "You spent two million dollars on a statue? Is it from a famous artist? Will the value increase? Who designed it?"

"Yes, no, probably not, and no one knows," Sergei answered as he sat back in the plush leather seat and looked at Dimitri. "It is absolutely beautiful, Dimitri. I will return your donation to you if you want, but I am keeping the statue."

Dimitri stared at Sergei's determined face and shook his head. Sure, they both could easily have paid a hundred times that amount, but having been poor once left Dimitri on the more conservative side. If it wasn't a good investment with a chance of increasing in value, he didn't invest.

Sergei sat in the plush leather seat looking out into the dark sky. His thoughts were on the impulsive purchase he had made. He frowned as he thought of the statue of the young woman. He didn't know who had been more surprised, him or Dimitri about the unexpected purchase. His plan had been to attend the auction and make a huge donation, then leave. When the statue had been unveiled, he had been mesmerized by it. The expression on the face of the statue held him spellbound. The combination of innocence, defiance, and steely determination made him almost believe in humanity again - almost.

He looked at Dimitri and told him what Simone had related to him while they waited for the statue to be set up on the stage. He had been unable to tear his eyes away from it. A shiver of apprehension had swept through him, as though warning him that his life was about to change.

"The statue was in the garden at St. Agnes Orphanage. The building was in terrible shape and the city was threatening to tear it down. I couldn't let that happen. It was my home for a short time after my parents were killed. I lived there for almost a year before they located my father's mother who took me in. The statue is of a young woman who lived there at one time. I don't remember exactly who she was but she is considered to be the guardian angel for all of the children who lived there. I know she helped me during the year I was there," Simone had quietly explained to him before the bidding started. "The garden is being redone into an interactive play area for the children. The architect in charge of the renovations decided the statue wouldn't fit in with the new design. The statue was donated to the auction to help raise funds for the new playground equipment."

"She is beautiful," he commented as he studied the delicate features of the bronze statue.

"From the little I remember, she was a very unusual woman for her time. I just know I always felt safe when I was at the orphanage, knowing she was watching over me," Simone said with a small smile.

"What happened to the woman?" Sergei asked, but Simone didn't reply as the auctioneer began speaking.

A sense of dread built in his stomach as he listened to the auctioneer give a brief history of the statue. He looked down at the program, curious to see who the artist was that designed the statue. He frowned when he found no mention of the artist or any information on where it had been cast. The work was too detailed to have been done by an unknown artist.

"All I know is that she was murdered by a man who tried to burn down the orphanage," Simone whispered as the bidding began. "There isn't a lot of information on her. Just that she lived there and gave her life protecting the children who lived at St. Agnes."

"So you paid two million dollars for a statue that no one knows anything about?" Dimitri asked in disbelief. "Because you thought it was pretty?"

Sergei frowned and drained his glass. "You'll understand when you see it. I'm having it shipped immediately. It should be delivered in the next week."

"You have lost your mind," Dimitri muttered under his breath. "Two million dollars. I hope Simone is happy."

"I told you, I'll reimburse you the funds if you want," Sergei bit out. "Wait until you see it, Dimitri. You'll see what I mean when I say I could not let the statue go to anyone else. Plus, it will give you something else to do. If anyone can find out who the artist is, it is you. You always were a sucker for a mystery."

Dimitri scowled at Sergei before he finally grunted in agreement.

"You better hope I turn up a very famous artist who makes this one of those one-of-a-kind finds that is considered a miracle."

Sergei's lips curved in an unusual genuine smile. "You know, I think it just might be."

"I hope your intuition is right again, my friend," Dimitri grumbled. "Two million dollars' worth of one-of-a-kind."

Chapter 4

Rune fumed silently as she looked around the tattered atrium. She didn't want to be staring at dried and withered plants that adorned the huge area that had at one time been beautiful. She wanted to watch the children as they ran circles around her while throwing snowballs. She wanted to hear their off-key singing as the excitement of the Christmas season approached.

Instead, she had been ripped away from the serenity of her former home. She had spent the last century watching over the children. The orphanage had changed dramatically over the years, but the children, despite the changing times, remained the same. She sent warmth to the new arrivals, listened to their hopes and dreams, and did what she could to make them feel safe and happy.

She grimaced as an older man brushed dry leaves aside so the workmen could set her up in the center of the marble platform. She listened as the men joked in a language she didn't understand.

She would have panicked when she felt herself start to topple over if she had cared what happened to her, but she was beyond caring now. She had been ripped away from the one place where she wanted to be. Until she was either pulled back to the plane where she existed in a world of nothingness or returned to her garden, she couldn't care less what happened around her.

"Be careful!" A sharp, deep voice snapped out. "I do not want the statue damaged."

Rune turned to glare at the male who had barked out a sharp command. She recognized his voice from the room where she had been put on display. He had purchased her for a ridiculous price. She could have told him that she wasn't worth two million dollars! She had tried to send out feelings of discouragement, but if anything, he had seemed more determined than ever to own her.

Not that he ever will, she thought defiantly.

She felt half a dozen hands straightening her before they finally stepped back. She watched as the men quickly gathered the packaging that she had been stored in for the long move. She had slept through most of it, unable to bear the horrible emptiness and darkness of the crate. She wanted to rant at them to not take it too far because she wouldn't be staying long. As soon as she could find a way to convince the horrid man that she was a bad luck omen, she planned on being shipped back to where she came from.

Just you wait, she thought as another man joined the first and looked at her with an unexpectedly possessive look. *I'll make you both wish you had never purchased me. You'll be happy to send me back to my garden.*

Touching Rune

ADDITIONAL BOOKS AND INFORMATION

If you loved this story by me (S.E. Smith) please leave a review! You can also take a look at additional books and sign up for my newsletter to hear about my latest releases at:

http://sesmithfl.com
http://sesmithya.com

or keep in touch using the following links:

http://sesmithfl.com/?s=newsletter
https://www.facebook.com/se.smith.5
https://twitter.com/sesmithfl
http://www.pinterest.com/sesmithfl/
http://sesmithfl.com/blog/
http://www.sesmithromance.com/forum/

The Full Booklist

Science Fiction / Romance

Cosmos' Gateway Series
Tilly Gets Her Man (Prequel)
Tink's Neverland (Book 1)
Hannah's Warrior (Book 2)
Tansy's Titan (Book 3)
Cosmos' Promise (Book 4)
Merrick's Maiden (Book 5)
Core's Attack (Book 6)
Saving Runt (Book 7)

Curizan Warrior Series
Ha'ven's Song (Book 1)

Dragon Lords of Valdier Series
Abducting Abby (Book 1)
Capturing Cara (Book 2)
Tracking Trisha (Book 3)
Dragon Lords of Valdier Boxset Books 1-3
Ambushing Ariel (Book 4)
For the Love of Tia Novella (Book 4.1)
Cornering Carmen (Book 5)
Paul's Pursuit (Book 6)
Twin Dragons (Book 7)
Jaguin's Love (Book 8)
The Old Dragon of the Mountain's Christmas (Book 9)
Pearl's Dragon Novella (Book 10)
Twin Dragons' Destiny (Book 11)

Marastin Dow Warriors Series
A Warrior's Heart Novella

Dragonlings of Valdier Novellas
A Dragonling's Easter
A Dragonling's Haunted Halloween
A Dragonling's Magical Christmas

Night of the Demented Symbiots (Halloween 2)
The Dragonlings' Very Special Valentine
The Dragonlings and the Magic Four-Leaf Clover

Lords of Kassis Series
River's Run (Book 1)
Star's Storm (Book 2)
Jo's Journey (Book 3)
Rescuing Mattie Novella (Book 3.1)
Ristéard's Unwilling Empress (Book 4)

Sarafin Warriors Series
Choosing Riley (Book 1)
Viper's Defiant Mate (Book 2)

The Alliance Series
Hunter's Claim (Book 1)
Razor's Traitorous Heart (Book 2)
Dagger's Hope (Book 3)
The Alliance Boxset Books 1-3
Challenging Saber (Book 4)
Destin's Hold (Book 5)
Edge of Insanity (Book 6)

Zion Warriors Series
Gracie's Touch (Book 1)
Krac's Firebrand (Book 2)

Magic, New Mexico Series
Touch of Frost (Book 1)

Paranormal / Fantasy / Romance

Magic, New Mexico Series
Taking on Tory (Book 2)

Alexandru's Kiss (Book 3)

Spirit Pass Series
Indiana Wild (Book 1)
Spirit Warrior (Book 2)

Second Chance Series
Lily's Cowboys (Book 1)
Touching Rune (Book 2)

More Than Human Series
Ella and the Beast (Book 1)

The Seven Kingdoms
The Dragon's Treasure (Book 1)
The Sea King's Lady (Book 2)
A Witch's Touch (Book 3)

The Fairy Tale Series
The Beast Prince Novella
*Free Audiobook of The Beast Prince is available:
https://soundcloud.com/sesmithfl/sets/the-beast-prince-the-fairy-tale-series

Epic Science Fiction / Action Adventure

Project Gliese 581G Series
Command Decision (Book 1)
First Awakenings (Book 2)
Survival Skills (Book 3)

New Adult

Breaking Free Series
Capture of the Defiance (Book 2)

Young Adult

Breaking Free Series
Voyage of the Defiance (Book 1)

The Dust Series
Dust: Before and After (Book 1)
Dust: A New World Order (Book 2)

Recommended Reading Order Lists:

http://sesmithfl.com/reading-list-by-events/
http://sesmithfl.com/reading-list-by-series/

ABOUT THE AUTHOR

S.E. Smith is a ***New York Times, USA TODAY, International, and Award-Winning*** Bestselling author of science fiction, romance, fantasy, paranormal, and contemporary works for adults, young adults, and children. She enjoys writing a wide variety of genres that pull her readers into worlds that take them away.

CPSIA information can be obtained
at www.ICGtesting.com
Printed in the USA
BVHW04s1642290418
514758BV00002B/155/P

9 781944 125158